1

http://www.personofnointerest.com

Follow the book on Facebook at

https://www.facebook.com/personofnointerestbook

Cover Design by Ebook Cover Design by

www.ebooklaunch.com

Edited by Cara Lockwood

ISBN-13: 978-0-9974549-1-8

ISBN-10: 0-9974549-1-1

For my wife, who constantly stands by me, my children, who never fail to put a smile on my face, and to friends and family, who have supported me the whole way through.

Contents

Prologue 7

POOF! 11

Blink 79

Stick Figure 119

HUD 147

Enhancements 195

Life 207

Loneliness 219

Setback 257

Philanthropy 275

Confrontation 307

War 333

Epilogue 403

Prologue

If works of fiction are true, there are typically three ways a person could acquire abilities or unnatural powers. One could be born with them and thus be a freak of nature. This person could be outed right away or have people around who care enough to keep the protagonist's unique traits a secret. Or perhaps one is not of this world, and instead belongs to an alien civilization or an ancient secretive cult or culture. Whatever the case, when it is time to make one's existence known to everyone, this hero will be well prepared and be surrounded by people who can provide wisdom and support.

Finally, one could be the result of a procedure or just an experiment that went horribly wrong. This hero will have a hard time understanding his or her ability, and will probably engage in a training montage and if the event was public enough, be subjected to plenty of government scrutiny. But, in all these situations, at least they know the cause of their predicament and have a foundation from which to start from.

My life is not a work of fiction. I was not born with the type of abilities that get infants thrown into fiery pits for being the incarnation of the devil or put up on a pedestal to be worshipped as a god. I was neither a scientist playing with dangerous chemicals nor a secret government project. To the best of my knowledge, and I have investigated this thoroughly, neither my parents nor those around me can be classified as anything but your normal average everyday human beings. And yet, I find myself in a situation that seems even less plausible in the real world.

See, in those comics, books or movies that we like to read and watch, a school-aged protagonist can easily be categorized in a few possible ways. He, and for the purposes of this example, let's assume that it's a male, may be a nerd, leading us to believe that he will one day become cool in the eyes of everyone around him while remaining true to his nerdy roots. He may be the popular jock in his grade, and chances are that he will have a realization that will change him profoundly and then, use his influence to change the views of all the dimwitted popular kids around him. Or he could also be shy and a loner, secretly in love with some girl. Circumstances will one day vote in his favor and we can all be confident that this girl or someone he had never noticed before but had always been there for him will be the mother of his six kids. Regardless of his categorization, his entire tale will eventually end with him fighting a supervillain he had coincidently crossed paths with before.

I must point out again that my life is not a work of fiction. Spoiler alert. I don't get the girl. There is no other person out there who becomes my arch nemesis. My story does not follow the stereotypical progression that I just outlined above. The truth is that while stereotypes do exist, most people, including school-going kids are average with nothing too interesting about their personalities or their lives. They are who they are and you cannot pick out one teenager from the next. I was such a person. There really wasn't anything special about me. I was good at certain things, not so good at others and merely okay at the rest. Those around me weren't that extraordinary either. Yes, there were some cool kids and others who were shy and nerdy. Even these kids who did fit into a stereotype were probably never going to amount to anything stellar. The majority of us will end up with modest jobs, leading decent lives, and having families. We'll experience love, heartbreak and joy and on occasion, excitement and nervousness. But like the general populace, we'll lead these lives, and eventually fade away, never having contributed anything noteworthy enough to be remembered for. It is depressing but it's true.

Up until the summer of 1997, I had believed that to be true for myself, at the very least. Then, one summer afternoon, I got off the school bus just like every other day and a couple of meaningless incidences led to the most unbelievable event that changed the course of my life. Thirteen years later, I'm here, jotting down my experiences.

It's safe to say that I experienced a very different type of puberty and it managed to mess me up quite a bit.

POOF!

Chapter 1

Excerpts from my Life

Time: Spring of 1997

Location: Hometown, getting off the bus

Event: The Great Discovery

I found the school bus to be relatively empty by the time it got to my stop. The two people I generally found myself talking to on my way home would also get off here. Much to the annoyance of the driver, we would already be up and moving towards the door before the vehicle came to a stop. Nothing was different that day and we continued to ignore the driver's threats of informing our parents about not following bus policies. We got off the bus and I felt a slight breeze in the air. There were no clouds in the sky to stop the blaze of the sun pouring down on us. Even though we squinted, the shape of the new sports car that had graced our neighborhood was undeniable. Up until now, we had only heard about one of our fellow neighbors having purchased a Porsche.

My dad had shown me a picture of it in the newspaper, and I had taken the clipping to school just the week before to share it amongst my friends. Now, we saw the real thing for the first time as we proceeded to walk towards the shiny new Boxster parked next to the sidewalk. It was hard to keep our eyes off it. It had a peculiar design, a rather brave one to be honest and it continued to drive us closer and closer to it. This was eye porn at its finest, the glare of the sun shining off the purple chassis continuously changing position and intensity as we drew nearer. My friend reached out and before I could stop him, his fingers were gliding over its body.

A bit of wisdom on our part would have warned us that a Porsche is an expensive car and owners of expensive cars are a tad more paranoid about the security of their roadsters than your common family sedan owner. The sound of the breeze blowing through the leaves mixed with a blaring car alarm, which showed no signs of switching off any time soon. The silence was broken and we expected some authority figure to show up shortly. We stared at each other nervously, trying to communicate our displeasure to our idiot friend who decided to touch the Porsche while trying to keep our snarky smiles in check. On the whole, the experience had been pretty awesome and we slowly turned around and started sprinting in the opposite direction, hoping no one would realize that we were the culprits behind disturbing everyone's afternoon.

But we weren't out of the woods yet. The sound of a blaring car alarm and the sight of teenage boys running was too much for a German shepherd who decided to play catch up as it darted our way, barking incessantly with every stride. In the foray of confusion, I wasn't totally sure about what was going on. We were quite far from the car now and I just noticed that my other friends had stopped running, holding their knees panting while laughing and trying to communicate with each other and gasping for air. They appeared to be ignoring this canine running our way at full speed and my eyes were locked on to it as if I was suffering from tunnel vision. I had never been too fond of dogs. I tried to gain some composure back, making an effort to access the rational part of my mind so it could inform me that the intent of this dog was nothing more than to join in on the fun. But I've noticed over the years that when your mind is already in a state of panic, you don't make the best decisions. So, I turned back around and continued to sprint, ignoring the calls from my buddies to stop and just pet the dog. They were right, of course. My insistence on running was only getting this dog more excited as it ran past my friend in its efforts to follow me to wherever I was leading it.

I cornered the street, turning right while looking back to see if it was still there. I caught a glimpse of the house I had just passed. It belonged to an older couple who dropped by our place every couple of weeks with a casserole or a baked good. The blood drained from my face as it dawned on me that this house was at a cul de sac and I had managed to corner myself between a dead end and my pursuer. Instincts continued to force me to run all the way to the end, placing my hands on the brick wall and moving them around like I would suddenly discover a secret door that had always been there. I was breathing hard, a combination of the sprint and a panic attack kicking in. I looked back at the direction I had just come from, watching as the German shepherd was halting its own sprint but continuing to bark aggressively in my direction. There was no shutting it up as it jumped and moved from side to side, waiting for me to take some action. I kept doing my part and continued banging on the wall, the only sound in my head now being that of this stupid animal yapping away. I screamed at it to go away and leave me alone between sobs. I was slowly giving up and I eventually just turned around to face my pursuer, pleading my case to it. The dog continued, halting once in a while to assess the situation but then continuing to torment me once more. I looked into its eyes and all I could see was an animal who had his sights set only on me. At no moment did he ever look away nor did I ever see him blink. My back was against the wall now, slowly sliding down till I was huddling my knees and clenching my eyes shut. My actions may seem overly dramatic but I really wasn't ready to get pounced on a third time. The barking continued to echo in my head and just when I thought that my heart could not beat any faster, I just wished for the entire thing to be over.

Ever woken up from your sleep when your eyes are still closed and you are still sort of dreaming? The dream feels very much like reality and sounds or smells from your reality make their way into your dreams? Suddenly, you realize you are awake and the dream just disappears and you look around the room, wondering how you just got there. Your brain plays that trick on you when you are transitioning from one thing to another from time to time. In this instance, I'm still not quite sure at what exact moment the barking of the dog merged with the sound of my mother providing ill and unsought advice to the person on the receiving end of that phone call.

It felt just like a dream where I've been cornered and somehow magically, my mother has ended up in this dream environment as well. But the more I concentrated on my mother's voice, the more distant the barking became till my mind eventually decided to set things straight for me. There was no barking. There was no Porsche alarm in the distance calling out to its owner to press a button on a keychain. There was no wind blowing through the leaves of the trees. There was, however, my mother's voice, the sound of the dishwasher putting in some work and a soap opera in the background that probably contained a more dramatic performance than the one I had put together just moments ago. Slowly, I opened my eyes and I found myself in my living room and the street that I thought I was on disappeared from existence.

Chapter 2

It may have felt as if I had just woken up from a dream but I knew this wasn't the case. Let's get some undeniable facts out of the way.

I had gone to school that day and I had definitely caught the bus home. Minutes before I had found myself listening to my mom talking on the phone, I was without a doubt chased by a dog. The finger pointing and laughs from my friends when I met them the next day all but confirmed the events from the previous day. I was also stranded at a cul de sac mere moments before I managed to find myself in my house without ever having moved from that one spot where I finally broke down.

I teleported. As ridiculous as that sounded, even to me, it was the simplest explanation. It was a surreal moment. In any other situation where your mind starts to drift towards a supernatural reason to explain a given situation, it snaps back to reality. However, this time around, my rational mind kept challenging this science fiction conclusion that it had formulated, trying to find various faults in its merits but the complete lack of any explanation, better or worse kept snapping me back to the opposite of what reality says is impossible.

Amazingly, this is not what bothered me the most. Of course, accepting what had happened never stopped me from questioning the occurrence in the first place. I was having a hard time understanding how and why any of that ever happened at all. There was no precedence for this situation. I couldn't understand what caused it or if it could even be replicated. I felt like I was in some science fiction adventure all alone. The worst part about this adventure was that the actual journey lasted a split second and its consequences were significant. The experience of what happened passed so quickly, I wasn't even sure if I had experienced it at all.

One would think that such an event would force you to recreate it right away if only to validate the supernatural conclusion you had come up with to the explain what happened. But, again, your mind doesn't think rationally at that moment. I'm sure my mom must have talked to me when she eventually saw me or offered me something to eat but I remember none of it. I was actually quite oblivious to my surroundings as I was fixated with what had happened. The only thing I wanted to do was to ensure that every detail regarding the incident, no matter how minor, was documented so I could explain how such an event could have even transpired. I was trying to recount every moment in my head again and again but each time I tried, it would be the same scenes, dialogues, smells and details regurgitating. Recounting the memories did not suddenly make me aware of a beam of light I might have seen, a button I may have pressed or a special catch phrase I might have recited. My mind refused to think of anything else until it had analyzed the events from every angle. The reality once again was that I was just replaying those memories in my head the same way repeatedly. There would be no breakthrough and each time anyone or anything distracted me from thinking about it (like being told to take out the garbage or being asked how school was) it would become distracting and frustrating and a reset switch would be activated. I was stuck in a loop for days.

I could not figure out how I teleported. I didn't even know why I teleported. It took a few days for me to snap out of it and finally take action. I started my attempts to teleport once more. I did not recreate the exact moments at first, relying more on doing what any person would do. I would tense my muscles, move my head in the direction of where I wanted to be, even push off with my toes a bit, as if physical cues like those would somehow activate that power again. When all those predictably failed, I tried recalling images in my head of places I wanted to be or fake strong emotions, hoping that either of those would be a trigger.

With more failures came more recounting of events. Had I thought about being back at home at the moment I transported? Possibly, but I wasn't sure. Maybe it was the adrenaline rush from running or being terrified. Was it a combination of the physical clues and the thoughts and emotions in my head? Maybe it was the time of day, what I wore, whom I was with or the air temperature. I had no idea.

Days became weeks and as each week passed, I knocked out 100s of combinations of variables that could have resulted in my very unnatural experience. I even decided to push my friend into the Porsche though this time, the dog was leashed and thankfully so. If I were chased once more, my nervous breakdown would have been imminent. My friend this time around was not amused and I found myself pushed back in return.

Sadly, I was running out of ideas and with each unsuccessful attempt, I grew more tired, helpless and sad. I was having trouble with the idea that this would go down in history as a one-time incident with no explanation associated to it and an event that would live and die with me. I really didn't want to continue living without having an answer to a question that I could not share with anyone else.

Chapter 3

Excerpts from my Life

Time: Summer of 1997

Location: Outside school, after an exam

Event: The re-occurrence

Suffice to say, my predicament had kept me distracted for the two months following the incident. Sixty days of one failed attempt after another had started to affect me in very undesirable ways. My head was often pre-occupied by this one obsession of mine and regularly consumed by it, unable to concentrate on routine interactions I may be having with others or the general environment. Such one-sided interactions had not gone unnoticed either. My family's impatience with my unspoken dilemma soon turned to legitimate concern and while I tried to keep them at bay with clichéd responses, I was now fighting this battle on multiple fronts. My teachers had expressed interest in speaking to my parents and the number of invitations I received from friends and acquaintances to partake in activities were diminishing. Though I guess in the case of the latter, I hadn't expressed much interest in hanging out with people anyway.

Today, I sat in class rereading question eleven for the umpteenth time. The use of the word reading was far too liberal. The words grew distant with each attempt. I wasn't in the mood to be sitting here filling out a piece of paper that will be used later to judge my aptitude. I stared up at the clock. It was 1:15, which I could have sworn was a half hour later than I had expected. I nervously turned the pages to count the questions left and started calculating the math in my head. I had about twenty-five seconds to read, assess the answer and pick the right choice on the answer sheet for each question moving forward. I felt my hand shake in fear, and the pencil I held in my hand started to leave undesirable marks on the sheet. I looked at the person next to me. I did not know him well but he was already on the last page and appeared to look far less jittery than I was. I kept looking at his paper, not with the intention of copying off it but because I was too nervous to look back at mine and see my lack of progress.

A sudden tap on my desk made my body unfreeze as I looked up to find Ms. Chapman looking down at me with a stern yet otherwise expressionless face. Her head leaned slightly as she raised her right eyebrow, trying to draw my attention to the pen she held in her hand. I looked down and she tapped twice more, this time on my answer sheet. The implication of her actions were clear and she did not have to make a point again. She started walking again, adjusting her woolen sweater as she passed the next desk. It was a subtle motion but she sneaked a quick scratch with her thumb before her arms straightened up again. I looked back at the clock to find out that my estimated twenty-five seconds per question was probably closer to ten now. I pushed the questions away and proceeded to fill out the answers randomly. With luck, I would get a few right.

As I walked out of that exam that day, I succumbed to a moment of clarity. My grades this semester would not be making my family very proud. As I walked down the steps of my school, I had a sinking feeling that I was in this downward spiral that would affect my very future. My concern for having to explain my grades in the next couple of weeks to my parents would put me in a difficult situation.

However, with my depression and a sense of helplessness kicking in, I could not see how I would ever recover and get back to living a normal life. Would walking in with a dismal report card become a recurring theme in my household? Would they eventually just kick me out of school or force me to relive the same grade again and again? I was obsessed with an insane incident that I was never going to let go of and it would eventually make me throw my life away, whether in terms of relationships or working towards any career I would decide to pursue. Keep in mind that I was thirteen and I was dealing with the situation like any thirteen year old would do--in an overly dramatic manner.

Still, I had never felt so lonely in my life. I had never felt so alone. I didn't know how long I had been walking or where I was going. I didn't recall if I had ignored anyone who may have approached me during this time. Frankly, I didn't even know where I was or where I was heading, literally and metaphorically. I was just sad. I just wanted to get away from everything and feel ... different. And as I felt the first set of tears roll down my eyes and my lips shrivel up, I wanted nothing more than to be somewhere else.

Reality set in again. Even when you have no idea what you are doing, you are usually aware of your general surroundings. I knew I was outside somewhere. I knew I had definitely not walked into any place or decided upon doing anything specific. I had totally ignored taking the bus home, and instead opted for aimlessly walking in a direction that I hoped would get me to my house at some point. Yet all of a sudden, I was once again questioning the tale that my eyes were painting for me.

One moment I was definitely outside in some unspecified location and all of a sudden, I felt claustrophobic, my eyes adjusting to a far darker environment. I instinctively turned my head to the right and light hit me, forcing me to shade my eyes right away till they adjusted to my new setting. I felt confused about what was going on but the adrenaline had already kicked in. It was undeniable that I had teleported once more. I turned my head away again and slowly opened my eyes, the bright light replaced with rows of seats sporadically occupied by individuals or couples. I turned my head back towards the light and my suspicions rang true. On the screen before me played the first major blockbuster of the summer. I stood in the middle of two rows, hands by my side.

I glanced at the faces of the few who were at the theater to see if anyone had noticed me. No one paid any attention to me. Everyone watched the screen.

I was simultaneously trying to remember everything that

happened in the last two or three minutes so I could recreate this situation again. If the audience noticed my sudden appearance, they kept quiet about it. Should I just sit down and continue to pretend to watch the movie to avoid further suspicion or slowly walk out? It was a simply yes or no decision that I had to make, yet much like my body, my mind had decided that it was temporarily checking out and not performing its decision-making duties. I predicted someone would eventually notice me standing and demand that I sit down.

I looked at the screen again. I recognized the actor running away from the massive explosion behind him and I realized I recognized the characters on screen. I had been anticipating this movie release for months. There was no way I was going to watch this after missing the entire beginning. The blood finally started circulating through my legs and I started running towards the exit, turning my eyes away from the screen to avoid any spoilers.

Not that I could think about that.

All I could think was: I had done it again.

But how?

As I extended my arm and pushed the exit door to the building open, the smell of popcorn and the sound of the racing arcade game at the entrance started to fade away. I looked around and noticed a familiar highway not too far from where I was. Quickly, I was acquainted with my surroundings. Ever since my parents trusted me to make it back home on my own in one piece,

I had spent many afternoons and evenings at this theater, alone or with friends. If I walked west and turned left at the second light, my house would be no more than a couple of miles away.

I walked around to the other side of the theater, where one would find an alleyway with a couple of emergency exit staircases and some large dumpsters. My pace was quick, with my body shuddering with confusion and excitement as I was busy asking myself countless questions. I would try to put the brakes on the different things going through my mind but they would keep racing back, making it difficult for me to focus or slowdown in any manner. I started taking long and deep breaths in the hope to calm myself down and regain some control and composure. I started walking slower, eventually moving closer to a wall and resting my back on it as I slid down. I felt my backpack as I touched the wall, suddenly reminded that I had been carrying it this entire time. It hit me for the first time that I had the ability to teleport things with me. After all, I'd teleported with my clothes on. What other discoveries I would make about my ability would have to wait for another day.

This realization was all I needed as I pulled the backpack to the front and opened the zip of the main pocket and found my notebook and a pen. It was time to jot down details like those, anything at all that felt relevant. Yet, I never did write a thing. I just held the pen in my hand as I stared at a blank page. The act of holding a pen made me feel like I had regained control over myself again and even though I had no idea what to make of anything or what to decipher, I knew it was a step in the right direction.

Ten minutes later, I finally closed the notebook and dumped it all back in my backpack before proceeding to walk again. I was heading in the direction of home, a walk that would take me a good half hour. This was a good thing. I could already feel that my head was now trying to trace back all the steps that led to me suddenly appearing where I was now. I could feel the amount of activity in my head rising but this time around, I had a lot more focus. This time around, I had a small smile on my face.

I wasn't crazy. I no longer had any reason ever to question the events from two months ago. The most important thing of all, what had happened to me wasn't a one-time event and somewhere within me, I had the capability of recreating it.

Chapter 4

I like going to movies with friends, but once the opening credits rolled, the only thing I was bonding with was the movie. On the afternoon of my second teleportation, I had wanted to feel safe again yet alone. Recounting the events, I had pretty much confirmed that I had definitely pictured myself in front of the big screen if only for a brief moment before I ended up teleporting there. While I cannot recount what location I had thought about the first time around, being back home was certainly high on the candidate list. It was safe to assume that I had sub consciously selected a location to teleport to on both of these occasions.

In addition to that, much like last time, my emotions were running high. But it was a completely different emotion. The first time I had been scared and petrified whereas this time around, I felt depressed and helpless. Were strong emotions a requirement for me to perform such a deed or did they serve as a catalyst? I did not know. And I didn't know what else might link the two teleportation experiences. By process of elimination, I had already determined that my attire, the company I was in, location, time of day and actual events did not dictate my ability to change location at will.

At will.

This had been my first moment of realization that I may have had control over this supernatural ability even if I hadn't yet completely figured out how to activate it. At the back of my head,

I had realized that I was once again walking down a dangerous path of fueling my obsession that had eventually saddened me and had made me feel alone; one that I had labeled as pretty much the end of my happy existence but now, I was excited. My experimenting was no longer based on undefined parameters.

More importantly, something even greater had happened. I no longer had a reason to question the events of the first day I transported. I was no longer confused and looking profusely to recreate them. I was a lot more confident that given time, the ability could be replicated once more. I just had to be patient and willing to take my time and put some more structure around how to go about grasping control over this skill. First things first, I had to make an effort to start acting a little more normal again. I could no longer be constantly distracted living in my own world. Much like eating, going to school or helping the family out with chores, my experimentation must now have its own designated allotment of time during the day. They could no longer interfere with a routine that is typical of a teenager.

I also had to make sure there was no one around when I decide to experiment, not just from the location that I was hoping to teleport from but where I eventually end up. Things would have gotten complicated quickly if I had teleported in front of a person who was intently trying to look at the screen. More so, I do not think my mother's heart would have held up if I had materialized in front of her. Since her transplant, her ability to absorb any kind of shock or trauma had severely lessened. Thus, to reduce the risk of accidentally getting discovered using my ability, these became the most important constraints that I had put upon myself as it allowed me to narrow in on the first big decision I made. My attempts to teleport would occur long after most people have turned in for the night. While this guaranteed that I had complete knowledge of my surroundings when teleporting, I was also minimizing the risk of appearing out of thin air in public.

The second issue to tackle was location. It made complete sense that the origin of my teleportation should be from my bedroom. But where should I transport? Not only could I not predict who may be there but it was important that I had intimate knowledge of the location where I will eventually materialize. I was suffering from the classic Star Trek dilemma. I could not teleport myself into another object. Who knows what might happen in such a scenario. I would imagine that when it comes to my body and a light pole trying to occupy the same space, my body appeared to be the more fragile of the two. It was evident to me that before any field trials were conducted, I put together a proper place and scope out potential candidates for my destination.

When I felt threatened the first time around, I found myself cowering in fear at my own home. The second time around, I ended up in another place where I was used to escaping to. Both of these locations had worked as safe havens for me. Home was no longer an option for me to teleport to as it is my point of origin, though if I had been smart about it back in the day, I would have realized that I could have simply transported from one point in my room to another. But my mind was thinking bigger back then and considering I was thirteen, I give myself a pass on that. Movie theaters can be crowded late at night, and I probably don't want to be caught by surveillance cameras. That was the problem with most public places. There was a high degree of chance that some prying eyes, whether human or technology would catch a glimpse of me. More private locations would probably be worse. The few safe havens would be the households of people I knew and I couldn't think of a creepier thing than being caught in the room of a girl I frequently find myself looking at during science class.

My problem rectified itself one day when I happened to be walking back home from a convenience store and cutting through the community park. Kids were playing on the swing while a few other people jogged. As I people watched, a red blur flew by my face while simultaneously, I heard an apology screamed in my direction. I looked in the woman's direction, realizing that her very young daughter still lacked the proper motor skills to throw a Frisbee with precision. She proceeded to giggle while her mother, still screaming out apologies to me prepared to discipline her offspring. Before the little girl could see the disapproving look of her mom, I called out to both of them that it was okay. The mom turned her face back at me as I pointed my finger towards the trees behind me. I started to sprint in the direction of the Frisbee, which had now made its way into the side of the park that was thicker with foliage. As I picked it up, I stopped and did a 360-degree whirl. For a brief moment, I was alone in this decently crowded open space, the tall pine trees blocking the view of an otherwise crowded park bustling with activity. I couldn't help but smile. This is the last place I would have ever even thought of.

The park.

True, who knows who might be jogging there late at night, grabbing a beer or trying desperately to make out with a significant other. But the park also contains trees and bushes with little chance of someone being in a position to see me suddenly appear out of thin air. I had good memories there too, spending my evenings there with other neighborhood kids when I was a bit younger. It would do splendidly as a safe haven. I hurried back to the family and threw the Frisbee back in their direction, not waiting to see if either of them caught it. I proceeded to run home, knowing I would be back out here tonight to mark my point of materialization.

I had a time.

I had a starting location.

I had a landing location.

And, so, the experimentations began and much to my surprise, there was absolutely nothing magical about how I pulled off my third successful attempt at transporting. There was no trick to it. Well, let me rephrase. There was definitely a trick to it, but not one that can just be described in words. Over time, I realized that the trick was nothing more than a clichéd response I would give to someone had I been open to them about my experiences. It came naturally to me.

Let's also be clear that I had no success whatsoever during the first couple of weeks of trying. I was even starting to lose hope again. I must have been trying too hard or over thinking the whole thing. Even that night when I was finally successful for the third time, I must have tried countless variations of inundating myself with emotions and even more variations of how I commanded myself to land up on the north side of the park. The usual flexing of muscles across my body, or timing my blink with the thought of teleporting yielded nothing. I tried to imagine the park in the most vivid way possible. I went as far as to make myself believe that my body was getting light and during the course of my eyes being closed, I was slowly moving in the general direction of the park. Once I opened my eyes though, all I could see was the ceiling fan oscillating at a speed that never gave me any joy. But sometime during the course of trying out different variations, I struck the right cord and I found myself lying down on the grass in between the trees, the light from the stars sneaking through branches. I had been expecting myself to be standing up though and it dawned on me that in all three occurrences, I had ended up at the final destination in the same posture and direction that I had been in prior to transporting. This felt important and another small victory. There was a pattern and once I was done dwelling on this, I had another oddly comforting yet frustrating realization. I had pulled off transporting this third time in a similar manner as the other two. I had done absolutely nothing noteworthy to warrant such an unbelievable event. I was still unable to identify a trigger.

There was no point in trying to find another location for transporting. The park became my staple focal point and it wasn't until I was in bed that I even attempted my new nightly rituals. At this point in time, adding and modifying variables did not feel important. I focused on mastering the skill and then worrying about variations. A few more unsuccessful attempts and I managed to teleport myself to the park again a few days later. Again, nothing noteworthy yet in an odd way, I was starting to feel more comfortable. Dare I say as I've already mentioned before, it was just growing on me. I even nicknamed my ability that time. As if I was appearing at the park surrounded by smoke, I started referring to the ability as poofing out of thin air.

Poof! I enjoyed saying that in a juvenile sort of way.

My fifth successful field test happened just a few days later and that time around, I had all but confirmed the following. Visualizing where I wanted to go was key. I could not manipulate my orientation and physical demeanor during the process. A desire to find myself in the other location was mandatory. I had the ability to teleport certain things with me. Could I move any object at all regardless of size or weight? I had to remind myself that currently, this was not my priority and a topic to be looked into later. Surprisingly, I was warming up to the idea that my personal emotions probably did not play a role though helped set up the required conditions for a successful teleport. With each attempt, I found myself calmer and more in control. I hypothesized that the proper channeling of my desire is probably what triggers the actual event. Easier said than done though. I had no idea what proper channeling meant.

Chapter 5

Excerpts from my Life

Time: Summer of 1997 - Attempt number 8

Location: Home

Event: Transporting at will

"There is enough left for a last serving. Would you like some so I could be spared from looking for a container with a matching lid?"

I was enjoying the food so I looked up to size up what the pot had to offer. The amount left was at that uncomfortable point where you knew you could finish the food but your body would curse you all night. I knew I had a long night ahead of me and politely declined the offer. My mother sighed and bent over the dishwasher, meticulously looking for a plastic lid that would ease her pain. From the corner of my eye, I noticed my dad looking at me. He didn't need to shake his head in disapproval. His eyes did the talking. He motioned for me to go give her a hand.

As I got up to help, my mom proclaimed that she didn't need my assistance and, being at that horrible teenage age, I looked at my dad and shrugged. This was my time to escape. That look from my dad returned.

"Nonsense. You go sit down. This ungrateful child of ours and I will take care of the kitchen tonight," my dad said, noticing the fact that my mom was not doing especially well tonight. I must have been too oblivious to notice. It wasn't that I didn't have a good grasp of my mom's condition but that my dad was correct in his description of me. I was indeed rather ungrateful and continuously ignored warnings signs that would impede on what I had planned for myself.

She took a moment to get up and slowly made her way to the couch. My dad waited till she was out and then turned to me and made it clear that when he had said "we," he had actually meant me. He was going to go and spend time with my mom. This time, my guilt kicked in and I did not argue. He walked over to the couch as well and as he sat down, my mother lifted her legs and rested them upon his. She hadn't even finished putting them down before my dad wrapped his hand around one of her ankle as he proceeded to rub her foot. I turned around at that moment to face the table. This was going to take a while to clean up.

As each dish was taken care of, my mind turned towards the task I had for tonight, and my family became a distant thought. I was particularly excited. This day would be the first day that I wouldn't be guessing if I would teleport or not. I knew it would happen.

That may have something to do with the fact that the last two nights I had managed to pull off two successful attempts back to back and the amount of time it took me to achieve this each night was lessening. At that point, I still wasn't completely clear on what I was doing right. But, I was less surprised each time I managed to land myself at the park. To be honest, I was now more frustrated by the idea that I had to walk back home in the middle of the night and sneak my way back into bed without anyone noticing. I considered that a good problem to have. By the time I was done in the kitchen, my parents had already retired to their bedroom and I made my way up to my room. As I laid down on my bed that night, I felt relatively stress free. I told myself to do what I always do and just go over the motions. Very soon, I will discover the secret sauce and the whole experience will feel like riding a bike.

I opened my eyes. That was it! No actually, that was not it but 'it' was almost it, I guess? I looked at my arm, moved it and realized that I did not know how my arm actually moved. It just did. Medical science tells me that at the moment of the movement, my brain had sent out electrical impulses to my arm and my arm just did what it was instructed to do. I do not know how the impulses were sent, or the route they took. But when I desired my hand to move, it did. All this time, I've been commanding myself to teleport yet I've been waiting for some external entity to magically cause this to happen or having a complete understanding of its mechanics. I had been going about this the wrong way.

I placed my head squarely on my pillow and closed my eyes. There was no precedence for what I was about to test however deep down inside, I knew that when I finally attempted to teleport this night, I would do so without a problem. I moved my right hand. I moved my left hand. And as I decided to move them both together, I told myself to partake in a third activity. I decided to teleport. As I felt the sensation of both my arms slowly rising up as I had intended, the feel of the air-conditioned room was suddenly replaced by that of fresh air as I sampled the different smells emanating from the dew in the grass. I opened my eyes and saw a starry night and the moon rabbit. The feeling of success was overshadowed by my sense of pride. I closed my eyes again.

POOF!

I did not have to open my eyes to know that I was back in bed and resting on a far more comfortable surface. In fact, I never bothered opening my eyes at all.

POOF!

The prickly feeling of the grass trying to pry through my clothes returned. This time around, my clothes managed to suck up enough dew to give my back the sensation of dampness. I stood up, brushing off the wet grains of grass from my shirt and looked to the right. I continued brushing off the wet green blades off my pants and sleeves. I looked around and honed in on a spot.

POOF! I was still in the park but three feet from where I had been standing a second ago. I was no longer attempting to teleport. I was simply doing it. I did not understand what caused it to happen, but I knew that as long as I treated the ability in a similar manner to how I sent instructions to my arms to move or my feet to jump, this new found ability of mine would respond to it. It felt very unreal. I had expected it to feel like changing the channels on a TV, where I press a button and some disconnected operation occurs thereby changing the actual channel for me. This was very different. The ability felt like a part of me, like a combination of a sixth sense and a phantom limb that I had complete control over. I was smiling and had a heavy sense of joy that I could not shake off. I rubbed my forehead to push off the drops of sweat that had been accumulating there and went beast mode.

POOF! POOF! POOF! I could teleport as quickly as I could send instructions to myself to do so. There was no reload time, with my only constraint being the amount of time it took me to visualize a new location and commit to teleporting there. As I kept changing locations within the small confines of the foliage, I laughed and screamed a little in joy. I could not get enough of this superpower and chances were I could have let this go on all night if I hadn't heard concerned voices approaching me. Before any bodies became visible, one final poof and I stood in the middle of my room. Tonight was the night I would no longer have to walk back from the park and sneak my way back to my bed.

The ability to transport myself was committed to the muscle memory of my brain. I could go where I wanted, when I wanted without giving it a second thought, and as I climbed back in bed in an attempt to fool myself into thinking that I would somehow fall asleep that night, the only thing I could dream of was how starting tomorrow, life as I know it would be very different.

"I wonder if all that teleporting today would have any side effects," I said to myself as the expression on my face turned to regret as I whispered to myself, "God dammit!" There was no chance in hell I would sleep tonight now.

Chapter 6

My life is not a work of fiction. Yet, I'd never heard of anyone in real life who could do what I did. In comic books, when our protagonist discovered special abilities, the story follows his discovery with a short montage of said protagonist gaining control over his newfound powers. The montage normally ended with him having the control he desired, a big grin on his face and a very visible feeling of freedom and limitless possibilities.

However, in the real world, when something new was discovered or invented that can now be utilized by all of the human race, this discovery or invention requires far more than a short montage. It required multiple trials to determine safety, quality control, operational environments and most importantly, rules and regulations. I did not have the benefit of working with a body of governance that could help establish these for me. I did not have the luxury of controlled experimentation and testing. If I was a piece of code, the only way to test what I was capable of was in production. And my production environment was the real world, a chaotic place where the wrong decision could get me killed, injured, arrested or worse—imprisoned and tortured for science. I could probably hurt someone else in the process as well. My power may come with a sticker that offered freedom and unlimited possibilities but my real world offered far too many constraints.

I have already alluded to the fact that my newfound abilities stirred a level of paranoia in me. One of my initial fears was if my constant teleportation would lead to undesired repercussions.

What happened if I accidentally teleported myself into another person or object? I had absolutely no way of knowing the configuration of the area I was going to teleport into without being able to monitor it in real time. Turned out, I hadn't gone far enough with my initial paranoia. There were so many factors. I had made the assumption that teleporting myself into another object was a safety issue and thus a top concern, and there was little I could do here other than perform some risky experiments. I was not ready for that. Plus, I was worried about what would happen if people found out about me. I didn't want government agents in black suits coming for me, like they did for comic book characters.

People, cameras and dead ends were prevalent everywhere or at the very least, all locations of interest. In the first few weeks of my newfound ability to travel from place to place, my movements were so constrained that I almost thought it was better not teleporting at all. I guess if I had been a little less risk averse, I would have been able to put a good portion of my paranoia to rest but that was a tale for a different day. Then again, I was patient. And I was content with being patient. It allowed me to create the necessary rules that would govern how I move around. It allowed me to create the rules I definitely needed when my life became far more complicated later on than simply teleporting and the risk that I carried with me to be exposed at any given time. But I'm jumping ahead.

There were other complications too. It was tempting to transport myself in an instance to the mall or the arcade but it would make people wonder how I got there and more so, how I got there so quickly. I could create a web of lies but at least works of fiction have taught me that they have a way of catching up to you. The first rule that was already established was that I could not use my ability in front of another person. Now I had a second rule. I could not utilize my ability to take part in any activity that was scheduled. I had to find traditional ways of transport if I was meant to be somewhere, at least till I wasn't a dependent thirteen year old without a driver's license. If I was to use my ability, it had to be for unscheduled and personal events only. Secretly, I hoped this would continue to nourish my existing relationship with my parents and not raise any red flags with them.

Which naturally lead to rule number three. With 'some' exceptions to the rule, I could not transport myself to areas I frequented or to those frequented by people who know me well. If people talked and information of my whereabouts were shared, I would once again be forced to come up with explanations on my methods of transportation and the speediness of my travels. No. For now, if distances could not be traversed through walking, teleportation would draw unwanted attention.

In the list of complications spawning from other

complications, I had to take timing and visibility into account. I learnt this lesson the hard way when I found myself having a lengthy debate with Ms. Farnsworth about whether I had gone out for soccer practice two weekends ago. An elderly woman whose knees no longer responded the way they used to, Ms. Farnsworth spent the majority of the summer sitting at her porch consumed by the day-to-day activities of what took place on our street. It is easy to label such a person as someone far too interested in other people's lives but I honestly did feel she was a bored woman with very little to do otherwise. That day, I had stayed behind after practice having spotted Brandis, a girl who was in my grade and probably my first secret crush. Somehow in my head, I had envisioned that our mutual presence on this field will somehow lead to us crossing paths, resulting in a conversation, sharing of ice cream on our way back home (in my little make belief land, I had assumed she lived right next to me), followed by many other planned encounters and eventually going 'steady'. Sadly, an important pre-requisite to all this was trying to initiate contact and I was too chicken to approach her. I ended up only watching her from a distance for a half hour and when it got too late, found a quiet spot and teleported back home.

Mrs. Farnsworth did not see me come home that day and later on, as I walked out to grab dinner with the entire family, she was still out there at the porch, her expression turning from concern to confusion.

"Well, I'll be, young boy. I have been out here all evening

because I never saw you come home. I would have walked over if it weren't for these legs. How did you sneak by without me being any wiser?"

My parents chuckled and I should have too. This matter could have been resolved easily. But when your conscience is guilty, it mounts a valiant defense.

"I came home at the same time as I always do, Ms. Farnsworth. You probably didn't see me because I came in through the back," I proclaimed, feeling rather proud of myself.

I was ready to sit in the car, when I noticed the look on my mom's face. I closed my eyes just as she started to question my story. She had been sitting in the backyard all afternoon and evening with her friends. Once again, the matter could have been resolved quickly but my friend Mr. Guilt here felt like it needed to up the ante. With each lie came more questions that could have been avoided if I had just kept my mouth shut. And with each question, a more fantastical explanation was provided. Eventually, my dad whose threshold for pointless and mundane conversations was zero, pointed out to us that retracing the exact manner in which I entered the house sounded terribly exciting but he was hungry for dinner.

I would love to say that this was an isolated incident. I had told myself I would keep my mouth shut if I ever run into a similar situation. But guilt mixed with paranoia is a horrible thing and thus, rule four was established. Time of travel and visibility, unless everyone was unaware of my movements, had to be respected.

With every passing day, a new scenario was unearthed and a rule was created. Some rules were deprecated quickly, and I modified others as life and times changed. I grew to understand the spirit of these first few rules but managed to find room for flexibility in them.

When it did come time to teleport myself, I went through varying degree of rituals. I was too afraid to show up at a location. So I always moved first to an area that was visible to me. After a quick check of the sky for low flying planes or people on ladders, I took to teleporting over to visible rooftops and continuing to keep moving from one to the next till I got to my destination. This helped avoid detection and landing on an otherwise occupied space. When I arrived at my destination, I would carefully peer over the edges to get a handle of my surroundings and make my way back to ground level. The whole experience was rather tedious but over time, it became second nature and I was able to find short cuts. If I took the same path multiple times, I would sometimes skip some of the stops I made in the hopes that the contents of various roofs had not changed.

While I did find this a cumbersome way to make my life a little more convenient, I was also wrestling with the elephant in the room. I had not forgotten about the fact that my condition did not exist in the real world. In fact, it had not existed at all till just a few months earlier. As much as I was interested in learning more about what I had become, I had no rational explanation for why this had happened to me. There was no accident. I was not injected with a mysterious serum. Nothing odd had happened that would warrant the current state of my life right now. Had I always been this way? It appeared unlikely which made me question the timing of why the spring of 1997 was the season I became a supernatural being. Nevertheless, my parents kept health records in the filing cabinets, documentation of every doctor's visit or lab test. When no one was around, I would look through them but find nothing odd. I looked through various places my family may be hiding something just in case they didn't want my condition made public.

After repeated unsuccessful attempts at finding any documentation around the house, cars and other personal spaces, I had built up the courage to confront my parents. The first night I ever approached the subject, my dad had been particularly proud of the soufflé he had prepared. His soufflé included ingredients no baked recipe should. He genuinely believed he had a masterpiece on his hands. My mother of course, would not touch it and understandably, my dad never forced her. But I got the chance to be the victim each time this episode occurred and as I continued to look at her, she smiled back in a mocking way, followed by a quick wink.

Maybe we won't have to eat anything if I just said something now. As I opened my mouth, no words came out. I realized I had never actually thought about what I was going to say. I was not about to reveal myself to them. My dad scooped out a large portion and placed it on my plate. The bottom side revealed a mixture of avocado and beans. I couldn't believe what I was looking at. Today was the day I was not going to play nice. I asked him why he thought those two ingredients belonged in there. He detected I wasn't impressed by dinner. It was my mom's turn to look at me but this was the last straw. Believe it or not, I had been subjected to a soufflé with meat, another with croutons and one that felt more like a potpie than a dessert. Avocado was the last straw.

"Dad, I could sit here and pretend to like it. If I had the ability to run at the speed of light or maybe teleport, I would dump this somewhere and come back to this chair, pretending like I enjoyed this... this thing to the fullest. But I don't have that luxury and I seriously do not wish to eat this," I said as I patiently waited to see their reaction.

Silence. Shock. Did they know about my powers? Did they have them, too? I turned to my mom to say something, then my dad but turned back to my mom. She was silent and shocked all right. But she looked angry, not like a person whose secret was suddenly discovered.

"Don't talk to your father that way," she scolded me.

"Teleport? Where do you get such nonsense?" my dad added, shaking his head. He looked sad, though, as if I'd really hurt his feelings, and I guess I had. "Eat your dinner and be grateful you have one."

My mom was still looking at me. I still had no answers

and I had somehow managed to break my dad's heart, a feat I had felt before today to have been impossible.

I would be subtler every time I would bring up that topic with them again. They were a dead end so I turned my attention to unfamiliar faces around me, gazing over the side frequently to see if I was ever being followed. I would look for the same unfamiliar faces in multiple locations yet if I was under some kind of surveillance, I had found no evidence to support this.

So how did this happen? I took a renewed interest in my family history, questioning my parents about our ancestries, and requesting stories they remember about their grandparents.

Everything checked out. If there were answers out there, I would have to look further than my parents and my surroundings. Sadly, I realized that I was still not ready to try investigating further such as hospital records or breaking into government facilities to find out if there was an active file on me. For now, there was not much more that I could do and I just had to accept myself for what I was and get back to playing around. In the meantime, I would still keep an eye out for any other oddities if they happened to present themselves.

So I started tinkering with the limits of my abilities. My orientation and physical demeanor could not be manipulated. Turned out that I also had no control over momentum either. Any momentum and directionality I started with had to be respected through the course of my teleporting experience. For now, I kept all movement limited to a horizontal plane.

It stands to reason that I have the ability to transport anything I'm in contact with due to the fact that I've never had an embarrassing episode of arriving naked at my destination. I've also never dropped my wallet or phone implying indirect contact is not a limiting factor either. However, the floor my feet stood on, the bed I had occupied every night during the early days had never moved with me either.

Nor have air and dust molecules ever occupied the same plane of existence where I appear. I hypothesized that my ability was very reminiscent of moving my hand. It not only moved when I wanted to but moved the way I expected it to. It was an underlying assumption for me to teleport with my clothes and so I did. I expect to hold on to my wallet during the course of these events and thus I did. I never considered air as occupying the same space during my first initial accidents or experiments. I never expected the floor to move with me. I was transporting the way I expected to have transported. If anything, through further experimentation, I discovered that I had to intentionally leave my wallet behind if I wanted to or show up without my clothes on, which became quite convenient before taking a shower.

By the end of the summer, I had such a great grasp of my ability that I became less interested in what it would allow me to do and more engrossed in how I could manipulate it. If indeed a lot of my power was based upon my desires and a certain expectation, did it warrant bending the rules?

August 15th. I finally decided to take a small leap of faith.

What I thought would take days, if not weeks of experimentation, turned into afternoon of countless discoveries.

Chapter 7

Excerpts from my Life

Time: August 25th 1997

Location: A random rooftop

Event: A leap of faith

Poof! Poof! Poof! This may have been the furthest I had ever traveled. At one point, I ran out of rooftops but my vantage point was so great, it was easy to spot the area around me. I was close to the edge of the city. What lay in front of me was an open road, fields of undeveloped land and an uneven topography. One more poof and I would have traveled a distance much further than I wanted. Behind me was an area that seemed safe. It had a suburban feel where most people were probably looking at their clocks counting down the time before they could make their way back home. My mind was racing, contemplating the unthinkable. Nervousness took over but at the same time, I could feel my knees shaking. I had gotten so comfortable and good with using my abilities. I was so confident. And, yet, day after day, I held myself back abiding by rules and restrictions I had set for myself. However, today felt just right. The road in front of me was empty. The sky was barren. If there were any eyes on the ground or air, they were lost to me. In front of me lay no sign of civilization other than basic rural infrastructure. I looked back at the direction I had just come from and accepted the fact that if I was to turn back around, I'd end up safe but I would also walk away with a feeling of regret. Without giving my mind a chance to debate this further, I took one final look at a clearing at a distance and closed my eyes.

I didn't have to open them back to know I was successfully teleported beyond the imaginary boundary of the city limits. I smiled, not because I felt the weight of some of my self-made chains slide off but because I had taken a calculated risk. I had just stepped onto the long wild grass and I could feel my shoes, socks and skin still intact. Unlike the grass I had encountered at the park that was neatly trimmed, this was much longer and definitely would have required coordination to ensure it didn't occupy the same space as myself had I not decided to throw caution to the wind. It was a gamble I admit, one that I had been avoiding from the first day I gained some control. I should have felt my adrenaline take over at the prospects this presented but instead, I felt a sense of calm and relief. I had taken a very unexpected step towards removing some very different chains that had been weighing me down. That feeling was now replaced with confidence and I had never felt more motivated to keep pushing on. I lifted my eyelids and the light from all around entered in, turning the blurry collage of colors into a more recognizable canvas. My eyes hadn't even finished adjusting but I had already spotted my next target that was covered in uneven topography and loose rock of variable sizes. Poof! I was there.

By all accounts, sharing the same space as a solid object

was a natural fear and my experiment should have failed. But it didn't. At that moment when I stood on the rooftop, I believed I would be fine and I was. I had then teleported myself to an area in the distance I did not recognize. I materialized in a clear spot. It occurred to me that I had simply provided a general area as my teleporting target. I had a hypothesis and I tried it out a few more times. Each time, I either landed in an area unoccupied by a solid object or it was something that I could easily displace.

My hypothesis may sound outlandish but it was simple and for me at least, the only explanation. The universe was somehow working with me, not against me. I expected the grass to move and it did. I expected the universe to drop me off in a safe spot and it did. I now expected water to displace itself if I happen to materialize in it. Hours later, I would confirm this to be true as well.

My gaze fell upon a branch and a thought crossed my mind. I paused for a second. Had my balls really grown three-fold since that moment on the rooftop that I'm even willing to consider this?

It's one thing to let the universe work with you. What would happen if I forced its hand? I got on my hands and knees. I curled all my fingers except the index on my right hand and placed it an inch away from this branch. This was a heavy branch, approximately five feet long with a sizable girth. My weight could not possibly displace it. I stared at my finger. How much of it was I truly willing to sacrifice if things go wrong? A portion of the tip that is barely noticeable. Yeah, that sounded about right. I stayed in that position for what felt like an eternity. I could hear the sounds of little critters making their way around somewhere under the leaves and the birds flying from one part of a tree to another like they just can't find a comfortable spot to rest on. I could feel the wind against the sweat that was rapidly accumulating on my forehead. I would close my eyes each time before I thought I was ready to do it only to realize that the possibility of screwing up were higher in those scenarios so I would snap them open, only to be confronted by the reality of what I was about to do. It was quite the conundrum. Just do it. I repeated that to myself countless times and it wasn't till I stopped screaming that to myself in my head that I felt the calmness come back. I looked at my finger and that branch again and this time, softly, whispered to myself once more.

Just do it.

And I did.

I had been so conservative about my approach that I was completely unsure about how it all turned out. Did the tip of my finger survive? Did the branch move? Did my finger only get as close to the branch that it could possibly can? In a moment of complete spontaneity and recklessness, I once again threw caution to the wind and told my body to move a whole two inches in the direction of the branch.

CRACK!

I stared in disbelief! I had not expected this. And the fact that I had not expected this only quantified my disbelief. For one thing, that crack was not the sound of my nimble bones breaking. My finger was clearly inside the branch and it wasn't snug. Did the branch just break or was I indeed able to now occupy space with another entity? Building on my recklessness, I teleported another few inches and the sound of multiple cracks and my entire hand inside the branch confirmed my initial findings. All around, the branch showed stress fractures. It felt good to have won that little battle with an inanimate object.

Two minutes later, my patience and cautiousness were replaced by a feeling of invulnerability as a nearby piece of rock lost round two. Then, I attacked a metal traffic barrier. It didn't matter what the surface was, my body not only managed to teleport to an otherwise occupied space but caused any object to displace. In the case of these solid objects, it normally resulted in tearing them apart. I looked up at a tree and wished to engage in an epic movie moment. I closed my eyes, and opened it up a couple of seconds later.

While my ears were completely overwhelmed by the sound of a tree exploding, time seemed to move excruciatingly slowly for my eyes as they watched the spectacle of tree barks fly in all direction. There were large pieces of bark, smaller splinters of wood and entire logs bending like a person's knees just gave way. The smaller pieces flew high up in the air while the larger pieces of wood flew more horizontally with speed, crashing into any object in their way. I now stood in the same location another living thing had occupied for decades. Years later, I regretted that I had killed a tree for no reason but at that moment, I was overwhelmed by the sheer awesomeness of my experience and petrified of what this implied. I was a freaking weapon. Under no circumstances could I ever do this to a person or an animal.

The day came to a close a few hours later but as I lay in bed that night, my elevated heart rate was noticeable. For the first time since acquiring my powers, I not only felt control but I also started to grasp the true nature of my capabilities. Tonight would be another sleepless night. School started in just a few short weeks and I had so much more to discover.

Chapter 8

Excerpts from my Life

Time: Back to school

Location: Walking home from the bus stop

Event: Exclusion protocol

The joys of being a teen. An entire summer had passed and one of us finally gained enough courage to speak up about what the majority of us boys now knew. The girls certainly looked a little different from the last time we had seen them. Our emotions were mixed. We had many questions but were more intrigued than anything else.

Mustafa and Manuj, the two idiots I shared the bus ride home with had not stopped expressing themselves and very little of what they said left anything up to the imagination. Manuj had started becoming a bit crass a while ago, a behavioral trait that appeared to have spawned as an attempt to get in with the cool crowd. Mustafa desired the same fate but he played more of a follower role, hoping he may become a permanent fixture in such a crowd by association. As Manuj attempted to use his hands to describe the many indecent thoughts in his head, one of the girls finally turned around and gave him a disgusted look. All three of us turned red and I attempted to distance myself from the other two. Once they were out of earshot though, I grabbed a twig off a branch and broke it, proceeding to smack Manuj with it.

The indecency returned. "Man, I feel just as stiff as that twig you're holding there." He laughed as I stared at the twig in my hand, feeling dirty. Before I had a chance to throw it away, Mustafa came in for the rescue.

"Of course you do. You and that little twig probably share the same girth." Manuj turned red once more. I smirked and walked a little faster, saying goodbye as the other two continued to exchange profanities with each other in an attempt to one up one another.

A short walk later, I entered my home proceeding to engage in routine exchanges with my family on the various notable moments of our day. Apparently, my dad had never noticed the new Italian restaurant on his way to work, the same one that had been open for business since May of last year. My mom offered to tell us about a very pleasant conversation she had with this man who dropped by her work. I decided not to bring up how much better the girls looked this semester. As discussions died down, The TV offered us some expected re-runs while I nibbled on snacks my mother didn't like. I always secretly thought her disapproval was a result of her inability to participate in snacking with us. It had been four years ago that we had found out that she needed an emergency heart transplant. Insurance came through but it hadn't been easy. During her operation, there were minor complications. Her life was saved but another surgery would be required to fix some of the blockages they hadn't taken into account. This time around, the insurance company said no and my mother has lived the last few years living a less adventurous life.

When it seemed evident that I was singlehandedly going to finish off a box of cookies on top of everything else I had already consumed, she walked over and snatched it away from my hands. I turned to protest but my dad, who was lying on the sofa, casually swung his foot into my face to discourage me from getting into an argument. At this moment, he was only interested in listening to conversations that were happening on the TV.

To my dad's joy, I took this as an opportune time to disperse to my sacred space setting expectations that we will once again reunite but not before dinner. I walked up the stairs and entered my room. It had been a tiring day and as I came to lay myself over my comforter, I heard a snap under my back.

The twig had broken in two. I must have brought it all the way home and deposited it on my bed along with my knapsack. I picked up the longer side and stared at it. It was pretty dry and lifeless, as all twigs should be. For a brief second, my mind drifted towards the comments made by my friends and I smirked. Dry and lifeless would probably also be another accurate comparison. My attention turned back to the twig. It wasn't particularly straight either, curving in different directions along its length. My eyes slowly moved to the door. It was closed. A peek outside the window confirmed no eyes were spying on me. I got out of bed and peeked through the window once more, just in case. It wasn't like I was going to leave the room. I didn't need to have a planned out agenda for this. In some kind of a ceremonial manner, I held the stick out and teleported myself a few feet to the left. The twig and I arrived at our destination intact, just as I had expected. I took a hard look at the twig again. I was not as confident about knowing the results of my next teleportation beforehand.

Poof!

The twig and myself were back to our original coordinates. I was less than pleased. This wasn't the outcome I wanted. I poofed again a couple of more times and history repeated itself. My trusty twig and I were joined to the hip it seemed. Another look at the twig, another heavy breath and poof.

I was closer to the window this time but a mere second after teleportation, I heard the gentle sound of the twig making its acquaintance with my bedroom carpet. I walked back to where I had been and picked up my little friend again. The experiment was repeated again with the same conclusion. I walked over and placed the twig in my pocket.

Poof.

I'm sure this time, the sound must have come a tad bit sooner but it all felt the same. I could still feel my keys and the plastic bag that I had been carrying my lunch in earlier today in my front pockets. I teleported once more, this time in the direction of my wardrobe and the clanging of the keys was undeniable as it hit the soft carpet underneath. The plastic bag was of course less noisy and a visual confirmation was required. I had just figured out how to manipulate the expected but I was not done. I picked up my keys and looked at them. I was not willing to risk the next experiment on them so I walked back over and picked up the twig. In a ceremonial way reminiscent of a few minutes ago, I held out the twig again. I looked at it intently to get a measure of its size. Approximately, eight inches sticking out from my hand I guessed if I was to ignore all the curvatures.

Poof.

The stick was still in my hand and yet, I heard an ever so slight sound of a weighted object hitting the cushiony carpet. That stick was not as long as I had remembered it. Maybe five inches at most?

I was not in the mood to repeat the experiment though. I was disturbed by what had happened. To be able to pick and choose what transports with me was one thing. To be able to decide how much of any object went along for the ride felt unnatural and the irony of this was not lost on me. Weeks ago, I had already decimated a tree by materializing inside it. Today, I was able to purposely teleport only a portion of an object. Tomorrow, could it be a person that managed to piss me off?

Today, I felt more dangerous than awesome. It was unsettling to know that I had the means to rip another person's body in half if I chose to. I would definitely get over this feeling in due time but that evening, I felt overwhelmed. Another thought occurred to me and to this day, I regret that I ever let it inside my head. I took the mangled twig and touched my desk.

I looked at the side of my desk to see a baseball bat resting on it. Dirty laundry covered the bottom of the baseball bat. I kept looking at this little chain I had formed in my head and poofed a few feet back. Everything moved with me though the bat lost its balance and fell. I teleported the table back and moved the rest by hand and then I sat on my bed in silence. If I was unsettled before, it was worse this time around.

As the night progressed, I found myself wrestling with the fact that ripping another person in two was the first thought that went through my mind upon making my new discovery. This was the complete opposite of how I wanted to approach my powers. More importantly though, the gravity of my last experiment was starting to hit me. You never realize it when you watch a movie or read a comic book or play a video game. But the simple fact that a superhero or a villain teleports with their clothes on should be a dead giveaway. If something I'm touching and anything that thing is touching can teleport with me, where does it end? I could end the world today by removing Earth from its orbit. I sat down with this single thought running through my head repeatedly. I sat there for hours but eventually, went back down for dinner as I was expected to and albeit a little quiet, I spent most of the night engaging in whatever activities the family seemed happy with doing. Eventually, I said goodnight to everyone and walked back up. My constant desire to teleport myself was overshadowed by one of those rare moments I've had since my life turned upside down where my only wish was to be normal again. I closed my eyes and then proceeded to stay awake till morning.

Chapter 9

The truth was there were many people on a daily basis that annoyed me. These same people could be annoying me while I was in the vicinity of a sharp object or a heavy blunt instrument. I had the ability at any given moment to take matters into my own hand and stab or bludgeon someone.

Teleporting didn't make me a murderer.

But, it could make me a *better* murderer. If I chose to be one.

I was quite sure that nine times out of ten, I could perform the deed before anyone stopped me. It would be so unexpected that no one around us would be able to react in time.

But those were silly thoughts. Irrational thoughts. Of course, I wouldn't actually ever *kill* anyone.

My power felt like an extension of myself; an extra limb as I'd once mentioned. From everything I'd investigated over this summer, it behaved in much the same way.

True, I could rip someone's body in two but I need not worry about doing such a thing accidentally. My powers obeyed me, and it was my will that caused things to happen. My experiments had also taught me that the universe was working with me and it would require a very intentional thought in my head for such an occurrence to happen. As for being able to destroy the world in an instant, that unimaginable weight never really lifted off me and as time went on, I simply managed to develop an ability to ignore the extent my powers could be utilized. Thankfully though, all this subsided my desire to be normal again and I was back to being that special teenager with some very dangerous capabilities. I still had no idea about my origins and once in a while, looked up in the sky waiting for someone far more special than I was to give me a sign. With time, I did that less and less as my calls for an answer never got responses.

I had spent the entire summer experimenting and testing the limits of my powers. I had then switched over to testing the limits of how much my powers could be manipulated. It felt like finding out that your favorite video game had various Easter eggs that you had no knowledge of, or discovering that a shelf in your home housed sequels to a cherished book.

Not till I was back in school and reaching the limits of my testing did I bother to explore what I wanted to do with these powers. Up to this point, I hadn't actually utilized my teleportation in any way to facilitate my life. I had just been tinkering with it substituting the time I would have otherwise spent on my video game console or watching TV. But little by little, I unconsciously started incorporating teleportation into my life. If no one was around, I would use it to avoid climbing stairs, transporting things far too heavy that required carrying, or step outside after dark if I just felt like being somewhere else. Sometimes I would forget to pick something up that I was supposed to bring with me and I would simply teleport back to fetch it. No biggie.

However, it was getting harder to respect the rules I had created for myself mainly due to the fact that I either felt they were becoming obsolete or the intent was of no concern to me anymore. Some of my rules had been created to protect myself but I no longer needed rules to control how I teleported anymore. I became less and less cautious over time. I no longer teleported from rooftop to rooftop to get to where I was going. I would simply teleport to my final location. However, at times, I was getting sloppy. There were times I materialized directly on the ground, taking people by surprised who happened to be walking in my direction. I never felt they would get hurt. Remember, the universe is working in my favor and I could never unintentionally teleport into another object or person. But people would only think that they weren't looking where they were going a few times. Eventually my luck would run and out the brains of those around me would no longer try to create a rational reason for my sudden appearance. My rules were important but I was unsure which ones were relevant and which ones had to go.

Keeping track of creating new rules, deprecating others or modifying them as circumstances changed proved cumbersome and hard to keep track of. As I discovered more and more about myself, I came to a point where I decided that rules will come and go but I needed to abide by three guiding principles. In essence, when I looked back, my rules had all been designed to satisfy these three requirements.

- My abilities could not be made public. My alternate life must remain a mystery.
- I could not let myself get hurt.
- I could not hurt another person.

It was so easy and simple, yet it took me so long to come to a point where I could articulate that to myself. And with those in place, I became far more liberal. My teleportation was no longer just something I messed around with or used as an aide. I was ready to explore and save time and money. Any time I was alone, I became a superhero, finding myself on top of vantage points taking in the world I lived in. I stood on the peak of the tallest hills and buildings and looked down at the city during the day and night if only to feel like the characters in the panels of the comic books I read growing up. Nooks and crannies were all within my reach, if only to have the knowledge that I had been able to access them for no practical reason whatsoever. I would do stupid things, like start the tub, go into my room, and lie down. When enough time had passed, I would teleport sans clothes straight into the tub and wait for the drops of water that were now high above me pause in the air for a brief second only to fall back on my body. I enjoyed feeling each one land on my face, a slightly different temperature than what I had only moments ago felt.

My family was led to believe that I had taken an interest in walking to where I wanted to go and that their chauffeur services were no longer required at all times. The truth was, I spent all that time exploring more and more of the city. There were abandoned warehouses with no security personnel or cameras. I would balance on the beams and slowly walk like a tight-rope walker, pushing the limits of the rusty steel till they would give way. I would teleport out just in time to watch them fall. And when I did not feel the need to see or experience things, it gave me extra time to get things done during the day. Commuting wasted far less time for me now. I was also far more motivated to go places. No more excuses for not joining someone at the movies or the mall because I didn't feel like convincing someone to drive me there or because it was miles away. I was becoming a lot more social now as well as productive.

But the fear of the unknown still continued to haunt me. There were a few occasions when I traversed much further from the city limits. The first time, I actually looked at a picture of a place I didn't know. To be honest, I still had no idea where that place was. But I started toying with the idea of trying to teleport to places I've only ever seen in an image or a video. So I looked at the picture intently as I tried to visualize the double leveled bricked street. I focused in on the emblem of this one shop and very quickly, I found myself in a strange foreign land, staring at the real emblem.

It was definitely nowhere close to where I lived. The change from bright daylight to a night only lit with street lamps confirmed this. It should have been exciting but I had just teleported myself into the middle of a crowded area. As I was still getting my bearings, an elderly couple crashed into me and uttered what appeared to be inappropriate words in an unrecognizable language. The crowd was walking around organically like a single entity and I had just managed to disrupt it all. As I backed away from the couple, I tripped over some object on the sidewalk, falling in the direct line of others making their way to the next bar it appeared. I heard concerned voices all around me, as a small crowd gathered to pull me up. My physical characteristics were much different from the crowd I was around which in itself was a point of curiosity for some.

My head was still confused trying to absorb all the details that it hadn't prepared itself for. I was already questioning my stupid decision to teleport here when another concerned citizen showed up, this time dressed up in a uniform. I should have played it cool but my instincts to protect myself kicked in and I pushed people aside as I began to run from this authority figure. I never looked back to see if I was followed or not but after running and making a scene for what appeared to be an eternity, I finally found a quiet spot for a brief moment.

Clearly, I had not thought this out too well and I made my way back to a friendlier setting. I had to remind myself that my rules and my guarded approach to using my powers had a reason and that incident in the foreign land was a testament to why I had created them. For a period of time, I lay in wait for the police to knock on our door, pull out a picture of me in the middle of some random nation and ask me to explain myself to them. For now, my mobility remained limited even if my desire to visit lands far away continued to resurface.

Limited in a 2D plane that is. The greatest thrill I discovered during this time was not teleporting to a particular place on a map but teleporting upwards. It started with small jumps, maybe two or three feet and I noticed something I had never been privy of before. For a brief moment, I was in a limbo state. The effects of gravity were not felt immediately. I teleported further, daring to go ten to twenty feet. Upon reaching such a grand height, I limited my air time to a second or two so I could avoid building up momentum on my way down. Surely, I could not survive a fall from twenty feet completely intact so I had to teleport myself back to a location before the force of acceleration got too strong. I started going higher and higher, completely disregarding the guiding principles I had just mentioned. I risked someone seeing me but it didn't matter during these moments. I risked getting the timing wrong and hurting myself but the view of the city, the feeling of being surrounded by clouds and then finally, witnessing them under me as I reached new heights made it all worth it. I played around too. Sometimes I took a running start, jumping a split second before teleporting right above the clouds, giving myself a couple of extra seconds to feel like I had just hopped over the moon. I got silly about it really quickly. Much like teleporting up into the sky, I would teleport into shallow water, usually up till chest level. Watching the water explode all around me never got old. Jumping head first and teleporting felt like a torpedo taking off. Looking back, I realize that while other kids were watching cartoons or getting enthralled by seventeen-inch monitors, I was developing a whole new set of pastimes.

My last six months had been a whirlwind. Everything in my life had changed. I had experienced every emotion in the book to its extreme. There were times when I just wanted everyone around me to disappear so I could spend my entire day playing with what I referred to as a new limb, though in retrospect, when you're new to being a teenager, one could have picked a better choice of words. And six months in, I felt like I was prepared. I felt like I could fully incorporate my teleportation into my daily life, maybe even explore opportunities on how I could use these for my financial benefit in the future, or to simply help out those in need. Who doesn't want to be a superhero?

Yup, I was definitely ready. But the universe that had worked with me up to this point begged to differ. It made that abundantly clear when it decided to throw another curve ball in my direction.

Blink

Chapter 10

Excerpts from my Life

Time: Fall 1997

Location: In my bedroom, yawning

Event: Heads up Display

Ugh! The worst thing about spending the entire night traversing across the city is that every morning, you curse yourself for taking those few extra stops on the way back home. I hadn't respected the seven-to-eight hours of minimum sleep recommendation you keep hearing about in schools and on TV. Needless to say, every morning of mine began with regrets. I could just get up and teleport myself to the bathroom but my aching joints and muscles preferred that I slowly make my way to the sink while I engaged in awkwardly stretching different parts of my body. Rubbing my eyes wasn't quite helping the different colors from mixing together as I navigated my way using foggy vision. I was quite sure my face stared back at me in the mirror but I continued rubbing my eyes, hoping for more clarity. Rapidly blinking a few more times felt a little bit better.

After splashing a little cold water on my face, I felt like I had just taken an espresso shot, or at least what I thought an espresso shot would feel like had I been of caffeine-consuming age. For that matter, if I could get past the horrid stench of coffee, maybe one day I would be able to validate my previous claim. As

I went about performing my morning bathroom rituals, my mind was preoccupied with the travels from yesterday. It had been a Sunday and I had traveled reasonably far to a waterpark. Before it opened, a quick teleport into the booth, a swipe of a wrist badge and back out. It had been a good day in the water though I had taken my first step into the world of crime. I was young. I thought little of it. While my buddies stood in line later on to collect their passes, I had already been inside first in line for many of the rides I had hoped to conquer.

I opened my dresser in the hopes of finding some clean underwear. My vision was all but cleared but I still felt like there were some white spots causing me to awkwardly move my head around to gain a better visual. I rubbed my eyes some more as I picked up a suitable pair of boxers. Then I searched for the least used pieces of clothing lying on the floor of my closet and I was ready for the day.

It was the usual breakfast this morning, not just in terms of the food but atmosphere as well. The morning news was playing on the TV babbling on about the latest thing we should all be paranoid about.

Sometimes I felt the entire economy of this world relied upon scare tactics, forcing the consumer to invest and buy things they'll never need, or help finance projects that benefited no one but those who requested the financing in the first place. I turned my gaze away from the TV and looked out the window, patiently waiting for the school bus to show up. I just wanted to get the day started or at least sit on a seat and nap for a bit.

Mom was on the phone gathering information on the happenings around the neighborhood so that when the time came later today, more unwarranted bad advice could be distributed amongst unsuspecting homemakers. Five dollars lay next to my plate of food indicating that today, there would be no packed lunch. I ate breakfast as Mom flipped through the TV channels to put on something more auspicious. When I heard the loud, tired engine of the bus in the distance, the separation rituals began. A quick peck on the cheek, a check to see if I had finished my assignments and frantic waving from the front door, I put the straps of my knapsack around my shoulders as I climbed up the bus, still incessantly rubbing my eyes. Through the window, I could see my dad discover that he could no longer hear the next thing in life to stress over and promptly switched the channel back to watch the smiling local news anchors. A look of satisfaction came over his face. I found a seat somewhere in the middle, sat down and started getting a little concerned about my vision. My eyes didn't normally take this long to clear up.

You know how you don't really notice something at all but when you do, you wonder how you had ever missed it in the first place? Once you see it, it can't be unseen. All this time, I thought I was suffering from white spots in my eye, due to being tired and groggy but those spots didn't normally have such finite shapes. It was definitely a spot, or like a spot— a circle if you will. There was only one yet I had been mistaking it for many. It was the roundest spot I had ever come across. But it wasn't blinding me or anything. It wasn't blurriness. The circle was just there. And it appeared to fading in and out. Is that what it was doing? Blinking.

Camera recorder! That was it. Except it was white instead of red. That was the best way of describing it. Whether you were using an old cassette-based video camera, a mini DV recorder or even a video capture device on your computer, the standard recording symbol is that red blinky thing. That was exactly what I was seeing and it wasn't an illusion. I stared at the spot or focused on it for a long period, not sure what it was or what to do with it. I kept trying to answer the question but later realized I was just repeating the same question repeatedly without trying to formulate a theory. I was getting a little tense. Abnormal characteristics that manifest themselves on me have known to result in unprecedented situations.

I had discovered teleportation purely by accident. It just suddenly happened one day without any previous provocation on my part. Mr. Blinky appeared to follow a very similar MO. Had I just acquired another ability? And if so, what was the symbolism behind the little blinking area in the corner of my eye? It would stand to reason that my eyes are my body's visual component and the blink reminded me of a camera. Were my eyes recording things? Because that would be pretty awesome. But where were the recordings going? My head, of course, you dummy. That wasn't the right question. Could I view these recordings? What resolution were we talking here? Was it recording everything? I focused on the blinking dot so did this mean the recording is focused on the dot and made everything else out of focus? Was this an endless recording? How did I switch this off? Was this some kind of passive ability that was always switched on?

I had no answers at all. I didn't even know if I was right. All I had was a blinking dot and the only level of control I could think of was to see if I could switch it off. After trying out the few obvious things that crossed my mind, all resulting in failure, I was reminded that my teleportation ability relied heavily on setting the right expectation and expecting the ability to respond accordingly. I told the white dot to stop recording, to switch off, to go away but much to my frustration, none of it was working.

Sigh. This was going to be another day where I was going to be distracted. By lunch, I had started and given up on using physical cues. I had tried closing my eyes, blinking as well as moving my eyeball towards Mr. Blinky, all to no avail. At one point, I was hoping to ignore it like one hopes to ignore an ambient sound in a room. But no matter how I occupied myself, at some point, Mr. Blinky would always become the center of attention. Was I going to spend the rest of my life with this stupid anomaly?

By the end of the school day, I started calling it my completely useless heads up display, providing me with absolutely no useful information whatsoever. It wouldn't go away no matter what I did and as my frustration became some kind of morbid amusement over my uncontrollable dilemma, I started finding it easier to ignore it from time to time or to be less distracted by it, a 180-degree attitude shift from what I had experienced during lunch. Time healed everything, I guess. I even managed to summon up the courage to sit next to Brandis, my secret crush, on the bus. We must have had some conversation but I was mostly busy just looking at her. Every time she would break eye contact and look away, I would sneak a peek at the rest of her. Those moments lasted split seconds but they were imprinted in my head for weeks to come. I would describe but in retrospect, these memories involved who at this point to me, is a child and considered inappropriate. I don't quite recall what I must have said but as she got off the bus, she handed me a little piece of paper with something that looked suspiciously like a phone number. I smiled at her as she took her final step off the bus, the shy smile on her face only briefly available before all I could see was her hair.

Before the bus even had a chance to move, Manuj had already made his way next to me and held his hand up in the air. High fives were shared all around, even though that first phone conversation with her would go nowhere as I would find out that coming weekend. But, hey, small steps.

The rest of the day followed the usual pattern other than the absence of any desire on my part to practice my teleportation. The curiosity around Mr. Blinky had gotten the best of me, even if it was less bothersome that late in the day. A part of me worried that this was some kind of a side effect, a thing that I had feared from the very early days of teleporting. Another part of me felt the need to dismiss that. All around me, it started getting dark and when I had all but forgotten about my little friend in the corner of my eye, I realized that its white color had not dimmed at all while everything around me was becoming a silhouette. I guess I was going to live with this forever. I wasn't annoyed anymore. I guess it was just one of those things that's always there, like a pain people complain about having for years. You just learn to accept it.

I accept you, Mr. Blinky.

Mr. Blinky disappeared.

That was rude. Just when it and I were becoming buddies.

Had I set the right expectation? Did I have to accept it? Hey, Mr. Blinky, come back. It didn't. It was gone. And before I go down the path of providing details on all the different things I tried to bring it back, I'll just come out and say that it never did return and that day was the first and last time I saw it.

At the end of the night, I lay on my bed confused and my mind was blank. I really wasn't sure what to contemplate even. Should this entire thing just be ignored? It's tough to deny it ever happened but at least it wasn't like the first time I teleported. It was a blinking dot. I did a quick check on my bed to see if I could still teleport just in case, you know, that little dot was a warning telling me I was about to lose my power. Everything was fine. I tossed myself to the side and stared at the wall, contemplating what my future had to hold. I looked at my night table and confirmed that the phone number I had acquired today was lying there safely. I adjusted myself again, getting into a more comfortable position. At some point, I fell asleep.

Chapter 11

Excerpts from my Life

Time: A week after Mr. Blinky

Location: Mall

Event: Disappearance

The mall was crowded. Way too many people and we were nowhere close to the Thanksgiving shopping season. With the weather starting to get slightly nippy now, I guess most people just preferred being indoors. It was 6:30 in the evening and I was running a little late. I assured my mom I'd meet up with her in about a half hour so I could try on some clothes and then, I ran off to the food court. My friends had already ordered without me and as revenge before I could be stopped, I decided to simply smooch nuggets off their plates. The food was quickly demolished, the money was placed on the table and we went over the plan one final time. Between the group of us, we had enough to buy four games or possibly five if there were enough used ones in stock.

Four games it was and with a bit of money left over, sundaes for all too! We each picked a game we wanted to play with the promise to trade whenever we were done. We all took one look at Mustafa. He groaned.

"Look, I like to enjoy myself when I play."

"Dude seriously. One week. If you're not done by then,

we're just going to come and take your game from your house," one of us replied. Mustafa continued to protest his treatment and Manuj smacked him in the head as I decided it was time for me to depart. The others decided to follow suit.

Goodbyes were shared in the form of hand signals as we each departed in different directions. I walked over to the usual stores my parents frequented, hoping against hope it wasn't one of those stores I disliked. Looking back, before the days everyone carried a cell phone, finding people was a nuisance. Not to imply I didn't have a phone. But every minute cost us money and texting wasn't quite popular back then.

They ended up being in a place that I had no interest in and much to my dismay, Mom held shirts. Mom babbled something about how she'd found the perfect thing for me to wear for some occasion I knew little about. I tossed my game to my dad who displayed some great dad reflexes in catching it mid-air, as I grabbed the clothes she had picked out and walked towards the changing room. From the corner of my eye, I could tell my dad was trying to check out if he would enjoy the game I had selected or not discreetly. He pretended like games were for kids but I'd come home on many occasions to find a different cartridge from the one I was playing previously in the console.

That shirt. I didn't even have to put it on. It personified everything that could go wrong with a shirt. Checkered. Seriously? Did she just finish watching *Clueless*? As much as I loved my family, I was counting down the days before I could legitimately move out, using college as an excuse. It would definitely remove a lot of constraints on my ability to travel using my very special medium. Being able to buy my own clothes would be another plus (note: It was not till I actually went to college did I realize that my mom could still ship me clothes whenever she wanted to. Paying for postage never turned out to be a barrier for her). I slowly put the shirt on with a look of disgust on my face and stared at myself in the mirror as I whispered, "Four more years."

I moved the curtains out of the way, turning back one last time to look at myself, shaking my head in helplessness. If I had been concentrating, I would have noticed the elevated step walking out of the changing room but I didn't, resulting in me tumbling over and almost crashing into a rack of clothes nearby.

"Oh crap, I hope no one saw that."

I was pretty loud. The sound of things slowly falling to the floor went on for a second or two after I had already found myself face to face with it. People turned around. They looked at the clothes on the ground that I had spilled with my hands while trying to regain control as I fell. The person who worked there looked annoyed as she looked around the clothes trying to find a culprit. Surprisingly, she completely glanced around me, looking very confused and eventually she stared in different directions as if to see if a child had run away. As she walked over, I tried to move my foot before she crashed into it but I was a little late. She stumbled slightly, but regained control right away, looking back in a half-hearted attempt to investigate what might have caused it. Everyone else went back about their business like I wasn't even there. I could hear the sound of my mom approaching, calling out if I was done changing so she could take a look. To this day, I'm glad I never said a word otherwise the situation would have gotten weird pretty quick. I slowly got up and as I thought she and I were about to lock eyes and she would notice I had been in an accident, she looked right past me at another rack, still trying to embarrass me by screaming out loudly if the shirt she picked out fit me or not. I wouldn't be surprised if the entire store now was somewhat curious, waiting for me to emerge out of the changing room to judge.

I did not fully comprehend what was going on but in the last few months, I had gotten used to oddities. The best thing to do was a reset. I climbed back into the changing room and mentioned to her that it will take another minute. I had a dilemma. Had I activated another power that had remained dormant until now? If so, I had to switch it off in the next minute. Common sense dictated that no one was able to see me during the little fiasco I pulled a moment earlier. I called out to my mom again, asking her some pointless question. Her response back to me confirmed that she could hear me. Was I just invisible? I told myself to stop being invisible and took a deep breath before stepping out. She turned around and gave that smile every teenager hates. The smile that says that the clothes looked just as amazing on me as she expected and just as horrible as I had foreseen. It was evident that other pieces of clothing similar to what I just tried on would now be picked out, tried on, taken to the cash register and eventually discarded as is tradition when shopping with my mother. By the end of it, we will walk out of this entire mall with only a handful of new things.

What happened over the next hour or so was a blur as I found myself very jittery and impatient. Another life changing event may have just occurred that I could not fully confirm. Teleporting was one thing. There was no denying that at one moment, I was on a street cornered by a dog and the next, in my living room. This was ambiguous. Maybe no one saw me. Maybe I was invisible and when I commanded that power to shut off, it did as I had expected. Or maybe nothing had happened at all. I was relying on the actions of others to determine if something had indeed transpired. Had I bothered looking in the mirror to see if I had a reflection? I may have but I was clearly not thinking. Maybe my subconscious wanted to avoid looking at that ghastly shirt again.

It took a while but my incessant calls for going home and feeling bored finally got to my dad, who told my mom we needed to go. Mom said if it wasn't for her, this family would be wearing the same thing all month and be an embarrassment but she took the cue and things started wrapping up. My mom spent the walk to the car muttering to herself as my dad juggled with the keys while explaining to my mom for what seemed like the hundredth time to realize the rest of us just didn't care as much about how we looked. The drive back may have been the longest one I ever had to endure.

Once I was home, like a good little boy, I told my mom that I would take the clothes up and hang them. I could see the subtle look of pride on her face as I walked up the stairs and then immediately darted to my room. With the door closed and the clothes deposited on my bed, I walked into the bathroom and stared at myself in the mirror. Even before I attempted anything, I was playing out the different scenarios in my head and setting up expectations of what I was going to see. I wasn't doing this on purpose. My mind was just working on overdrive. I cleared my head of these thoughts and decided to put on my disappearing act.

I'd mentioned a few times that teleporting now came naturally to me. It was second nature. I knew how to command myself to utilize this ability now and as long as I knew what I was doing, it all just worked. So while I had been preparing myself to spend the next few weeks figuring out how to use my invisibility cloak, it came as a bit of a surprise that my first attempt produced immediate results.

I almost fell backwards. Not only had I not prepared myself to achieve results so quickly, I was not prepared for what disappearing entailed. I just faded in an instant. But more so, my mind could not grasp the reality of what was happening. I could see my hands, my body, my clothes, yet there was no reflection. I lost control of my limbs and had to steady myself to stay up and stare at the mirror, which showed me nothing of value. My eyes just darted around hoping to catch something from the corner of my eye, but try as I might, there was no reflection. I did not exist as far as this mirror was concerned. My breathing became heavier and my heart raced. This wasn't excitement but a panic attack. It's not that I couldn't handle being invisible. But this experience was just too surreal that my brain was having a hard time accepting it as reality. Ever heard of the hollow mask illusion? As a hollow mask spins, your mind automatically auto corrects itself and visualizes both sides of the mask as convex forcing the image to stick out even though it knows one side is concave. Your mind has trouble accepting something as a reality even when presented with the necessary evidence.

My disappearance only lasted mere seconds as I told myself to stop being invisible or risk driving myself mad. I was back and I fell to the ground. Seeing myself appear out of nowhere was just as bizarre.

I spent the next few minutes just listening to the sounds of my breathing. Soon, my chest expanding in and out was the only thing I could feel. I finally moved, only to wipe the sweat that had accumulated on my temples. I was not ready to try again but in those few seconds during my first attempt, I had learnt a lot. I could see myself but only through my eyes. Much like teleportation, my clothes along with my possessions became invisible with me, yet the floor I stood on did not. I did not even want to imagine the vertigo I would feel if I intentionally tried to make the floor disappear with me. I had no reflection in the mirror either. Could I interact with things? I had not thought about that. I got back up and looked at the mirror to confirm if I was invisible again. Same dizziness took over and I closed my eyes but maintained my invisibility. I opened my eyes but did not look at my lack of a reflection this time. Instead, I picked up my toothbrush. There it was, in my hands. Slowly, I gathered the courage to look at the mirror again, setting up the wildest expectations so I had some semblance of being prepared. I gazed back up and there it was, a floating toothbrush. I managed to keep my composure but none of this was making sense to my brain at all. As it continued to deny everything that it was witnessing in front of me, I pre-emptively leaned in to support myself before disaster struck. I looked at the reflection of the toothbrush again, ignoring the fact that there was no hand holding it. I focused in on it. A second later, I gave the command and the toothbrush disappeared. This was insane. This was crazy.

This was fantastic. I let go of the brush and its reflection returned as it raced its way to the tiled floor. I picked it back up and looked at the mirror again. I transported myself three feet back. My reflection was none the wiser. I made the toothbrush visible again and teleported. The toothbrush became a low budget special effect from some straight to video movie. The child in me began laughing, thinking of all the ways this could have been used to scare the bejesus out of everyone. The toothbrush of death!

I put it back on the vanity, forgetting the fact that it had been on the floor a few moments ago and that tomorrow morning, it would find its way back in my mouth. As I walked passed my bed, I remembered to put the clothes away before my mom's pride evolved into disappointment. A thought crossed my mind and I stopped walking.

I proceeded to fade out again and then poofed into the living room, which was at that moment occupied by every member of the family. They continued to talk, completely unaware that they were being watched. I didn't stay too long though at the risk of having someone crash into me. Invisibility did not grant me the ability of being undetectable. I teleported back into my room and realized that teleportation was about to get a whole lot simpler. Cameras and inquisitive eyes were no longer going to act as barriers for travel anymore. The boundaries of how far I was willing to go were about to expand.

Chapter 12

I was a teenager. I could teleport. I could become invisible. Let's get it out of the way. Within days of mastering my new ability, I did what every boy my age would do. The local college was located in our town and I made my way to the girls' volleyball practice with no real desire to watch how much they've been improving their game over the semester.

Fifteen minutes went by and the girls finally decided to call it quits. I felt my heart race a little more, the reality of what I was about to do setting in. I was finally about to do what every guy standing around the field right now was only dreaming about. I teleported in the direction of the building the girls were heading in and eventually made my way inside.

They didn't waste any time after entering the locker area. Before I even teleported in, the bench was lined with discarded sweaty shorts and girls, ranging from the shortest to the tallest, toned to the slightly more voluptuous. They all stood talking and messing around with each other in different stages of undress. I was a horny little boy in a playground, unable to choose which ride to experience first. My eyes simply darted from the blonde to the redhead; from the one who still hadn't draped her towel to the star of the team who stood confidently lecturing the other girls. Then, I saw Beth.

Beth had dropped by the house many times. My mother and her dad were part of the same book club and with no one to look after her at home, her dad would often bring her along. I would say that I'm going to bed but in recent years, I would rest at the top of the staircase and in the most precarious way, try to catch glimpses of her. Today however, jackpot.

The sounds of everyone else around me became a distant hum. The majority of her body was currently exposed in front of me and I felt like my legs were frozen in place. No matter. I didn't need my legs to move anymore. As Beth grabbed a towel and proceeded to make her way to the shower, I silently teleported.

Her top was off and I stared at her back, waiting any moment now for all my wishes to come through. Images of Brandis that were imprinted in my brain were slowly disappearing, making way for whole new albums. She finally turned and I... just stared. The pounding sound of my heart was becoming deafening. She stood under the shower, the water quickly moistening her hair and forcing a sliver of it down her neck, helping it create a path for the rest of the droplets to follow. I was still in disbelief. Night after night when she would come to our house, I would be happy if she came into view for a brief second, fully clothed. Now here I was completely violating her. I did not think I was during that time but I'm much older now and I can't make any excuses for my behavior or actions.

As I continued to move my eyes from the top of her hair all the way to the blue tiled floor where she slowly turned her feet as she showered, I failed to notice the slight commotion behind me. Beth was far more in tune with her surroundings and looked over. For what felt like an eternity, our eyes locked and the pounding in my heart, which I thought could not get any stronger was about to pierce through my chest.

How did she know I was there? Who alerted her? What is going on behind me?

I turned around only to find a couple of other goddesses in their birthday suits staring directly at me with a quirky inquisitive smile and a confused look on their faces. My palms felt sweaty till I realized it wasn't sweat at all.

I raised my hands and looked at them. Moisture.

Moisture all over me. I brushed it off and the girls jumped back, watching the show of water magically dispersing itself in various directions. I stopped what I was doing and once again, just stood there, in a state of shock. I heard footsteps behind me and I turned around just in time to see Beth's body moving towards me. She was just as curious as the rest and moved her hand towards the floating moisture in the air. I jumped back, almost crashing into another girl. I lost my footing and as I fell, I reached out to anything I could hold. A redhead's towel came off as I pulled on it in an attempt to break my fall. What started off as innocent inquisitiveness turned into a bizarre event for everyone involved. I had seen all I needed to see, no pun intended and made a quick escape. I was back in my room, my heart still racing but not because of the wonders I had witnessed that afternoon.

Nevertheless, I can't deny that I enjoyed the experience.

However, it wasn't lost on me that out of all the different ways I could blow my cover, that may have possibly been one of the worst ways the world could find **outabout** me. What do I do with my gifts? Stare at unsuspecting girls like a pervert. I would be lying to you if I said the want to go back into a girl's locker room hadn't crossed my mind, but I avoided doing so for a good few months.

My experiences, of course, weren't limited to that one little incident. Much like teleportation, I experimented a lot with my new power and what I was quick to learn was that invisibility behaved in a manner that followed little logic. If I had my keys in my pocket and became invisible, I had the ability to make my clothes and my keys invisible. By virtue of that, it would stand to reason that I could make everything around me invisible as well. However, this was not the case. Unlike teleportation whose rules I was able to manipulate, invisibility had a lot more restrictions. I could not create an infinite amount of daisy chains with it. Looks like I could change the entire orbit of Earth but not make it invisible in the process.

However, I could still pull off making objects invisible through indirect contact if there was a real expectation for them to go invisible. An item inside a box would go invisible if I held it. Multiple layers of clothing would disappear along with me, and so would all the laundry I had stacked in my hands even if I wasn't touching every single layer. I could touch a table and make everything vanish on top of it, yet I could not touch a keyboard on a desk and make the desk disappear. There was no mathematical formula to this. The only criteria it followed was for me to find the results of an invisibility episode reasonable in my head. That sounds vague but that is pretty much how it worked. This was one of those times you would hope that your mind did not think logically.

Also, unlike teleportation, there wasn't much to experiment with my little disappearing act. I learnt the majority of what there was to learn very quickly and most of the lessons learnt were pretty straight-forward. I've all but covered them. You see me or you don't. Of the things I could make disappear, I could selectively choose to make one or many reappear back. That was about it.

One would think with these powers, I could sneak into any place in the world, unravel the secrets of Area 51, make my way to the Toys R Us warehouse and get early access to the latest movie merchandise, get the inside scoop on important information, whether it was something that impacted things on a national level, or simply finding out the results of a test. The truth however was that I had the ability to run away with no way to be traced if I chose to and I could disappear at will. But I was still not undetectable. My principle guideline of always remaining a mystery was my highest priority.

My alternate self did not exist in the minds of others and that condition must remain that way. Yet, randomly opening doors, things suddenly disappearing or moving, and sounds that had no source of origin would create panic and suspicion. Suspicions created investigations. Investigations revealed mistakes, such as DNA, hair and fingerprints. My physical presence exists in any place I venture to even if I could not be seen and I must respect my limits. So, I continued to operate in a manner where I would not raise any red flags yet decided to broaden my horizons. I continued to use my powers to further explore the world, now leaving the confines of my city and using photographs, TV images and such to navigate the country. I remained invisible during these moments to avoid any video evidence of my whereabouts in an area I couldn't have possibly travelled to on foot. I walked on remote empty beaches at night as I took in the smell of the wet sand, felt the wind in my air and listened to the calming sounds of the waves crashing into each other. I walked in the water, to avoid footprints. This new-found freedom made me discover new ways to use my abilities! The first day when I was about to return back from a beach, I noticed the sand all over me. I wasn't too sure how I would explain this and I realized I did not need to transport any of the sand back with me. It hit me that I was thinking too small. I could choose not to bring back anything outwardly touching my clothes. Instant laundry!

I stood on rooftops of major cities, taking in the lights and sounds. I would try to walk briefly amongst the people to see how they interacted and what they did. I sampled food at famous restaurants I had heard about straight from the plates that were ready to be carried out. Some patrons would not get their money's worth those nights. I swiped my first beer, too, and regretted that action right away. I still think all children should be made to try some. I can't think of a better deterrent than actually being forced to taste that stuff for the first time.

I took to watching midnight shows at the local theaters where the seats were empty and ended up saving a bunch of money. Sometimes, though, in order to keep my social life intact, I was sometimes forced to watch the same movie twice while pretending to be completely blown away at certain moments. I still remember two years later when I watched The Sixth Sense. I should have been nominated for an Oscar for the performance I gave when the twist was revealed to me for the second time.

The more I discovered the world, the more of it I wanted to experience. Nights were getting limiting. Not everything was open and it was dark outside. I enjoyed people watching and unless I was in a more metropolitan setting, those out and about were few. I switched over to traveling during the day for brief periods when I knew I would be alone and uninterrupted. These moments never lasted long but I enjoyed the five or ten minutes of escape. I was rather amused as a fly on the wall when I ventured into Wall Street and observed the happenings at the stock exchange.

An entire method of business that made you infinite amounts of money or made you lose it all, not because of the performance of an actual service or product but by mere speculation. I didn't get it. I also started observing how things were made. I would go to factories all over the country, sometimes watching the manufacturing process of a car on an assembly line or completely switching gears and observing how pharmaceutical companies test out their life saving products.

I eventually ventured into more international territory and once that happened, there was no going back. Traveling halfway across the world was very convenient, with my nights coinciding with their days. If I thought the beaches I'd seen here were great, the ones in Asia were beyond amazing. I saw natural marvels I hadn't even dreamed existed, random rock formations sprouting out of the water or forests so thick, I could walk the entirety of them by simply jumping from one canopy to the next. It was like being in a video game or a cartoon where the artist could make any world they wanted to except that the world that I was witnessing was real and everyone I knew along with myself had been oblivious to its existence. Pictures and videos around me limited my inspiration so I started frequenting the library, heading straight for any books with photographs of this beautiful world. Books on nature and engineering feats were the best and anything I liked (and usually, I liked everything), I committed to memory or checked the book out so I could bring it home. Some nights, I would go to ten different places, experiencing the streets of Paris for a few minutes and then heading off to the Panama Canal. I made a quick trip to see an artist perform a street show in Morocco and then made a detour to Alton Towers, and rode the latest roller coaster on an empty seat. I was left speechless one day when I accidentally happened to chance on the Maeslantkering. I did not even know what it was when I saw it. I was in the Netherlands to see the windmills I had to study about in my books in school but I teleported to the top of the barrier and felt it swing all the way. Humans had outdone themselves with this invention.

And then there were nights when I may have planned to make multiple stops across the world but then decided to get completely mesmerized with something such as the Northern Lights. I made more discoveries, such as the fact that invisible or not, I was not immune to the environment around me. Man was not designed to stay in -30 for extended periods of time, whether Celsius or Fahrenheit.

But some of the best moments I ever spent were in the savannahs of Africa. The timing was tricky but I often made my way to a different country during the wee hours of the morning to observe a hunt. It wasn't easy finding the big cats and I would have to teleport from one location to another countless times before I found a lone cheetah or a pride of lions out and about. I always had to remind myself that I was still physically present so I would find barren branches from which to observe from, if one was available, still keeping an eye out for a snake or a monkey that had lost its way. I made connections with certain animals that I would frequently observe. The bonds became strong and in hindsight, maybe irresponsible. The more you care about the world, your intentions for limiting interference is truly tested.

I once saw a pride of lions get dangerously close to a family of warthogs I had been following for a while, and I became involved. The pair had recently had a litter of piglets and I'd be damned if I let anything happen to them. The mom and dad were on guard while I observed the movement of each lioness. My heart thumped and I was ready to teleport the babies and the parents away at a moment's notice. This thankfully did not come to pass that day but I would be lying if I hadn't once in a while teleported a weaker animal away from the range of a larger predator to avoid confrontation.

In a few days, I had conquered every continent. I had stood on top of Everest (or at least I think I did. The pictures never gave me a clear indication of the summit). I had rolled in the deserts of the Sahara and taken a dip in the Devil's pool in Victoria Falls. I stood in the middle of the Ali and Nino statue in Georgia as they passed through each other night after night. I marveled at men and women in wingsuits as they jumped off cliffs and experienced their own adrenaline rushes. I was fourteen and had seen more of the world than almost anyone else had.

The question of how and why I had these abilities remained unanswered, though I continued to search for answers.

I started tracking my family sometimes to see if they'd say something or go somewhere that might reveal a huge family secret. I learnt things about them and their habits I wish I didn't but nothing that hinted at a family history of superpowers. I kept an eye on my physician as well and my teachers. But there was no suspicious activity to report back.

In case I was somehow being tracked, I sometimes would walk into an alley and suddenly disappear, hoping to see if anyone walked behind me to investigate. As usual, my attempts to find more information about myself yielded nothing and all I could do was hope for these feelings to subside. They eventually would.

So I went about my business as usual. Every day, a new city. Every night, a new country. The world was my playground and I would hand back the video games my friends and I had pooled in money for without ever playing them. All those things seemed so trivial to me now. I maintained the minimum requirement for a social life and ensured that my grades were in order. But I had far more important things to do than figure out which universities I was working towards applying for or what my career would be. I had already found my calling.

Chapter 13

Excerpts from my Life

Time: Fall of 1997

Location: Philippines

Event: Confrontation

I can't get into the events that took place that day without providing some more context regarding my guiding principles and my paranoia. One day, I knew this would happen and when it did, I would break down a barrier I had set up for myself not only to avoid detection but also to block myself from manipulating world events. My mistakes along the way would catch up to me and I would be outed or worse, cause unintended consequences.

It's understandable that if you're reading this, you're probably sitting and wondering why I was being so overly cautious. The probability of me getting caught in one of those acts was unlikely considering no one is out there really looking for an entity such as myself. My face on a traffic cam in Chicago was of no consequence. It's sort of true but I was not worried about the immediate consequences of my actions. I was worried about where I felt my life would eventually take me.

Even during the first few days when I started exploring, I had seen things that I did not like. I had seen people do things that I did not like. Petty crimes here and there and people generally being assholes to one another. I stayed out of it. But much like preparing to rescue those piglets, I had known that if I ever encountered something that I couldn't ignore, I'd have a decision to make. And so, every day, I prepared myself. I could remain incognito if people didn't believe that a magical being had interfered. I could remain a secret if people weren't even sure what happened. What would drive suspicion was if I also deliberately left evidence around to give plausibility to their stories. No one believed a person when they talk about an object moving on its own or the same person being in two places at the same time. But people get suspicious if some precedent has been set that can be corroborated by a certain threshold number of people or by documented evidence. If random acts could eventually be quantified as a pattern (and they have a tendency to do so over time), anything could be made to sound plausible.

And thus my paranoia.

Things changed for me in the Philippines. I went to the yearly Masskara festival in the city of Bacolod. It was pretty and colorful. It was rhythmic. It rose from a terrible tragedy involving the sinking of an inter-island vessel. Dubbed the festival of smiles to cheer up the population, the festival now occurs yearly, allowing people to don masks and dance on the streets.

It was a great pick me up after a long day, though it was still daytime here. I watched the festival for a while, taking in the sounds and listening to the people speak without having any knowledge on what they were going on about. Conversations were being had not just on the streets but amongst those participating and at some point, I stopped watching the festivities and turned my attention to the city itself. It was a decent metropolis, inundated with life and a general sense of joy. I started moving in between different rooftops to explore what it had to offer. It was not the oldest of cities, yet it still offered a lot in terms of historic buildings and artifacts. Shops littered the entire city grid and just as I was teleporting from one roof to another, trying to discover what the next alley had to offer, I had to pause for a second and look back. I felt uneasy about what I may have caught from the corner of my eye. I teleported back and peered over the edge of a building. Below me were the back entrances of some commercial shops, almost deserted due to the festivities currently underway. Almost deserted. The three youths towering over the smaller one were the only signs of life and those three really didn't seem to be friendly. I moved in closer, teleporting to lower ledges, ensuring I didn't lose my balance or knock something over.

I could not understand the words but the tones were definitely aggressive. The little guy was holding his ground but barely. He was clearly intimidated and at any time, would not be able to hold his rebellious composure anymore. The voices got louder and with that, the possible victim here attempted to be more defiant, even as his voice cracked.

I climbed down to an even lower edge, preparing myself for the worst. The three grew closer and more threatening and the kid finally seceded. I was hoping this was the end of it, and that the thuggish individuals would walk away knowing they had somehow won a symbolic victory. But the hope for that diminished when they started getting ready for a more hands-on lesson. The one on the right grabbed the young boy's collar as the kid went into a state of panic, blurting out what sounded like apologies or cries to let him go. In mere seconds, he was completely broken down and I felt myself grow angry. They played around with him, slapping him or lightly kicking his shins. My fingers clenched up but I held together. They screamed at him. His protests were dying down, a look of hopelessness set in, and his otherwise silence only broken with heavy sobbing. He attempted to voice some words as he cried, yet no tangible word came out.

It was an image that I had not forgotten to this day. His face marred me forever, getting recalled at the most random of moments to change my mood, no matter what the setting. I saw it each time I saw injustice in the world.

I was ready to scream but instead, I just closed my eyes. I had already decided what was going to happen next. I looked up and teleported to a higher rooftop. They were kicking him now but I had to ignore it to keep my sanity and to ensure I didn't end up killing myself. The timing had to be precise and I could not afford an injury. I looked back down, not at them but right below. I tried estimating the timing and the drop but I gave up. I had to rely on pure instincts. I jumped.

I waited to gain more momentum than needed to make a bigger impact. Two seconds went by. Three seconds. Any faster and I think I would have risked having to come up with excuses that I would be sharing with a doctor. Poof! I materialized above two of them. I had a split second to brace myself.

I lay on the ground, limbs a little shocked from the fall but moving as expected. Muscles were a little sore, too, but nothing I couldn't walk off once the adrenaline wore off. I had rolled off those two older boys mere moments ago. Poor souls. They had no idea what had happened. The kid they were picking on was still cowering and hurt and was not aware of anything that had just happened. But the third guy was at a loss for words. He would start asking his pals something numerous times and then just stop, having a hard time processing why his friends fell to the ground in such an odd fashion. The other two were slowly getting up, looking around. Clearly, they had felt a tackle and were naturally looking around to see if anyone was there. There were no words being shared, just random grunts, sighs and sounds of pain. I sat in standby mode, ready to pounce if the beatings resumed. A couple of questions were finally uttered around what happened and if everything was okay. No coherent or sensible answer was provided.

Our kid here had finally looked up, yet he was still unable to do much. He did not look like he was in good shape but was now aware of the situation that he was no longer the primary point of interest. In a stupid move, he tried to slowly drag himself away, putting a bit of distance between him and his antagonists in the dire hope that they will forget about him. That wasn't going to happen. Soon, his shuffling movements caught their attention again and they proceeded in his direction, as if to take the anger out on him for the stunt I pulled. I was not going to let this happen. I got up and ran, my footsteps distracting all four to turn in my general direction. A few feet from them, I jumped and teleported in their near vicinity, knocking them down. Confusion now rose all around me as the three tried pushing each other off, each blaming the other and questioning why they're knocking each other to the ground. I guess an invisible entity running the show here was not even an option.

I wasn't sure if this would be the end of it so I pre-emptively tried one final thing. I grabbed a stick lying on the tarmac next to me and banged it against a piece of metal. That got their attention. I teleport to the next piece of metal I could find which happened to be behind them and banged on it! They turned around again. Third time's a charm and they turned once more but this time, I saw fear in their eyes. Gone was the confusion and look of pain. They looked like gazelles aware of the fact that they were getting stalked but not sure where the danger lay. The kid was scared as well but I hoped he knew the theatrics weren't meant for him.

I stopped what I was doing, allowing for a split second of silence. I grabbed another piece of metal and teleported within a yard of them. I waited till they were somewhat looking in my direction and banged the two pieces together. Clang! One of them ran. Another stumbled and backed away. The third probably shit his pants. Less than a minute later, my invisible self was left on the street with just the cowering boy.

I did not do anything after this to help him. I may have traumatized this kid enough. I did not know anything about the Filipino culture but I hoped he believed in some deity who intervened. I had taken a big gamble with what I had just done and this was going to be a test of my theories. I started teleporting back and forth, trying to keep an eye on the thugs while tracking the slow movements of this boy as well. I needed to know where they lived. It was obvious I had to monitor them over the next few days and see how this unfolded, even if I could not understand anything they said to anyone. But I worked with what I had and for now, I was mainly interested in watching the interactions, reading the body language and hoping no one would be led back to the spot where I had decided to grace these boys with my presence.

I slept late that day as I kept a watchful eye on the first four people I had deliberately exposed myself to in any capacity. None of them seemed to understand what had happened to them. The kid talked to a few people who were concerned about his condition but their attention was focused on taking care of the child, not investigating any claims of a ghost haunting an inconsequential back alley. As for the other three, I never saw them use hand gestures or speak of an altercation, probably out of embarrassment. To the best of my knowledge, over the next few days, neither the kid nor those bullies ever made it back to that alley nor was the kid bothered by those antagonizing him. A week passed and I was finally breathing easy again.

The guiding principles seemed more important than ever to me now. I could totally feel the adrenaline pumping through my body. I may not be very big but I knew I had the ability to help others. I was almost looking forward to my next encounter and that scared me a bit. Did I really want to help others or did I enjoy the thrill of putting people in their place? Did I find some comfort in exercising my brand of justice, to essentially be the hand of God without having to justify or check with another if my actions were just? I had trouble differentiating between my intentions and it was obvious to me that I had to make it a priority not to pursue them or to do so sparingly. If during my travels and adventures I happened to come across a situation that required interference, then so be it. Otherwise, it was too dangerous for me to go seek it out. I could already feel the effects of getting desynthesized to such acts and the last thing I wanted was to feel a certain sense of thrill in them. I was not ready. It didn't stop me from remaining cautious. I always kept a watchful eye over those I've interacted with and this kid was no different. Over the years, I followed his life and it appeared he either forgot the incident ever took place or stopped dwelling on it. Nothing special became of his life but so far, he's led a happy one. That was all that mattered to me.

Stick Figure

Chapter 14

Approximately one year ago, I discovered my ability to teleport from one location to another. Give or take a few weeks, I discovered about six months later that I gained another ability, one that allowed me to become invisible. I could combine these two abilities in various different ways. For the one year that I had access to what people only dream about, it may look on the surface that I did not have a lot to show for myself. It was not like I tried to change the world in any way, as is expected of people in the works of fiction I grew up reading though I may have impacted the lives of certain people and creatures from time to time.

No, the year had been about self-discovery and opening myself up to possibilities I had never imagined. When people my age were thinking about becoming doctors, architects, movie stars or just doing well enough to get a decent job, I was slowly giving up on a lot of that and was only interested in learning more about the world. I wanted to know what it looked like. I wanted to observe the natural world, and marvel at how an entire eco system managed to live in perfect harmony. I wanted to know about the people, how they interacted and lived and why was it that a person in a developed world living in a villa on the beach had trouble making do with so much while a family in an impoverished corner of the world that had never practiced proper birth control continued to provide for itself and remained content with the simple lives they led. I wanted to see the beauty that existed everywhere around us and slowly, I was warming up to not turning away from the filth as well. As much as the incident in the Philippines pained me, it was impossible for me to assess and understand the world if I only looked at it through a single lens. I was definitely curious and currently, not sure about what I wanted to do with this knowledge. But I knew that this lifestyle would now define me and that was okay. I didn't need a high paying job or a social status to validate myself. I had more than anyone could imagine.

And, yet, with these powers, even as I broadened my horizons, I continued to create barriers for myself to ensure I was able to respect my guiding principles. I was still too afraid to do some things. Even with my abilities, there were some places I wouldn't or couldn't venture to at the risk of injury or certain death. It was important to remember that not only was I detectable but also vulnerable.

Life was about to change once again for me, though. I was about to gain a lot more and this time around the gravity of what ends up happening to me did not take weeks or months to realize and fathom but an instant. Looking back, I remembered how every few months, my life kept changing but I don't think anything was ever as important as what was about to happen. I would no longer live in a world of restrictions. As long as I did not do something stupid, I would have no reason to fear eyes, cameras, people or objects running into me. Most important of all, I would no longer have to worry about hurting myself. For the first time ever, I would truly be able to operate in full anonymity.

Chapter 15

Excerpts from my Life

Time: Spring of 1998

Location: Home

Event: The return of the HUD

Approximately one year since I first teleported.

About six months since I learnt to vanish into thin air.

And on this day, it returned!

Well, it didn't really return. This wasn't Mr. Blinky but my eyes were definitely seeing something again. It started off as a white spot just like last time till I was able to recall that day during the fall. I had to remind myself not to accept its existence. If I did, it may go away like last time.

It was early morning again and I had just climbed out of bed. This time, I did not make it all the way to the bus. I was staring at myself in the mirror when I noticed the little thing in the corner of my eye, like some kind of a prompt waiting for me to take action. The problem was, I was genuinely groggy from last night's adventures on an uninhabited island in the pacific that I had decided to hike. It was a small island and it had taken a couple of hours to get from one corner to the next. Every so often, I would break away from the hike to follow a random lizard about. I was exhausted this morning.

I splashed water on my face, trying desperately to show

some semblance of being fully conscious. The blurriness around what I thought was still Mr. Blinky was slowly fading but not fast enough. In a few minutes, I would hear the calls from downstairs to come and eat what could only be described as a lazy breakfast and that would mean an endless amount of distractions. Why couldn't these things happen on a weekend?

Six months. While I waited, I started wondering if this was happening according to some kind of a timeline? Was I going to get gifted with some new ability twice a year? I wasn't totally sure if the appearance of Mr. Blinky was a precursor to an ability. In reality I had only seen it once before and I had no confirmation that this lead to anything. But it felt right to think something was about to happen. And something did. Two things actually and I was not happy with the timing at all.

I left the bathroom and sat down on the bed. I was finally able to properly focus on the dot in my vision. It wasn't Mr. Blinky. It was something else. It was some kind of a person with a broken limb? Wtf does that imply? I was having trouble concentrating on any of this as my dad's dreaded calls to come downstairs kept getting louder. I eventually gave in and climbed down the stairs.

It was a lazy breakfast as expected. No effort had gone into it because Dad had made it. My mother had decided to sleep in. This day of the week was when she went to her part-time job even though she was advised against doing so. But a woman like her, who had spent her entire life being active, needed more to do than just sit around the house. It came at the price of resting a little more before going to work and that meant Dad was in charge in the kitchen.

Dad should never be in charge in the kitchen.

As I munched and tried to concentrate, I kept getting interrupted by my dad in his hopeless attempt to bond. It wasn't so much that he desperately wanted to be much closer to his son. My dad was a bit of character. At that moment while we sat on the table, he probably wanted nothing more than to not get into a conversation with me but now that he was assigned the label of a dad, he felt no choice but to take part in such social norms. Don't get me wrong. He loved me to death but he wasn't much to make small talk.

He asked me if I was still interested in the vacation plans we had been making forever. Pfft. If only he knew what I considered vacations now. I must have committed to a lot of stuff I would probably regret later but I solely concentrated on figuring out this stick figure person. My dad appeared frustrated. He had clearly made the attempt to bond with me like dads should. On the one hand, it made him happy that he could get back to his usual routine. On the other hand, it probably made him feel that he would be judged as a horrible parent. From the corner of my eye, I noticed that he simply shrugged and went back to his newspaper. I went back to obsessing over my little friend.

It was the oddest thing ever. Why was there a dislocated limb? The prospects of what that implied concerned me. My intentions of not wanting to accept this stick figure were reaffirmed for the moment.

I heard the bus in the distance and promptly took off, not waiting to clean up after myself. I heard the door shut loosely behind me as I made my way to the large yellow vehicle, which was still a bit of a distance away from my house, currently picking up Manuj. I decided to continue walking over instead of waiting on the sidewalk. I hoped there wasn't anyone chatty on the ride over to school today. I found an empty row and sat down. Manuj took a bit of offense to the fact that I did not sit next to him but Mr. Cool decided to act all aloof, like it didn't matter. I wasn't interested in how he felt. I wanted to be left alone. For the moment, I placed my knapsack on the seat next to me to subtly encourage anyone walking in to find another place to sit.

I looked at Mr. Stick again. It was definitely a stick figure. It was white … no … not really white. At least not as white as that dismembered limb. There was something off about it. The white was there but there was something else that kept changing. I focused and noticed it was nothing more than the color of the seat in front of me. Was the stick figure kind of Opaque? I turned my face. Still white and now a touch of blue, letting through the color of another student's school bag. This stick figure definitely appeared to be see through. I wasn't sure what that meant. The dismembered limb no longer looked like a limb though. My stick figure had two arms and two feet. Maybe this disjointed thing was just a stick? Why was it moving back and forth?

It dawned on me then that Mr. Blinky was not so much blinking as just disappearing and appearing back. I kept thinking it was something implying a recording. Yet, a couple of weeks afterwards I discovered I could become invisible. I wondered again if this was a precursor to a new power? Did I have the ability to now become see through? I may scare a lot of people but I'm unsure how that helped. What was that little stick trying to do, though? I followed its movement. It kept going around the stick figure in a continuous rotation. This wasn't making any sense at all. Desperate to solve the puzzle, I got reckless again and started commanding a magical stick to show up. I told myself to become see through. None of it was working and the stick figure remained. I chuckled, somewhat mortified at the next possible explanation I was about to test out. I imagined what it would be like to only occupy a 2-D plane. Nope, that didn't work but it would have been hilarious and mind boggling had that been my new ability. Jumping and crouching would be my only means of avoiding … wait a minute.

That stick wasn't going around the stick figure. It was going through it. I just assumed for some reason that it was going around. Maybe I didn't like the idea of anything hurting me. But, at the same time, the stick figure was opaque. My heart raced once more. If this meant what I thought it meant, it was the answer to most of the problems I had been running into all this time. *How convenient.* Almost too convenient.

The stick could not have any power. If anything, all

power was displayed by me. If I was to assume that in this eight-bit representation, that stick figure personifies me, then it was safe to assume that I had the ability to pass through things.

That was the end of it. My little friend in the corner of my eye disappeared. Had I guessed the power correctly? All of a sudden, I had the presence of mind again to realize that I was still on the bus. I wanted to be reckless and give it a shot but now, someone was sitting next to me and any open experimentation or weird behavior was not going to go unnoticed. My eyes fell on my knapsack and I pretended that I needed something from it so I picked it up and stuck my hand in. I lay my hand on whatever I could find. My fingers ended up grasping a book, probably one from my geography class. I lay my palm flat and closed my eyes, like somehow that would make a difference. I issued a command to pass through that book.

It was the weirdest feeling. One second, I could feel the book against my sweaty palm. The next second, I still felt like my palm was lying on top of something yet I could also feel it wasn't there. Nervously, I moved my hand towards what would have been pushing against the book but I felt no resistance. I stopped and stared. A portion of my finger appeared to protrude out of the bag.

My shaky movements caused my finger to glide, like the surface of the bag was some kind of a holographic image. I jumped a little, pushing my hand back into the bag in the process and receiving a startled, yet stern stare from my seat mate. I waited for him to look away and proceeded to peer inside my bag only to jump back again in a state of panic. A quick jolt, a subliminal thought and my bag went flying while pieces of literature found their way across the floor, people's hair and empty seats. The guy next to me was genuinely frightened. As people recovered and looked around, trying to find the origination of the disturbance, all eyes eventually turned to me. No one was quite sure what happened and how it happened and I only had a moment to devise a response.

"Dude! Who the hell dropped fireworks in my bag? This isn't funny!"

Yet, I said that with an ever so slight grin on my face and the combination of my smile and the unbelievable story I had implied in those few words resulted in laughs all around as looks of confusion were now replaced with everyone thinking something awesome just happened on the bus. Nobody could get over why the book exploded. Everyone turned to each other as if dropping fireworks in my bag was a very plausible activity conducted by one of the pranksters on the bus. Accusations were thrown around and as much as everyone deep down inside wanted to pretend that they were the mastermind behind this antic, no one came forward as the culprit.

Someone picked up my bag and threw more things around, others joked about what excuse I would have to come up with during class and I decided to play along and join in on the fun. By the end of it, good times were shared by all. Jokes would be made for the next few days and years later, during a chance meeting with someone I hadn't met in ages, they'd bring up this very story.

As we got off the bus, I checked my schedule for the day. I had a few classes and labs, but nothing to submit and no tests to take. I took a trip down to the nurse's room and faked an ache in more than one part of my body. A quick call to my parents and my mom rushed over to pick me up. She looked concern as most moms would and pulled her phone out of her purse as she proceeded to drive the car with one hand.

"Mom, what are you doing?"

She didn't feel it was important for her to go to work today. This was of course, unacceptable to me.

"Oh my God! Can you stop treating me like a little child! I can take care of myself!"

She turned to me and said, "Of course you can," and she put her phone down. However, the look in her eyes didn't match her words. I could read that she herself didn't feel like going to work today. Her movements looked tense, like they usually do when her chest is in pain. A level of guilt kicked in but only for a moment. I was a bit of an asshole son. I stopped looking at her and stared ahead for the rest of the trip home, not giving her a reason to reconsider staying.

I've taken many such actions in my life during my teen years that made me want to go back and slap myself.

We finally made it back home and miraculously, I was

feeling marginally better. After providing enough assurances that I could get through the rest of the day without her supervision, my mom left for her job albeit sadly, leaving me in an empty house with an infinite amount of questions. After verifying she had left the driveway, my day began.

I was pleasantly surprised that I did not fade or become transparent when I utilized my new ability. But, if I felt weird about teleportation or vanishing, this was a completely new level of unnatural. I passed my entire hand through a wall followed by throwing things up in the air and letting them fall on me. They passed right through and fell on the ground. Much like invisibility, my mind initially had a hard time comprehending what was happening. When I decided to walk through the wall, instead of a panic attack, I felt nausea take over and was forced to throw up in the sink in the kitchen. I proceeded to clean up the mess I had made when my gaze fell over a knife. I picked it up and without a second thought placed it over my finger. I was feeling nauseous anyway and was right by the sink. If an accident occurred or I got sick again, I was already ready. The knife went right through, or at least it tried to as there was nothing actually there for it to pierce. My body, though visible, was clearly not there, like it was occupying another plane of existence.

Yet, I held the knife. It made sense. I wanted to hold the knife yet wanted my other hand to be gifted with my new ability. I could selectively choose which part of my body was experiencing this effect. I looked down and phased my feet out of existence. I still stood where I was, not falling through the floor. I commanded myself to go through the floor and I did. The shock was overwhelming and thankfully, instead of phasing back in, I teleported. That was some quick thinking. Otherwise, I'd be trying to explain why the laminate in the kitchen was torn to shreds.

Years later, I came to call this ability "going ethereal" after playing countless video games where characters manifested such powers. It worked remarkably well with my other abilities too. I spent my day transporting, going invisible and ethereal all at once. I filled up the tub and tried walking on water. No splashes. The water passed right through. Another trip to the girl's locker room was already in the works now.

It was amazing. As long as I remained ethereal and invisible, I was undetectable. I had no boundaries. I still had limitations. I could still leave fingerprints if I decided to phase back into what I started referring to as existence, but as long as I remained ethereal, this would not happen. I could not interact with another soul either but I could be anywhere I wanted to be and no one would know. And just to be sure, I stood up on a weighing scale. It registered nothing. I stood next to a mirror and breathed out. No fog. I poofed outside and ran aggressively towards a bird. It did not move. It had neither seen me, felt me nor heard me. As far as it was concerned, no one was watching it. I walked back to the house, realized it was locked and teleported back in. I stared at the wall again. By now, my mind should have gotten used to this.

What would it be like if I successfully walked right through it this time? What would my eyes see if I wasn't preoccupied by blowing chunks of breakfast out of my mouth? I was afraid. I had no idea what to expect but I needed to know. Slowly, I made my way towards it as I pre-emptively calmed myself down. No matter what happened, I had to tell myself to not phase back in. Just teleport. I went invisible just in case I teleported without thinking. My foot went through followed by my knee. I raised my hands up. I had moved the majority of my body through. I rested my face against the wall, having not gone completely ethereal. I rested all my weight and phased, eyes open. I didn't see anything. It was just black, like someone had turned the lights off. I kept moving, losing my bearings. My face appeared through the other side and I could see the kitchen cabinet, from the inside with the plates. My eyes were not completely through so it felt like being in a buggy video game where your character gets caught in a wall. I passed all the way through and just stared at myself for a while. I was having trouble processing what I had just been through, literally and figuratively but I was dealing with the situation far better than last time.

I looked out through the kitchen window. The bird, still drinking from the fountain outside was none the wiser at what had transpired moments ago. I teleported back outside, inches from where it was.

"Boo!" I said.

The bird did not react. I took a moment and looked around to ensure there was no one in the vicinity. Still, to be more cautious, this time, I repeated my experiment with a gentler voice. The bird almost crashed into the sides of the bird bath as it tried desperately to fly away. Excellent. It appeared that much like selectively choosing which part of my body remains ethereal, I could do the same with any sound coming out of my mouth.

Till my mom came home, I kept experimenting though there was not much more to learn. Mostly, I was having fun instead of wondering how I would utilize my new power. I already knew that tonight would be a very different night. I had been gathering a list of places to check out for a while now and barring unforeseen circumstances, what was in those places would no longer be a mystery to me.

Chapter 16

It's fair to say that I did suffer a bit of disappointment. Area 51 had been a bust. In retrospect, it actually offered a lot of amazing things to see and an abundance of picture and video opportunities to share that would have made me millions but I was out there looking for something more relatable. A supernatural or an alien presence. I found neither. The personnel who worked there didn't mind the Area 51 conspiracy theories either. A single myth allowed tourism for an entire area and fueled countless plot points for movies and TV. They genuinely seemed like they were happy to help keep the myth going, unofficially of course.

It also turned out that the majority of celebrities lived like everyone else with the exception being their line of work and the amount of money they had. Their houses were beautiful and their cars were speedy, yet their lives were a bore, characterized by the same mundane conversations and rituals I would find in my own home. In some cases, I did come across a more than usual amount of drugs and sex but this stereotype was perpetuated by a select crowd.

Speaking of sex, I did spy on the opposite sex once more. It was thrilling at first, a boy's fantasy, but halfway through, I felt a sense of guilt. I did not feel like I was engaging in an activity that was right and even at fourteen, I didn't just feel like I was violating someone's personal space but possibly betraying them, even if they didn't know who I was. A year into observing people without their knowledge, what hit me was how unsuspecting people were when they are in their most vulnerable state almost like transmitting a message out there that if you happen to come in their vicinity. I felt like I needed to do the right thing and look away. I kept getting that vibe, as if not turning around put a stamp of a pervert or a creeper on me. By definition, it did. The thrill left me that night but my desire to engage in this activity respawned from time to time. All those nights ended in much the same way and if anything, the duration of these engagements only grew shorter. Looking back, I'm glad I eventually took the high road even if it took me some time to get to there. I won't lie though. The urge to violate that trust does creep up from time to time but I learned to control it.

My new powers only made me more determined to find out who I was. I finally had the means necessary to move around without drawing suspicion yet I was met with more failures. I regularly faked the need to see my family doctor again and again and after my appointments, monitored their activities. I wore gloves and sneaked files out of their drawers without ever opening them, spending hours every night reading for any details I may find that indicated the doctor's interest in me. I broke into the hospital I was born in as well and did the same. I never found anything noteworthy.

Computer files were much harder to get. I would distract employees and then utilize their unlocked PCs to navigate. These moments were brief and usually, I had no idea where to look so I finally took to looking over their shoulders and noting down their passwords, hoping to come back at a later time and work uninterrupted. I would spend nights scurrying through the databases, searching for my name or anything related to my likeness. My efforts bore no fruit. Thankfully, I never had the government show up at my doorstep. If I was indeed special, a sudden interest from employees at the medical center trying to find information on me would have drawn attention. I was relieved and frustrated at the same time.

I ran into the same trouble trying to spy on government agencies. In fact, they were worse. I neither knew where to look or when to look. If all else failed, I had hoped to gather intel about things hidden from the general public. But the government workers were just as boring as celebrities, constantly concerned about budgets, power and covering their asses. This fourteen year old was not interested in any of this. As a last ditch effort, I visited Area 51 once again along with other quarantined off areas under government protection to see if anyone or anything there would shed light on my existence. Everywhere I looked, I would hit a brick wall.

I was often depressed, unable to rationalize my own existence. The manner in which I gained my new powers was too structured. The way my powers were complimenting each other was too methodical. Yet, there was no evidence so far of any external force unless you looked up in the sky and wondered if it was Him. I was impressionable and at this point, I was not ready to be dismissive of a higher lifeform. Hell, I was sure there would be people laughing at anyone claiming they had manifested the type of powers I had without showing proof. I could no longer turn my face away from the prospect of considering that something even more supernatural than me existed. God would be a hard one to prove but I could at least change the focus of my investigation to try to seek out alien life.

I started frequenting newsstands with the goal of trying to read up on the less believable stories of the day. I could not engage anyone directly but I would travel to the locations where the stories originated from, making it a point to visit the local precincts and governmental buildings. I would follow people of interest around, hoping to uncover a secret door or a hatch that would provide the answer to all my questions once I stepped inside them. Suspicious facilities were toured illegally by me. Restricted area signs were not respected and at night, I would watch the movement of any cargo going in and out of the facilities.

And time after time, I kept teleporting back to my room completely empty handed. Some of the stories I followed turned out to be hoaxes immediately, others showed no evidence of the claims and sometimes, I would run into a nut-job. I would give them the benefit of the doubt though. I would follow them for months on end to see if they had any other experiences or try to find a familiar pattern amongst them. There would never be anything concrete and thus I would continue sitting in my room staring at the wall after every trip wondering what to make of all this. Maybe this was a good thing. Sure, if I discovered something, it would explain what I was but it would also intrinsically tie me to a larger design laid down by others. Maybe having the freedom to decide what I wanted to be came at the price of never truly understanding why I was subjected to this predicament in the first place.

And just as the previous times I had passionately pursued learning about myself only to show nothing for it, I managed to eventually lay the matter to rest and look towards what brought me joy. For months, I'd spent my time sitting amongst the trees, experiencing the African safaris from a safe distance. Now I walked amongst the herds of animals, letting them pass right through me as they went about on the yearly migrations. My ethereal powers allowed me not to get subjected to environmental conditions such as a slippery floor or harsh temperatures. I would find myself sitting on icebergs, watching the larger sea mammals feeding for hours on end and gracing me with a breach from the salty water from time to time.

It was at this time that I experimented with my powers even more. I found myself in West Bay, Roatan, one of the calmest beaches I had ever come across. The visibility in the water was great. The salinity was high as well, pushing your body back up and minimizing the amount of effort you needed to continue floating at the top. This was a good location in case something went wrong or at least it made me feel that way psychologically. I walked in, not feeling the water at all. I kept walking as the water rose over my knee and up to my waist. Being in water was always an uncanny feeling. I was surrounded by something very familiar, yet, it was like a hologram, something I could see and hear but neither touch nor smell. My feet felt the same way. I could feel I was walking on something yet I could never distinguish one surface from another. The floor and this beach felt the same.

The water was up to my neck now but I did not stop and kept going. I was a step away from breathing underwater and I was preparing myself for nothing to happen or to push myself up in the water as I gagged and choked on water that was far too salty. I experienced neither as my body, due to natural reflexes, decided to hold its breath. It took me a couple of seconds but I slowly pushed all the air back out till I had none left in my lungs. The moment of truth was upon me and I breathed in again. I kept breathing in and out yet what I was taking in and pushing out was unknown to me. No water had gone in. There was no air around me either. Was my body just responding to an action it had performed all its life? I tried to hold my breath again but this time, intentionally and as expected, I could not hold it for more than half a minute. My breathing was performing an intended function yet when ethereal, my environment did not create limitations to this act. For the life of me, I could not figure out the science behind what was transpiring.

Something swum by me. My head darted to the left,

hoping to catch the tail end of whatever I saw. As I should have anticipated, my vision was completely blurred out as it should be under water. Something else swum by I thought. No, it was just sand from the sea bed rising as I dislodged a rock. My visibilities was severely impaired and I smiled and teleported away, knowing that next time, I needed to bring some more equipment with me.

The next time came and as I teleported directly underwater, I had a scuba mask on and much like discovering all the beauty I had seen on land, I now understood why countless people on tropical islands spent an hour putting on their heavy gear two to three times a day to submerge themselves and put their lives in danger. The world was far more colorful and vivid under the ocean than it was above. A few more dives in, I realized that if I only kept my head ethereal, I could still feel the water all around me. That felt a lot more natural though I was unable to do this at greater depths due to pressure build up. During those times, remaining completely ethereal was the only option. I continued to breathe fine and did not experience any decompression sickness, nitrogen narcosis or all the other things divers worry about.

I touched a manta ray swimming by near the Big Island in Hawaii. I watched the cleaner fish eat parasites off a large Mola Mola as they would visit the reef, like it was some kind of a regular check-up. Below these oceans, an ecosystem existed that ninety-nine percent of the population would never bother experiencing. Over the years, I would see more fish, crustacean, and sea mammal known to man. I would also see the deterioration of these reefs that I would come to love. When I looked back, my need to change the world probably started with my need and ability to start cleaning up the reefs around the world. It made sense. There were few around to see what I was doing. There were even fewer who would ever wonder where those sunken treasures went.

So a couple of times a week, I would visit various different areas of a particular reef and start cleaning, picking out anything that did not naturally or intentionally belong in there. A quick touch and I would teleport out, standing in my ethereal form over Mount Redoubt in Alaska. The items were deposited into the volcano never to be seen or heard from again. It was during this time that I also discovered that my powers did have another limitation. I could certainly transport an object of any size and mass but I could not lift it if it was too heavy. The physics appeared to stay intact. I could transport a truck fifty feet in the air but upon materializing, I would no longer be able to carry the weight and the object would obey the rules of gravity, whether or not I was ethereal.

During the cleanup process, I also discovered that I was not invincible in my ethereal form. While I could not feel the water around me or the sand between my feet, this was not the case for any object that had accompanied me into the ethereal plane. I was technically able to stab myself with a knife if I chose to as long as that part of me and that knife shared the same plane of existence. I had a very close call once when I tried to remove a large piece of debris from a coral formation in Palau. Once I teleported myself to hover for a second over the volcano, my hands lost all grip and the debris fell before I could move away. I lost contact with it but not before it slightly grazed me on my leg before entering back into the real world. I transported myself back out. I found this all too morbid. I had the ability to walk in a sea of lava yet if I decided to let the surrounding lava join me in ethereal form, I would be vaporized in an instance.

In this manner, I traversed more of the world, above and below the land and water. I made my way to places where was I no longer worried for my safety, like walking on steep narrow ledges on the side of a mountain or finding myself in the middle of a raging river experiencing an angrier flow of water due to the melting ice or a monsoon season. I engaged in other activities, too, that would have made every nature documentary maker very jealous. I bet they've never had a chance to be in the midst of a lion pride as they jumped in for the kill. What a great shot it would make if I had held a camera as I stood in the path of a Cheetah running sixty miles per hour while chasing a gazelle.

The months since I had acquired my new power were flying by in a blink of an eye. It was almost fall again and I was impatiently waiting to see if Mr. Stick and Mr. Blinky would be joined by another friend. I took many guesses as to what it could be but it was impossible to predict what would happen. I tried not to get my hopes up. There was no guarantee that the universe would shine its light on me once more. That didn't stop me though from getting rather impatient every morning during the months of August and September, as I wondered what might be coming my way.

HUD

Chapter 17

Excerpts from my Life

Time: Fall of 1998

Location: Park

Event: The great sensory overload

My new friend that had shown up in the corner of my eye this morning did not play nice. I had spent the last two months awaiting its arrival and I was definitely excited this morning when I woke up to find it right there. I was also excited that this time around, it showed up on a weekend. The symbol this time around was a couple of half crescents around a circle. Was it an ever watchful eye? Sight beyond sight? An opportunity to pilot a show on CBS?

I could not decipher what it meant though and as the hours ticked by where I utilized the age old technique of trial and error, I continued going about my day as if it was any other, only stopping for a split second from time to time to take another guess. Morning became afternoon and the afternoon slowly slipped into the evening. I had landed up at a park just as my friends and I had planned a week ago. The leaves were well on their way to changing colors, a few giving up and finding their resting place amongst the grass. I sat amongst them, tired of trying to guess my new power. I had exhausted all options and unless something magically came to me, I was not about to solve this new puzzle. I was a little distracted by it but I was also distracted by the crowd near me.

My ability to remain completely undetected now allowed me to walk amongst the people I knew without them ever knowing about my presence. I had discovered dirty laundry, hidden skeletons, awkward secrets and unholy desires of many of them when I had made a decision to learn more about their lives. I had found the good in many that no one ever saw because they were too shy or had never gotten a chance to shine. I had taken those who were held up on a pedestal and stripped them down. I had taken others who would otherwise go unnoticed and had been able to isolate aspects of them that shined.

My friend Mustafa, as an example, wrote poetry in his free time. I didn't, and still don't care much for it but he was passionate about writing. Some of his poems made their way over to the arts department at school and now, the head of the department personally mentors him.

There was Sandy, an overbearing girl who constantly demanded attention, even if the majority of us didn't care to reciprocate. At home, she kept a book with an entry on each person she met at school. I would like to say she merely kept information about each of us in there to get back at us but there were stories about us that were completely untrue. Lord only knows how she planned on using it, but I made it a point to drop the book in between her mom's pile of paperwork. I never saw her with another diary again.

Vicki was a popular girl but kept her personal life a secret. Like a story out of a TV movie, she went home every day and took care of her younger sibling. Her parents weren't drunks or abused them in anyway. They were just ignorant. She made a real attempt to study as well but the girl only had enough time during the day. On various occasions, I would read over the contents of a test or exam beforehand. Later, before we walked into class, I would coincidentally think out aloud about subjects that would make their way to the test while she was in earshot. I felt she deserved a little extra boost.

Having this personal information on people, as much as it was an invasion of personal privacy, allowed me to remain social enough at a time when my social interactions remained largely limited due to my alter ego. I had gained a sense of confidence and became that relatable guy. I was popular, not just amongst those who were popular to begin with but others who felt I could connect with them on a different level. Funny how knowing things about people and using it to mold your conversations and interactions with them could make them like you all the more.

Today, however, I wasn't invisible.

The crowd today was a melting pot of people I had helped bring more to the limelight, jocks who now felt more human and girls who showed me far more attention this year. I had been telling tales about questionable rituals from countries all over, pretending like I had heard stories of these from reliable yet unnamed sources and that I swore this was all true. I could have said I read it in some book, but nerdy is not what I was trying to go for here. People laughed, with a few calling me out for talking bull. But my stories were well picked, knowing someone in the crowd knew what I was talking about by having observed them. Those anecdotes were soon seconded and it was clear that I was pretty knowledgeable without being uncool. The fact that I could also empathize with the right person at the right time as well as spontaneously retort with great innocent comebacks (even though I had prepared them well in advance) continued to shoot me up the popularity ladder. Looking back, was I really much more different than Sandy?

The eye was still there and I continued to ignore it. This social gathering would soon come to a close and I would decide to just accept it. For now, people were done with stories. A Frisbee smashed into the side of my face. A couple of shout outs, a few laughs, and one extremely overdone laugh from a girl who had only joined the school this year. I looked over and she quickly looked away. I had seen her a couple of times at school but hadn't had the chance to actually speak with her. She looked cute in a slightly dorky sort of way. I picked up the Frisbee and threw it in her direction. She looked a little shocked, like she wasn't ready to be the center of attention, yet she was somewhat happy that my personal attention was diverted towards her. As she got up to chase me, I took off in the other direction, hiding behind a picnic table that had seen better days. Today was turning out to be a fantastic.

The games continued for a while longer. Once a couple of people decided it was time to leave, the floodgates of goodbyes began and the ever-present eye slowly started to dominate my thoughts again. The park was mostly clear and as I waited to get into a secluded location from where I could just teleport back home, I decided it was time to just accept my new friend into the mix. Note to self: I should wait a few more seconds to ensure I will be all alone instead of accepting my powers in public.

What followed right after the weird symbolic eye disappeared was nothing short of the feeling that I was going to have an aneurysm. My eyesight flickered and felt distorted like they were recalibrating from something. Colors changed and just when I thought my vision completely cleared up, I was seeing far more than just the grass, the sky and the kid's playground in the distance. There was far too much data flooding my eyes, as if I was having sensory overload.

My eyeballs must have been darting around everywhere trying to make sense of all the extra things covering up the real estate that was my vision. There were so many symbols, boxes and random words just showing up that I could not read due to my eyes lacking the ability to prioritize what to focus on. I was even unsure if this medley of unwelcomed information were overlays on my eyes or actually part of the living scenery. I may have reached out to grab a few but I was grasping at air. I felt a gentle tap on my shoulder. It was her, the girl who had looked all too happy when I had assaulted her with the Frisbee a short while ago. Why was she here? More importantly, why was I seeing bits of information about her suddenly show up as though my eyes were analyzing her entire face and shoulders. If the bits of pieces of information moved out of the way, maybe I would have been able to observe those things myself.

"Hi," I managed to say to her while twisting and jerking my head a little in an attempt to get a better look at her. Monosyllabic responses worked as well. The less my mouth got used, the less the chance of me purging all over here from the nausea that was building up.

"It's getting a bit dark. Feel like walking me home?"

You've got to be kidding me. I just stared at her. Could the timing be any worse? Here I was struggling to bring one of my senses back into control and of all the times the universe could have picked for me to walk a fun and pretty girl home, this had to be the moment. She started looking at me awkwardly too and for a brief minute, I snapped out of it and responded. "You don't need to ask me twice." I immediately regretted my choice of words.

She looked relieved, as if she may have questioned the wisdom behind being so forthcoming with her offer. There was an awkward silence as we walked. I was appreciative but had to keep reminding myself that guys my age only dream about bold girls approaching them.

"Caroline right? How's school treating you?"

As she started to speak, I prayed for her to just talk about herself. Please, please talk about yourself. Keep this a one-sided conversation. I didn't even care to understand what was happening to my vision. I just wanted it all to stop. I felt like I was trying to hold all this together while my head was spinning and I was one step away from letting my nausea get the best of me. I was probably smiling a lot and nodding my head. My responses continued to be limited to monosyllabic statements. I closed my eyes for long durations as we walked, memorizing at least the next ten steps in front of me. Whatever was impairing my vision seemed to disappear when I did this. I guided myself by feeling the fall wind against me providing me with directionality on where I was heading. I could hear her sniffle a bit from the chill in the air. If this was any other occasion, I would have wanted to slip my hand into hers, but I wanted to give little indication of wanting to prolong this walk home. Once in a while, I would feel her eyes looking at me and I would snap my eyes back open, letting the monsters back in.

I had gathered that I had gained some kind of a gaming Heads Up Display, where information was being provided to me about various different things and my surroundings as I looked from one place to the next. It was all too much for me to take in. I tried desperately to switch it off but it wouldn't happen. This ability may be completely passive and probably gets better over time. I looked over at her, picking up on random pieces of information like color labels, measurements and such. All I really wanted was to look at her.

Goddammit how far does she live? We had definitely walked a couple of miles and I was seeing no end in sight. We were close to the limit of how far I was allowed to venture out on my own. I continued to smile. I did not want to blow anything and she continued to be oblivious at how jittery and awkward I was being. How was she not noticing the state I was in right now? Could it be that she was being just as nervous and shy as I am when I'm around girls? She was behaving exactly how I would. Was she trying to impress me? She WAS trying to impress me. She had no idea what was going on with me because she was too pre-occupied making sure I didn't think negatively of her. Oh, how the tables have turned. It just made me love her even more, which is probably the type of reaction that would continue to reinforce negative male stereotypes.

The walk continued and I questioned her parents' style of upbringing. We had closed in on an hour and it was going to be completely dark soon. I was also a little concerned. Sure, I could teleport back home in an instant but the time was fast approaching when my parents would take notice of my absence. I had little time before the concerned phone calls to my friends' homes would begin. My hour-long absence after we had all dispersed would be difficult to explain. Sure my parents would enjoy my tale of how I walked a girl home but a name would be insisted upon and if the location of her humble abode was ever discovered, the logistics of my movements would be brought into question. Well, they probably wouldn't but I believe I've already discussed my paranoia.

Out of pure chance, I managed to rectify some of my issues. At some point, I realized that within the clutter that my sight was now navigating through, was a round circle. I had to avoid focusing in on it. Every time I would, it appeared to activate and distort my vision by resizing things. There was a rectangle there too. I wasn't sure what that was doing. I saw subtle arrows with what appeared to be measurements of some kind. An empty drop box. This HUD was not as cluttered as I had originally experienced now that I was not constantly activating that round circle. There was still writing showing up and I picked up words from time to time. It was surreal because the words I picked up more often than not seemed to compliment some random thought that entered my head. I didn't have the clarity to figure out the exact relationship but it would come to me soon. The nausea was still there but I was less likely to blow chunks at this point. My conversations with her were reaching a point of normalcy and as my communication skills improved, the less shy she seemed to become, like it was some acknowledgement of my interest in her.

But more importantly, I was now able to really look at her for the first time. Before I was solicited into this walk, I hadn't bothered to actually observe her. She was shorter than I was and very nimble. Her hair was short, and as she swayed her head, the hair moved just enough to reveal the studs she wore on her ears.

Her voice cracked a lot but in an innocent cute sort of way, like she was shy but also, not attempting to sound different.

An hour and ten minutes later and we were finally at her place. None of it resulted in any physical contact between us as we said goodbye due to the presence of her older sister outside questioning her about her whereabouts. She seemed more disappointed than I was. I was personally not expecting anything. My first encounters with girls never really result in anything, much less the second or third. I turned around once pretending like I was trying to get my bearings but hoping to catch her from the corner of my eye. She was still outside trying to subtly catch a glimpse of me too. My eyes displayed an arrow pointed towards her with the number "27" on it. I would realize soon that it represented the relative distance between the two of us.

I turned around and walked away, trying to find a secluded spot on this very busy street. I may have gotten used to this new ability but I was left far too disoriented to continue functioning for long. Once I got home, I still had to look forward to more family chit-chat.

Calls hadn't been made yet. My mom however did notice there was something wrong. I played along. I needed to rest. It had been a long day. She completely agreed and let me go. I was alone but I still couldn't focus. Turns out I wasn't playing along and had not lied to my mom at all. I was genuinely tired and exhausted, at least mentally, and I was glad to find myself in the restroom. I threw up, loud enough for the family to come and check. I was tucked into bed but not before my temperature was checked. I didn't resist. My abilities could wait till tomorrow. At that moment, keeping my eyes closed meant those new demon friends of mine would stay away. I dozed off.

Chapter 18

I was slowly turning into a video game RPG character. I'm unsure how my leveling worked but with time, I have been gaining one ability after another and now, I had a fully functioning Heads Up Display or as gamers like to refer to it, a HUD. My eyes were providing me with information that it felt I required or was requesting. It took another day after gaining the ability to stop feeling the disorientation and a few days more for it to no longer be a distraction.

The HUD itself was pretty cool. It took a while but I learnt to control the little circle that had almost ruined my impromptu date with Caroline a few nights ago. It allowed me to zoom in on anything I wanted to get a better look. If the numbers on top of the rotating circle was to be believed, it provided me with information on the zoom factor. I It appeared that I was capable of up to a 120x zoom with no noticeable loss in quality. My eyes also provided me with constant measurements, whether it was providing a metric on distance or dimensions of a particular object. I could look at something and place a label on it, acting as a memory marker that followed the object or person around, always available for me to see every time it came back into view. The rectangle worked a lot hand in hand with the circle. It was a sort of a picture in picture box, providing me with another window to follow the zoomed in object around so I could focus onto it if I chose to while still continuing to see the world as my eyes intended. It also had a locked on feature. If I zoomed in to see an ant, as long as the ant was in my field of vision and regardless of which one of us moved, the frame followed the ant around, never losing sight of it. I wish real cameras had that ability. My eyes could focus in and out of any frame it wished to.

And, then, finally, there was what I had termed the search function, in more ways than one. I could think of anything I wanted to search, or define parameters for a larger search and within a radius of what appeared to be three miles, I could find it as long as I looked in that direction. I could limit the amount of results it found or set filters to get more specific. Walls, tree, metal and buildings, none of them were a barrier for me. I couldn't physically see what I was looking for if it was obstructed but I could see markers on their exact spot indicating its location as well as my distance from it. In such situations, the zoom in ability really came handy. I could specifically search for anyone or anything I had originally put a marker on as well and the ability worked in much the same way.

It is hard for me to explain how sophisticated my HUD was. The search feature alone was a behemoth. It could read my mind and provide me with lists and drop boxes to further filter results. I could dynamically filter on colors, sizes and other characteristics and I won't lie if I said that it took me till almost my six-month power cycle to make it second nature to use this gift of mine. It also inventoried everything I had ever put a label on, allowing me to keep the filter active or inactive.

Needless to say, over the years, I never lost my keys, wallet or phone. It was impossible to hide anything at all from me anymore as long as I was looking for it. And, yes, I once again did a complete sweep of the house, my parents' work places, the doctor's office, the hospital and various government buildings across the nation to find a document with my name or my likeness. I searched for my own face everywhere I went, hoping to lock in on a photograph lying around in a place I would not expect. I visited pharmaceutical companies, military contractors, and old abandoned sites around major countries in the hopes that I may have been the reason for their sudden closure. As usual, nothing turned up and it was around this time that I started to firmly believe that I was an anomaly no one had any knowledge of. Was I just an accidental natural freak of nature? The methodical and systematic manner in which I gained my abilities said otherwise. But, for now, it was safe to assume that I was also not some kind of a man made construct. This limited the cause of my powers to a list of very few possibilities that made me very uncomfortable.

More importantly, though, it made me feel truly alone in this world and if I was ever discovered, the world had no contingency plan for me whatsoever. Worse, I had no contingency plans for the world. The reaction would be total chaos.

If Mr. Blinky had indeed resulted in being some kind of a recording feature, then I could have become the exclusive supplier of wildlife footage to the National Geographic channel. Alas, that ability never manifested. For now, not only could I get up close to any creature I wanted to or dive to the furthest depths of the ocean, I could also locate what people spend days looking for as well as observe the smallest of what nature had to offer and keep a steady cam on it. I would certainly bring down the budget for a David Attenborough special. Should I follow documentarians around and somehow point them in the right direction? It seemed complicated. If I really had to direct people towards the right place to look for something, I figured I could probably provide a better service that benefitted everyone more.

I was already providing a service to the world by cleaning up the oceans where possible. Now, I could be a better Samaritan by helping look for things that were now lost. It started with cars and home invasions. I frequented the precincts around the country and looked at the police reports. I looked specifically for pictures or identifiable information that would allow for better filtering.

And then, my hunts would begin. I would scan a radius of three miles at a time, gridding out the cities and looking for a match. I had a good success rate in finding things, too, but it wasn't a 100%. Missing cars were simple. I would simply relocate them to an area in the view of the original owners or a place frequented by the local law enforcement. I definitely helped them get some easy wins. Car jackings and burglaries were harder to deal with. Finding what was missing was not the issue but I could not leave people's belongings or cars in convenient locations. Once again, that would draw too much suspicion. I had to lead the cops to it and in doing so, even close down the illegal operation. At times, this was easy enough.

I'd wait around for the cops to pass by the location of interest and I would stir up some commotion like a loud noise or an unavoidable disturbance. Other times, it was harder. I took to following the criminals in question, planting evidence of their stolen goods in the car itself. These people were sketchy enough to warrant a search. I would wait till they were close enough to cops to give them a probable cause. Sometimes, all it took was breaking a tail light. Sometimes, I would cause the cars to swerve. Anything to grab the cop's attention. Turns out the majority of the cops responded. A search would reveal a portion of stolen goods, leading to plea deals in exchange for information on entire operations, a reduction in crime (at least temporarily whenever I concentrated on certain areas) and drinks at the local cop bar where observations were made about the lowering IQ of the criminal masterminds.

I felt good about myself. My powers had provided me with an infinite playground to work with and, now, I was in a position where I was giving something back, either to the world itself or to the people in it. My personal gains were now finally being balanced off with community service. I did not have to go out of my way to fix the injustices in the world. Sometimes, fixing injustice meant simply helping out without being confrontational.

I liked that and I knew over the course of the next few years, I will be able to find other domains I felt comfortable taking action in too.

As I mentioned once before, however, the universe may be working with me but sometimes, it had its own agenda. My hands-off strategy to save the world only lasted for a few more days.

Chapter 19

Time: Feb 1999

Location: My friend's birthday

Event: The six year old

Now that my friends and I were older, we considered ourselves adults, able to attend a birthday party unsupervised. However, a birthday party itself at our age was bound to get you picked on, even if deep down inside, we all wanted to go to one or validate our popularity by hosting one on our very own special day. So here I was, at the birthday party of someone whom I wouldn't consider any closer than an acquaintance. Promises of cake had been made earlier that week and I was planning on holding this individual to that promise.

I had mentioned earlier that while popular now, my social interactions with people remained at a socially acceptable minimum limit. Apparently, this acceptable minimum limit was not the same when you may be unofficially dating. Ever since I walked her home from the park that day, it was evident that Caroline definitely liked me but my other activities still continued to take precedence. We would have a great time hanging out, conveniently cornering ourselves off so we could have a lot more alone time when we were out with others. We've been able to date here and there but I use the word date very loosely. My situation did not allow me to be overly committed. I didn't want someone getting too close to me and finding out my secret. Thus, I never took the reins of this relationship. She was too shy and I'm sure I sent her mixed signals. Nevertheless, there was still something there and my only reason for being at this birthday was her presence, and the cake, of course. Time to see if the two of us could pretend that we just decided to speak to each other by chance only to spend the entire afternoon secluding ourselves from everyone else.

We talked about classes, movies and music. She talked about her hopes and dreams in a sort of light-hearted way. The conversation was gradually gravitating towards me providing my hopes and dreams as well and it was something that I wished to avoid. I excused myself to grab another soda, asking her if I could grab her one as well. She smiled and accepted the offer and I walked over to the backdoor while acknowledging looks of approvals from my friends. Being subtle was something that did not come naturally to any of them. I must have blushed but kept walking, sure that she must have caught that little exchange between me and the guys standing next to the barbeque.

There were some parents inside. Some of them had decided to bring along the younger siblings and thus, additional supervision was required. Some parents just happened to be good friends with the hosts. At least they all knew not to come outside and respect the invisible boundaries between them and us teenagers. A friendly smile from a random mom and I made my way to the kitchen. Gossiping was afoot. Something about a new neighbor down the street. I picked up on one of the dads starting up his own business with the wife. Another talked about the ruckus made by some family cat. and then something about a girl.

I stopped. This was different. This didn't have the same tone as all the other conversations. The conversation was short but it was enough to make the corner of the room where it was happening a lot more edgy and more solemn. Some missing child? A friend of a friend? I was only catching snippets of the conversation and by the time I moved in closer, the circle had already dissipated. One parent looked more concerned than the rest and I casually followed him. As expected, he shared the story with his wife who looked heartbroken by the end of it. Other parents took interest and soon it turned into a topic of discussion. The words were being shared cautiously, so as to ensure the kids won't hear. No eyes were on me and I took this moment to conduct my disappearing act. Now I was able to move within their midst.

They were talking about a six year old girl. She lived three streets over and the incident took place outside some bank at a strip mall over the previous weekend. The child's parents were devastated and desperate as a few days have already gone by and the leads were drying up. No contact had been made and all clues pointed towards something far more sinister than just a ransom. The conversation turned to the state of society, debates about ample security and some parents naively claiming how they would have never allowed it. Those parents did not realize how the others slowly distanced themselves away from them at that moment. Empathy was one thing. Some people liked to take any tragedy and make it about themselves. The discussion carried on but I had already moved on. Words flew around me but I was no longer listening.

Something ticked inside me. I had the ability to find this child. I may be greatly risking myself here but, dammit, it was a kid. I could not ignore that. I aimlessly walked back outside sodas in tow, stopping only temporarily to become visible again in a quiet corner upon realizing I was still ethereal and invisible. Caroline was no longer sitting where I had left her but hanging out with a few buddies of mine. I walked over but my contribution to any discussion left a lot to be desired. I did my very best to keep up pretenses but inside, I was very disturbed. It had already been a few days. This child could be anywhere and I had the ability to find her was the only thought that still kept racing through my mind. Was I so desperate to finally kiss this girl that I continued to put this child's life at risk by delaying on the actions I should be taking right now?

I was not but it didn't change the fact that I had to be patient. I scanned the area for conversations and finally overheard someone talking about leaving. I asked if I could bum a ride off them and said my goodbyes. She looked disappointed but she was getting very used to this. How long could I keep this going before she realizes there were far better people out there than me who are interested in her as well? Today wasn't the day I was going to wait around to find out. I'd let fate decide how far my relationship with her would go.

The ride back home was short and no one was at home. I sprung to action. By now I was a frequent visitor of the local precinct and finding the files on the girl was not hard. The case was hot and currently being discussed. I did not need the file itself. I needed a name, a picture and some details. Turns out the kidnapping only took place two days ago and not the previous weekend, as the parents had been claiming. The police didn't have any leads or any indications of her whereabouts. There were no suspects either. There was nothing more that the precinct could help me with and I began a ritual I had started once I embarked on looking for stolen cars.

I teleported to the first coordinate in the grid I had created for my city. The entire city could be traversed and scanned by me within fourteen minutes if I stuck to the intricate route that I had structured for myself. I stood on top of the first building and entered in my search criteria. The mental picture of the girl was the only thing that I needed.

The image of the girl showed up in my HUD and my search began instantaneously. She had the face of a poster girl, with a smile that belonged at the end of a dental commercial. I pushed out the thought of how her family must be feeling right now out of my head. I spun my head 360 degrees and came up empty prompting me to teleport to the next location and restart. The results came back negative again. Each scan allowed me to cover a 28.27 square mile area. Fourteen minutes later, I was done, having covered the gaps I had left behind. The girl was not in the city and my worst fears had materialized. Another twenty minutes and I had finished a thorough sweep of the area around the city. The girl had definitely been transported out to another location. The success of my next move would come down to luck. I teleported back to my house to verify if anyone had come home. Upon finding an empty house, I made a decision. I picked the less traveled highway leaving the city and started traversing it, pausing every three miles to survey the land, creating the necessary overlap to ensure I wasn't missing anything. Sixty miles out and I found a vantage point. I zoomed in on the land and looked for stray buildings. Nothing. I headed back out and covered more area before arriving at the next major city. A three-mile sweep was not enough. A quick teleport 2,000 feet up in the air and I understood the general layout. I began at a corner of one of the suburbs on the outskirts and gridded the city out, putting a marker on each building I've used for scouting as an indicator of a place I had been to. The city was swept in record time and yet, there was no luck. Since I started, it had been less than fifty minutes and yet, I felt dejected. I fanned out another 500 miles on that same highway, knowing full well that any connecting highway or exit lessens my probability of picking the right route and dimming the chances of recovering this child. I was looking for a needle in a haystack.

I was investigating another town when I stopped and

wondered how generic my search could get. Could it account for types of people and automatically decipher people's intent? I began a new search.

Thief.

Nothing happened. I shook my head in defeat and returned back to find my dad pulling into the driveway. I walked out to say hello and helped him carry the groceries in. In the mental map that I had created in my head, I was still thinking about any gaps that I had missed in my search and making a note to go check them out tonight however I already knew I was grasping at straws.

I had a depressing dinner while I listened to sad news in general on the TV. Here I was, the most powerful being on the planet and I had failed this child. I had failed this child in under an hour and it was eating me up inside. My dad noticed something was wrong but I kept brushing him off. I finally just snapped and left the table, saying something to the effect of going out somewhere to be with other people. I was fifteen or thereabouts. My family was used to my typical teenage behavior. I kept walking for a while till I could go invisible without being seen. I couldn't give up so quickly. I teleported outside the city and started a circular scouting pattern. Each time I covered an entire 360-degree area, I moved out more, expanding my circle. I was resolute that I was going to do this all night if necessary.

And I did that for hours. I had created a massive blip not just around my city but three more at a distance. It was two in the morning and I was exhausted. It was too dark to use visual cues so I convinced myself to go to the next city. I told myself to try one more. By 3:45 AM I was pretty confident that tomorrow could be survived on a two-hour sleep. I closed my eyes and teleported to another unfamiliar metropolitan. I was not going to give up.

Chapter 20

I did not find that child that night. I did not find that child the night after that either. A week passed and neither I, nor the police, could find a trace of her. Her pictures were plastered all over the community, the same one I had used for my HUD. The public outcry at the incident could be felt everywhere but due to my own failure and that of the law enforcement agencies, the visibility around her disappearance slowly started to dissipate. Pictures of her around the community started to come off. The news about her drifted off the front page of the newspaper, replaced by more current news.

When you're a young teenager, something like that stays with you and haunts you, much like the face of the boy in the Philippines. You never forget it. I had left a permanent filter on my HUD to look for her wherever I went. And while that was a passive ability I had switched on, I can remember the countless times I teleported to a new location around the world and still spun my head 360 in the hopes of spotting her. Even if the media and the town had decided to move on, I hoped my relentless need to find her would never make her forgotten.

I would eventually find her by chance almost two years later. I almost wish I didn't. For the purposes of my own sanity, I'd rather not relive these details. It was hard to imagine the life she had lived, given the horrible condition that I found her in. That girl never really totally recovered and finding a way to bring her back to her family had been less than trivial. I was brought to tears to see the disbelief and joy on the face of her dad as he held her for the first time in years, completely breaking down and not letting her go. But the girl was scarred and the parents soon came to terms with this, their hysterical joy turning to despair as they watched their daughter struggle to adjust to a normal life. I had mentioned that there were certain lives I followed through the course of my years and hers was one of them, as much as I wanted to ignore it. It took years for her to learn to trust again and it's only in recent memory she attempted to make something of her life, even if it was cautiously. The happy ending here is that even if her life didn't turn out to be ideal, it could have been much worse.

Still, my failure that week resulted in my bringing tears of joys to many others. For a short period of time, my obsession around missing children grew and I ensured other kids and their loved ones would not suffer a similar fate.

I had accumulated much power and while I had been using it to entertain myself so far, I'd do more with it. I was going to go out there and save children in need.

Chapter 21

Excerpts from my Life

Time: Mar 1999

Location: A small town in Wisconsin

Event: Another kidnapping

I was no longer just chasing stolen cars or jewelry. I would look out for reports on kidnappings all over the country. Since my failure in finding that first child, I had determined that speed was key. The quicker I could respond; the less time I gave someone to escape my scans.

I never failed a kid since that night. My diligence resulted in finding all the kids within minutes of conducting my searches. The harder part, other than watching the sobbing faces of heartbroken caregivers was getting the authorities to look in the right place. But I would persevere, children would be saved and on many occasions, a larger kidnapping ring would be unearthed and shut down. In a matter of months, I had made many people very happy.

But this particular day was different. I would not get a chance to guide the police down the right path. The child was kidnapped no more than an hour ago from outside the mall. When I visited the scene, the mother was still standing there, holding on to the set of colored pencils and coloring books they had just bought for her together. I avoided the mother, who kept asking again and again where her little baby was. It was too much for me to bear. I glanced at the picture the cop was holding. I had what I needed and did not wait to get a name. I looked around for the tallest building and started my own investigation.

I had done a sweep of the area and found nothing there. Dammit. I didn't want this to be a repeat of my first experience. I created my circular search pattern again but gave precedence to the roads, exploring them out first before returning to cover the other glaring gaps. This time around, I made the right call as the marker I had set up for this child showed up and it was moving.

I teleported to find an old gray van which I marked right away as well. How typical. I followed, in the hopes to find a highway patrol car. I teleported into the vehicle to check on the child. She was very young, probably seven years of age. She was unconscious, but breathing. I could find no obvious evidence of physical harm either. I teleported out and continued looking for a patrol car. I was having no luck. The car drove for another twenty minutes and eventually pulled into a field in the middle of nowhere. It was a good spot to hide something or someone.

Trees and uneven ground gave it a bit of a camouflage. There were more cars there and a small building that appeared to be losing its battle against time and nature. Ensuring that the child was being deposited there, I teleported away to locate the closest semblance of civilization. I found none that I would consider close by. This child was on her own and I had decisions to make. I teleported back, assessing the situation in order to decide if I was going to engage or not. There were five of them and they carried guns. Not that arsenal mattered to me at all but I was surprised to find so many of them. In my experience, this was usually a one or two person operation at this stage.

Three of them were getting ready to leave soon, when I tuned in on the conversation. They wanted the girl to join the rest of the cargo before tomorrow night. There were more and apparently, they were to be smuggled out very soon. I felt my face grow hot with anger as I heard this. The three shared a very untasteful joke on their way out to the car. Leave, you sons of bitches!

I traveled back out to the road leading to this safe house. With my filters switched on, I looked for all the signage on the street. I found one with a name of a location and hoped it was recognizable. I grabbed it and tore it apart by simply making it ethereal with me. I left the sign in the grass hidden from plain view and switched my filters on again. I looked for a cell phone. Fortunately, one of them was carrying one. These, of course, were the good old days before people purchased disposable untraceable ones.

My timing here had to be perfect. I relied on the general mistrust between criminals that most Hollywood movies convinced me existed. When one was right behind the other, I punched the guy in front with all the strength I had. The guy at the back had no idea what happened but the one whose ears were probably ringing had already formulated an opinion. Shit was about to get real. A little too real for me. I had neither planned nor prepared for this.

He drew a gun, much to the surprise of the other guy. Accusations were thrown out with an equal number of defensive comments. Apparently, I created a situation where the accused was being treated as a double agent. Things escalated quickly and a shot was fired, hitting the man in the stomach. With whatever strength he had left, our completely innocent friend (well, innocent in terms of the recent accusation) took his own gun out and fired back. Man down.

I stood there in shock. They were child kidnappers. I should feel no pity. But, I had never seen people die before much less shot to death. Slowly, our friend took his last few breaths and perished as well. I can't let a child see this! And, yet, I had no choice. As disturbing as the moments from a few seconds ago were, the situation could not have played out much better than this. None of this was staged.

After standing around for what felt like an eternity, I walked over and took the phone out. I stood over the girl and said sorry. I nudged her with my foot a few times before she snapped out of whatever drug was given to her. She was scared and petrified, not just because she found herself around dead bodies, but she had no idea where she was and how she got there. She also looked a little out of her senses, and I hoped that she was unable to grasp the true situation that had transpired to and around her. I toyed with the idea of revealing myself. This is not the type of situation a little girl should be put in. Thankfully, before I made any decision in my head, she spotted the phone that I had placed next to her. I hope this seven year old knew her number or how to dial 911. She called her home but was mostly unintelligible. She narrowly missed going into a shock.

The cops must have been at the house. As she was being calmed down, her behavior indicated that she was being instructed to do things. She stepped out of the house and noticed the sign. The girl found the word on the signage too hard so she spelt it out. She continued looking. I felt frustrated thinking the sign was of little help. I teleported up to see what else I could find and there happened to be a car working its way in the general direction of the girl. I had a few minutes but no more. Using whatever sounds I could make, I directed the little girl towards the road. The cops appeared to be encouraging this behavior, too.

The car was almost there and now I had to hope whoever was driving it would notice her and stop. The girl was flailing her hands about and a very concerned citizen stepped out. The girl begged for help, shoving the phone into his hands and the good samaritan was briefed on the situation. In shock, he held the girl tight, in disbelief that he had found himself in these circumstances.

It took a moment, but he managed to gather his composure too while providing instructions to the police on where he was. He took her to the car and offered her water. After I had confirmed he was not going to harm her in any way, I bid adieu. As much as I wanted to ensure she got home safe and under my watch, there were apparently other children whose lives were hanging in a balance. I looked at my watch. It had been forty minutes since the other three had departed and they had headed back towards the small town where the girl lived. I took off in that direction, too, unsure about what my next steps were.

Chapter 22

Excerpts from my Life

Time: Mar 1999 - Minutes later

Location: A small town in Wisconsin

Event: The pursuit

Locating the men had not been hard at all but I was not sure how I could figure out where those other children were. If these three return back to that safe house, I doubt they would even bother going back to where the rest of the "cargo" was. I tailed them as closely as possible, listening in on every word that might provide me with an indication of where all those other innocent lives were.

It was not lost on me that less than an hour ago, an incident instigated by me resulted in the death of two people. Very bad people, but still. This haunted me and I was having trouble not dwelling on this fact. Part of me suffered from shock and if it hadn't been for my need to find these children, my adrenaline would have never reached the required levels I needed to allow me to keep going for the rest of the day. My attention kept drifting back to the conversations taking place but every few seconds, I would go back to picturing those dead faces. Could I have handled the situation a little differently? What worried me was that a part of me wanted to just say good riddance. Did that make me a murderer?

I heard a name of a location and tuned back in. Chicago. They were definitely talking about being in Chicago tomorrow. Some discussion was had about stopping by a local burger joint after the drop off. I wanted to phase back in and slap them right there but I kept my disgust buried. They were about to walk into a diner and much to my surprise, there was someone waiting for them. They sat down at the table and a few pleasantries were exchanged while the waiter hovered around the table. Disposing of the waiter with some quick orders, they wasted no time. The three were briefed on the situation in the city in regards to the missing girl. It appeared the information was now outdated considering the police were already on their way to her. Satisfied that their bases were covered, attention turned towards the rest of the day. They weren't planning on waiting till tomorrow. The trip to Chicago was taking place tonight. My luck changed when one of them confirmed the basic directions to the drop off location. Apparently, the traditional route they took was marred by a construction nightmare. The alternative route was confirmed through nods and I teleported to Chicago looking for a convenience store, but not without committing their faces to memory. They would not be let off so lightly.

I "borrowed" a map and looked for the address. Without the ability to ask anyone, this was turning into an exercise in futility. I teleported back home to map the location on the internet. Mapping sites were very new then and this was before the days of satellite imagery, and pictures. I took down directions on a piece of paper and worked my way through the route. Years later, I would learn never to utilize my own personal PC to conduct such searches.

I wasn't really in Chicago. I was around the outskirts in an area that was far more industrial in nature. It was still daylight with a lot of hustle and bustle, but this one area was largely empty. My filters were on, looking for a human child under the age of ten. I found them scattered around but a couple of areas provided high densities. One appeared to be deep within these old dilapidated buildings.

Another teleportation and I witnessed another horror I knew I would never forget. The children wore shackles and chains. There was crying, sweat and dirt. A few had hung their heads, so frightened that they were unable to even move. Others were screaming out to anyone who would hear them and family members. Above all, it was dark and moist and the rage inside me knew no bounds. The only thing keeping me from tearing up was my need to hang those responsible from the tallest buildings so the world would witness and know that a new sheriff was in town. The children were all alone in here. I did not want to imagine what they must be thinking of their predicament or if they even understood what it was. Some were too little in my opinion to comprehend what was happening. They just wanted to be in the safety of anyone willing to give them some love.

I could free them right now. I didn't care much about blowing my cover at this point. I could teleport them out. But how many more such children existed bounded up in some random abandoned warehouse? Where were they being sent? And If I just let these kids loose, where would they go? It made sense to figure out a way to get the authorities involved. I left the room, whispering a sorry for abandoning them temporarily to assess the situation. I scanned the building, finding only three other life signs. They were sitting in a room, playing cards. They did absolutely nothing noteworthy while I was in their presence.

I debated my options. I could wait. I could wait till they hear about the delivery cancellation tonight. I could wait till tomorrow or the day after to find out where these kids were supposed to be taken. I would receive invaluable information about the entire network. I would bring the whole thing down and end the suffering for many.

But I could not wait. The images of the dead bodies in the building outside Wisconsin were replaced with that of one child or the other just a few yards away from me. My tears had found a way of breaking through and I tried convincing myself to not be so hasty. I looked away to compose myself, desperately trying to think of another solution. One of the guys got up and placed a mask over his face. He picked up a bat and a pair of keys and proceeded to walk towards the prison room. He opened it and I heard the sounds of children briefly coming to life, some anticipating this was a rescue, others pleading to be taken home, while others cowered in horror, having been there longer and more used to the routine. My heart skipped a beat listening to the tragedy unfolding in front of me. The littlest of them stared up and reached out, in the hopes that this fine gentleman with a mask on his face and a bat in his hand was somehow there to make everything right. The debate was over. The decision was made for me.

Thankfully, the man had not gone in there to perform a beating of any kind. I took solace in the fact that while the children looked a little roughed up, none of them showed signs of serious physical harm. A few threats were uttered to put them all back in their place while he proceeded to unshackle one and walk her out of the room, leading her towards a toilet. She complied as best as she could. He proceeded to lock the door behind her but I shoved my finger where the lock would go, just enough to not secure but enough to give the impression that the key was turned.

I teleported back to the other two and looked above. There was heavy equipment above them on shelves and I decided it was time for the supports to give way. I held a vertical piece of wood and went ethereal. The equipment fell, crashing all over the room and on top of the kidnappers. The biggest impact came from the TV, which I happily maneuvered during its fall to take one of them out. The other tripped over him and, as he fell, I took the liberty to drop the filing cabinet on him. He was battered though not completely out. I walked through the door, where the third guy peered through the corridor, a terrified girl in his arm and his hands around her mouth. He was nervous and scared but he did call out to his friends. He heard a muffled reply back and he proceeded to walk over to the room. I was running out of coincidences to set up. I looked outside and could see people walking, probably to a nearby parking lot, glad that today's shift had ended. Before the guy could walk in, I teleported into the window, smashing the entire thing into pieces. I had tested this out before and knew I would suffer no cuts or bruises.

The guy walked in and looked in horror at the condition of the room. He dodged the pieces of glass that had just shattered and thankfully, covered this girl as well with his body. His gaze fell upon the gaping hole, which used to be the window and in a moment of panic, he dragged the girl with him as he decided to peer outside for a possible assailant. I crossed my fingers and hoped. She was clearly visible through the hole in the wall as he held her threateningly with one hand around her throat and the other gripping her wrists. More importantly, she was able to look outside and she noticed them. A shrilling scream and the entire population of workers standing outside were alerted. The response from them was quick as there was little doubt in their mind what the situation appeared to be. Instructions were barked to one to run back and call the police. The rest ran towards the gate and memories of my recent horror were replaced by the coming together of a community that had one noble goal in mind. Our kidnapper looked all around the room, waiting for something or someone to tell him what to do. He screamed at his friend to get up, who slowly crawled up to his knees. He was mobile, but barely. Considering him a liability, he grabbed the girl tighter as he ran out of the room, presumably to find a deadlier weapon or an exit. The girl's life was at risk and I mirrored his movement, trying to find an opening so I could separate the two out and more importantly, ensure he did not find his way to a gun. There was nothing available and at the chance of hurting the girl, I teleported in front and stuck my leg out and phasing it back in while keeping the rest of my body ethereal.

It was a legendary trip. He lost his grip on the girl as she fell on the floor right next to me, shaken but not hurt, an acknowledgement in her eyes that this may be a positive step towards freedom. He went flying, landing on his arm and by the looks of him clutching his forearm and the cries of pain, it was evident that something was broken. The girl had regained her senses and slowly backed away before turning and running. He tried to give chase but thought better of it. He did not have much time and escape seemed like his only option.

He was an idiot, though. The building was securely locked. The workers had climbed the fence to get in but were still stuck outside the door. Another woman had been dispatched to get tools to break in while they smashed and kicked at the padlock. A couple had decided to run around the building to find another entrance, a sound strategy, considering the kidnapper was unlocking it in order to make a daring escape. He was cornered and moments later, I wasn't the only one who got to witness the most horror one would ever see in their lives. Children, still shackled, pleaded and reached out like they must have done countless times before and this time, they were greeted with shock and disbelief initially, which soon turned to hugs, warmth and words of consolation.

An hour later, it was a circus. The neighborhood, which was probably normally empty after dark was now crowded with ambulances, cop cars, fire trucks and media vans. The children came out covered in blankets and surrounded by caregivers, ensuring the media would get nowhere close to them. Some were carried out. I watched from a distance as I could not hold back the tears anymore. I must have been bawling at the moment, not just because I was glad they were all safe, but also because I felt guilty. I knew there were others and I had the opportunity to take the whole network down. Sure, these three would talk but their knowledge of how far this goes would be limited.

A couple of hours later nothing had calmed down. The attention briefly turned away from the children and this unknown kidnapping ring to the heroes of the day, who were still visibly shaken by the entire ordeal. I smiled, glad to see the good in people when all day I had experienced nothing but the worst in humankind. The story had gone national with our heroes being praised, our children being shown empathy and our law breakers being judged. I was gently reminded that I had plans for tonight. I returned to that little town in Wisconsin and did a sweep. Everyone I was looking for was still there. It appeared they were caught up to speed on the happenings of today. There would be no delivery tonight. There would only be a sleepless night. After the news, they had not made any calls. They had not gotten in touch with anyone or each other. The guy they had met at the burger joint appeared to throw his phone into the river. I was going to get nothing out of these people. They had broken off all communication and I returned home.

I had witnessed too much that day. In my brief time in this world, nothing had compared to it. The worst part was I could bitch about the events all day or claim how haunted I was but my trauma came nowhere close to those children whose faces I saw and was never going to forget. The rage continued to burn inside me and as I noticed on my watch that it was well past midnight, I made a final visitation to that town in Wisconsin. One by one, I went to the place of slumber of each of these four individuals who were destined to suffer my wrath. When I saw the first man lying on the bed with bottles of beers next to him on the night table, I stood for a while, unsure of my next move. Finally, I touched him lightly with a single finger, much like I would touch the other three a few minutes later tonight and teleported.

I did not leave them together. But I left each of them in similar circumstances. Once they woke up, they had to find a way to navigate the elaborate mazes I had frequented in my travels these past few years. They would not be screaming in joy at what would be awaiting them. The mazes of forests or steep mountain paths would eventually give break to a seemingly welcome place but there will be no escape from where they would find themselves. They would never see another person again either. The only thing waiting for them on the other side would be a lifetime of fear, however short that life may have become for them now. I wasn't ready to cause more deaths. One death indirectly attributed to me was enough. Yet, I knew that was just twisted thinking. By simply teleporting to where I did, I could lie to myself all I wanted but I knew deep down inside that they'd die because of me.

Chapter 23

I would love to say that I was a changed man after some of these incidents. How could one continue living knowing the injustices that are taking place in the world and not do anything about them when you have nothing to lose?

I would also be lying if for the first few days of disbanding the kidnapping ring, I hadn't believed that I had found a new calling. There was no gray area in situations like these. There was only good and evil, black and white. And the more I planned on how I would take on kidnappers, the rapists and the murderers of the world, the more I felt angry and out of control, and I succumbed to the fact that I wasn't ready. Sure, I would take them out but was I going to continue jeopardizing people's safety in the long run? How long before someone decided that so many coincidences did not just take place? Would I lose my ability to help?

It was hard to fathom my train of thought. It would appear that I had little justification to not make the world right and my will to protect my powers and my identity was a sorry excuse. It's partially true, though. I was young and while a part of me wanted to go out and truly behave like the most powerful entity in the world, a selfish part of me wanted to continue being me. I wanted to learn more about this planet, and experience new things. I did not know what new powers were awaiting me and how they would change me fundamentally.

But I also disliked the rage. I had passed judgement of those four men and while I had no remorse, I knew I'd killed them. I have mentioned before about setting precedence to avoid these exact scenarios. My lack of remorse indicated what I had always feared would happen. Even in my teens, I believed that no one person got to decide another's fate so blatantly as I had done and if I was to pursue these obsessions of mine, many others will follow the same fate. How soon before the situation was no longer as black and white? How soon before it was simply guilty by association or a lack of action? This was not unjustified paranoia to me. In just the last two years, I'd cross lines I had told myself I wouldn't cross. Hell, two people had died and another four would probably not have lasted long in the new lives I had gifted them.

And so I gave it all a rest for a few more days. I let my emotions calm down. I worked on staying in control of myself instead of letting my emotions dictate my actions and I went back to using the powers for myself and to engage in passive help. Thefts across the country remained in check. Abductions were swiftly handled and with a lot of care. I helped out with a lot of fires, accidents and natural disasters all over the world. But I did not go out there with the express intent of getting my hands dirty. I wanted to continue affecting the lives of many individuals but it was still important to me that I remained anonymous to the world. As far as the world was concerned, there was no supernatural being walking the earth.

Enhancements

Chapter 24

The 2000s felt like a very different time than the '90s, and not just because of the rapid improvements in technology. The widespread use of cable internet connections and the wealth of knowledge definitely changed my life quite a bit. I no longer had to walk to a library or read a random article to find my next source of inspiration. I could now search the world not just through words but through pictures. Internet cafes were everywhere and frequent trips there in the late hours allowed me to find new places to travel or rituals to observe.

My world also changed because I reached a new stage in my life. I was older, no longer needing my parents as an excuse to move around. I had an old beat-up car that cost nothing, yet was believable enough that it could transport me around just fine. I barely registered any mileage on it. I was no longer living with my parents, either. I had moved out of state away from many who knew me, which worked out very well. I had less restrictions now on my time of travel and less people around me to whom I needed to explain my whereabouts. Cell phones were far more common and featured heavily but I never took one during my travels so it mostly stayed at home collecting voice mails. Even in the early 2000s, I understood that cell phones could be tracked.

It was 2003. I had seen every inch of the world but now I followed events. I would wait till July to catch the whale sharks at Holbox or watch the bears come out of hibernation, following the treks of the cubs and helping them along the ice each year as the ice got thinner and more scarce. I would attend the festivals each country had to offer and I would go there every year too because I was now less interested in ticking off something from a checklist but watching what I loved year after year.

I would also revisit the same places to engross myself in the lives of the people or to simply follow some indigenous species. I once spent a whole winter following the progress of Narwhals in the ice thickets as they waited for ice to melt in various locations to continue along their journey. I had trouble believing that they would congregate along narrow waterways in sheets of ice, waiting and having faith that what lay ahead would melt in time for them to continue their trek. I lived within a family of gorillas, observing first-hand how the social hierarchy worked. In some instances, I wasn't the only one there. Other humans would come to observe or to film a documentary. I smiled as they remained at a distance while I sat against the same tree as the alpha male. Tool use within gorillas was far more widespread and varied than most of these researchers had even imagined.

I followed the news online to track any recent discoveries as well, allowing me to be one of the first one to observe them as they happened. I was in Isla Escudo de Veraguas to watch the pygmy three-toed sloth upon its discovery. I mapped out the ruins of Herakleion in Egypt before the first set of divers could start to fully explore it. I even spent countless days in Son Doong Cave years before someone finally traversed it. I still do, as it is a sight like no other. Nothing like lying in a forest, yet still finding yourself covered on all sides with rock.

The acquisition of new abilities continued, though they felt more like incremental improvements on existing abilities. The six-month cycles were not respected either. The update to my skill set was slightly more sporadic. Pretty much all these enhancements I speak of in one way or the other addressed either complaints that I had about my current abilities or complimented my guiding principles.

I don't use the word incremental lightly. It is almost like these new enhancements was the universe's way of fine tuning what I already had, like a version 1.1. As I mentioned earlier, the universe was patching up existing issues that I may have struggled or complained about and this was evident as soon as I acquired the first power since gaining my HUD. At the beginning, it almost went undetected because it was an improvement to the existing HUD. I was able to scan an area now that was 4.5 miles in size, an improvement of fifty percent, making it far easier to look for something across a larger area. My zoom improved, allowing for a 150x magnification. This allowed me to take a renewed interest in the lives of insects. The interface itself saw adjustments, making it less cluttered and allowing for more fluid accessibility. My picture-in-picture ability now allowed for multiple frames, tracking multiple subjects at the same time.

I definitely welcomed the increased range that I had received. The search feature was by far the most used function of my HUD and some of the new changes definitely enhanced this experience. Surveillance became a lot easier when I was trying to navigate or follow multiple things at the same time. I could follow many things of interest all at once without losing sight or focus. I could situate myself far away so my ability could track things over a large area without being impaired in anyway. When I was in a jungle, I no longer needed to follow a single animal. I could keep an eye on all of them from afar, like a security guy watching multiple monitors. All these changes were most welcome, but all in all, I was a little disappointed. A part of me had been waiting for a completely new ability to spawn like being able to make things move with my mind or heating up an object with my hand. Neither of those were ever realized.

A few months later, I was greeted with another tweak and a familiar friend. A new version of Mr. Blinky returned. I did not know what its purpose was as I had just finished accepting the latest change, one that I had not identified. Mr. Blinky turned out to be another enhancement, an indicator letting me know when it was safe to become invisible or visible without the watchful eye of people and cameras. It was one of the most perplexing abilities. It ignored animals around me, but it would stop blinking when my movement could be noticed by a person. I utilized this power to confirm if there was anything following me around, to see if I wasn't just a freak of nature. The results appeared to be the same as they had been since 1997. Even when visiting government and private corporations working on top secret stuff, I discovered large moments of time when there was absolutely no one around looking in my direction, organic or technological. This enhancement definitely allowed me to plan my movements far less as I relied on it to tell me when to appear and disappear but it was largely useless as during my journeys, I would remain invisible and ethereal for the majority portion.

While on the subject of my ethereal power, that saw multiple enhancements as well. One of them allowed me to travel to multiple ethereal plains, so much so that my body could also occupy multiple plains at the same time. The usefulness of such an ability did not dawn on me at all, until I figured out the true purpose of what the other prompt had to offer.

The other prompt had once again provided me with a passive ability, one that I was not even aware of till the right circumstances presented themselves. In the summer of 2001, I was cleaning up debris from a building collapse in Nepal. I had not gained my ability to detect when no one was looking at me by then so I had to be careful about how I moved the large slabs around. I was mostly cleaning out the smaller rubble, trying to create the required passages for someone to pull out trapped people or important belongings. At one point however, a number of rescuers ran towards a disturbance. I looked up to see one of the rescuers trying to flag people to come towards him. There were definitely multiple people trapped underneath, but the slab covering them was way too big to budge without a large machine at their disposal. As the brave crowd used their might to lift the large piece of rubble, more and more people joined in. A woman ran right by them, finding an empty spot to provide whatever strength she could muster up in the precarious bit of room left available to her. I had to step in when even more people joined, creating a rather dangerous situation in case anyone stumbled. I teleported under the rubble, which was probably my first mistake. The family was a few feet below me, holding each other as they listened to the rescuers cheer each other on and shout out words of comfort and encouragement to the ones that were trapped. I placed my hand on the slab and inch it, enough to not destroy everyone's' hands but to merely push them out of the way as well. I did this slowly till a tiny opening was created. This caused the slab to move on its own and on impulse, I went ethereal. I was still touching the slab however, which became ethereal with me. My body took on the entire weight of the large cement block for a brief second, causing scratches and bruising.

It was at this moment that my new passive power kicked in. It appeared that if at any point my powers perceived undesired physical stress, they automatically made me turn ethereal and in the situation where I was already ethereal, made me phase into another ethereal plain. The bruises and scratch were gone, as if my body had just finished regenerating. The stone, no longer influenced by my power, entered reality again and got lodged in an unstable position. This could have all resulted in a disaster and only a miracle somehow ensured no one was hurt. Since then I've discovered I can enter up to 5 ethereal plains that are independent of one another. I've never personally used more than 2 except on rare occasions and wasn't sure what the significance behind 5 was supposed to be.

I also gained the ability to feel when I was ethereal, though this came a while later. Before, I could not feel the carpet, the tiles or the sand underneath me. Now I could experience any feeling without showing any signs of actually disturbing the grounds I walked on or the surfaces I rested on. It was probably an enhancement that I least understood. I felt like this version 1.1 release patched up a bug that I had despised, yet the patch made no sense at all. I had no clue how this ability simulated the feeling without actually showing my footprints in the sand or creases on the bed. It worked on living things too. I could pet a cat, feel the fur between my fingers yet the cat had no knowledge that I was violating its personal space. I had dubbed this power 'The Creeper.'

And while more abilities were not gained that complimented it, I did discover ample ways in which to utilize my ethereal powers. The idea came to me once when I was playing around with sharp objects and another experiment was devised. What if I allowed myself to experience the physical stress and drove the stake I was holding through me? And so I did and it pierced right through my skin and came out the other side. Yet, I was alive and well, experiencing nothing more than an itch.

I had always known I could selectively apply my ethereal ability on different parts of my body, but had not fully utilized its power in practice. While running this experiment, I had kept the top most layer of my skin non-ethereal while everything inside no longer shared the same plane. My skin did not behave like a paper mache though, devoid of support. My body was still there supporting it. The amount of power required to pierce through had not lessened (another anomaly much like gaining the sense of feeling) due to how I had configured my body. Neither did anything about it feel strange and, so, I continued through most of my life in this configuration, to avoid getting hurt and later, to avoid an unfortunate incident by accidentally displaying my powers during a physical altercation with a living thing or object.

That was about it I think. I know, it sounds odd. One would think I kept track of everything, but the truth is that once the abilities were just being improved upon, they did not feel like new powers. It's been so many years and the improvements were so incremental that I lost track of when a new enhancement arrived or if it had been part of the original power. I also have trouble remembering if something was an enhancement or an ability I just learnt to use better over time. For example, I have forgotten how some of the discoveries I later made regarding my teleportation ability started off as. But that was all for the best. I found those discoveries so unsettling, I avoided utilizing them at all costs.

By early 2002, I got no indication that I was going to receive any more upgrades so I resigned myself to believe that my transcendence to whatever I should call myself had now reached completion. There were going to be no more improvements and all I had left was to master whatever skills I had that I had not become an expert at manipulating. I was not bothered by this. By this time, there was no goal I could set for myself that I was incapable of hitting or achieving and the only thing that stood between me and those were how well I had prepared myself.

I had used the possibility of gaining an ability as an excuse to live life in a holding pattern, rather than figure out the life I wanted to live.

Now, I had no more excuses. It was time I figured out what to do with myself and the very generous powers the universe granted me.

Life

Chapter 25

Excerpts from my Life

Time: Summer of 2002

Location: Dominican Republic

Event: Freebies

I had been to this resort before. It was one of the nicer ones. There was more to do here than just sit all day by the beach, sipping on bottomless drinks and shoving mediocre buffet food into my mouth. They offered a lot of activities that would allow exploration of the nearby area. The beach was covered in fine grains of sand and in the distance, I could see a wreck, no doubt purposely sunk so close to the beach to allow avid divers to explore. I had visited it once and it didn't boast a lot of chambers accessible to divers, however, I had made it a point to go inside and seen some fish residing there. They must have gotten through little holes in the hull. It wasn't a spectacular wreck but it was easily accessible and thus, a popular stop for many divers.

The resort also offered food that was far superior to most of the other ones on this strip of the beach and that was what had drawn my attention to it. I was particularly interested in the buffet, which was not limited to the choice of pizzas, burgers and pasta but dared to offer a lot more. It helped that the menu changed from time to time, a rarity amongst all-inclusive resorts as there was no need for such a thing. I had sampled the food many years ago and only recently returned to sample it once again so I could decide if this resort would make the cut or not.

During the first day of the evaluation, I spent a bit of time sampling all that this place had to offer. Some time was spent at the reception, observing the behavior of the receptionists as they checked people in and out and to see what they did during their downtime. I visited the empty rooms before choosing one I liked.

The next few days were more boring and far more tiring, having spent entire nights in the corridors of the rooms I had selected as good candidates. I had to select multiple rooms as there may not always be availability for the one that turned out to be the prime candidate. All these rooms were currently empty and as expected, during the later hours of the evening and through the night, the foot traffic was minimal. The balconies offered tremendous views as well. Checking off the rooms was not much of a problem for me.

I next tackled the issue of the buffet again. I didn't like the idea of stealing food, but when I found out how much they threw away every day, my conscience was clear. On the third day when I was all but sure that there was ample amounts of wastage in this buffet business, I grabbed a handful of shrimps and walked over to the beach, where I nibbled on this delicacy while watching a honeymooning couple parasail for the first time. He was clearly not doing well while she didn't seem to take notice. I regretted having zoomed in on his face as he proceeded to purge the contents of his stomach, almost making me regurgitate the half-eaten shrimp in my mouth. I was laughing, choking and a little sickened at the same time. My appetite had been lost.

The following day, I decided to finally conduct a true field test. It was 8:30 PM at night and I double-checked the room multiple times, fueling my own paranoia. This room offered photo-worthy views of the ocean though it didn't matter much right now. It was definitely going to be unoccupied tonight and I decided to turn the shower on and wait. After ten minutes when no one decided to come and investigate, I finally stepped in and enjoyed the high volume spray. One wouldn't need to scrub themselves with this type of pressure I thought. I didn't really require showers, either, as I had the ability to just transport from one location to another, leaving the accumulations of the day behind at the spot I had previously been in. But I enjoyed the feel of the scorching water smashing against my skin. It was a psychological thing. I finally stepped back out fifteen minutes later, feeling rejuvenated and made my way to bed, passing a mirror along the way. I, of course, had no reflection but over the years, it always reassured me to know that my powers were still working.

It had been forty-five minutes since I had made my way to this room and no one had questioned there being a light on in an unoccupied suite. This gave me comfort. I did wake up a few times during that night, every time I heard a sound, fearing something had come in my room. But everything had gone smoothly and my first field test was a success. I returned subsequent nights and grew more comfortable. I braved switching on the television as well and catching up on local news and sitcoms. In the morning, I would sit on the balcony, enjoying the freshly brewed coffee from somewhere in the world that I had decided to pick it up from. Eventually, before the hustle and bustle on the beach picked up, I would make my exit. There would be no trace of my existence at all.

Dominican Republic was checked off and over the next coming weeks, it would be joined by a resort or villa in Zanzibar, Jakarta, Chiang Mai, New Zealand, Cuba, The Grand Caymans and a luxurious hotel resting just on top of a cliff in Dominica.

Chapter 26

Since the summer of 1997, I had broken quite a few laws. Even if, for the moment I ignored encounters I'd had with the scums of the earth and focused strictly on all other escapades, I had broken far too many serious laws that would put a normal person in jail. If anyone was aware of them, there would probably be an arrest warrant out for me as well in multiple countries, if not all of them.

See every time I crossed borders, I'd violated countless border crossing laws. There are visa requirements to consider, official port of entries, immigration and customs processes, the amounts of goods and services being imported in and your vaccination records need to be kept up to date. A few of those obviously did not apply to me at all but the law does not discriminate. The penalty for violating such a law was not a simple slap on the wrist. Consequences were far more serious.

I'd also visited several unauthorized locations over the years and while most of them were inconsequential, I did hold in my head intimate knowledge on others that I could sell to a reporter for a decent amount of cash. I'd violated privacy laws, protection laws across multiple industries and spied on personal, corporate and governmental entities. My sentence during a trial would be pretty severe and I could see countries across the world demanding extradition so they may deal with me the best way they can. Maybe they didn't even want to punish me but simply extract all the information I had in my head. Once they were done, then I'd go to prison.

Though I doubt I would ever go to jail. If I could be taken alive, one would expect experimentation. If I was too dangerous, lethal force would be utilized followed by dissection. I was worried about neither. If I was to be discovered, no power on this planet could stand up to me. In addition, what I'd done had never bothered me in the slightest. My conscience was clear. I'd never felt I broke any law that resulted in anyone getting hurt. I understand why these laws exist but given my situation, I'd always felt that they didn't apply to me. Voicing that out aloud however did make me sound like a villain who justifies why they are somehow above the rest.

It was also not lost on me that many people who did horrible things had the same exact sentiment and I made no excuses. But I knew I wasn't a villain.

Though don't get me wrong. I had definitely done 'some' things that I was not proud of. In my teens, I'd used my powers to sneak money out of my dad's wallet. As I grew a little older and realized that taking money from my dad still meant I was using money that would otherwise be spent on the family in the first place, I changed my habits and targeted larger businesses for my cash flow. Even then, I had ethics. I could have loaded up on money, gold, precious stones and worldly possessions but I only took what I needed. Twenty dollars here and there. It was still robbing, but my intentions were to never get rich, just get through life without having to worry about my financial situation.

But as the years went on, the guilt of such actions caught up with me and my career as a low level thief came to an end. However, it didn't change the fact though that once I hit university and had a far more flexible life with fewer eyes watching over me and a certain level of independence, I utilized my powers to cut corners. Saving on transportation was a big win for me right from the start. I went into the business of building custom computers for other students at the campus and as my reputation grew, so did my business. My mobility allowed me to serve the larger metropolitan area and I became quite known for providing speedy and quality service. My ethereal ability allowed me to assemble these computers fast as well and for a one-man operation, my throughput was unmatched.

As people slowly moved away from bulky desktops to the more portable laptops, I found my niche in gaming. I was a popular figure on gaming forums and my builds had a following. I catered to orders across the country and whereas I could have delivered all of those by hand, that would have drawn far too much attention. Sadly, I had to allow third-party delivery companies into the mix and compromise. Still, my venture had been so successful and worked so well with my schedule that this business of mine survives till today.

Serving the entire world, legendary builds. I didn't mean to imply that I assembled hundreds of these in a day. These were custom orders with people willing to pay the extra buck. I also had little need for money, with the true purpose of having a job to show anyone who wishes to audit my more public lifestyle that I had a reasonable source of income to cover my meagre to modest expenses. There were no red flags to be raised.

I kept my expenses at a minimum too. My place of residence was primarily utilized for the purposes of sleeping and during the day, doubling up as my workshop. This was where I stored all my inventory. I utilized little gas and to keep up appearances, I'd continued to keep the beat- up car I bought myself while in college, the mileage on it pretty much the same as it was back in 2002.

I had a cheap phone with a cheap plan. I had few long-term friends and the phone was mainly utilized for family or clients. It also encouraged me to ensure that I would never carry it around during my travels so as to not get tracked around the world. Hence, it spent the majority of its time on my desk accumulating voice and text messages

Today, I still maintain a small place of residence, with a car parked out on the street that barely ever moves. I have a stash of cash lying deep within the Lechuguilla Cave, along with some other very personal belongings. Yet, outside of doing my work, I barely ever reside in my city anymore, choosing to take up temporary residence in various beachfront properties around the world or in some isolated rainforest retreat overlooking the mountains. I could live anywhere but I chose these because even though I could transport to wherever my heart desired at a moment's notice, I enjoyed being in a single place from time to time. I enjoy waking up and walking out on a patio while sipping some coffee and spending a relaxing hour or two there before getting on with my work or other travels. I felt no guilt in living in these places as the rooms were empty. I felt no guilt in eating from their buffets. The food was always cooked in excess.

I lived the life of the most well-to-do hermit in the world.

Loneliness

Chapter 27

I turned twenty-six. Under normal circumstances, one could say that I still had a long way to go as far as gaining life experiences were concerned. But my life never amounted to an amalgamation of normal circumstances. I had, in fact, lived a very special life. At my age and with the number of years I spent with my abilities, I evolved not just in terms of my attributes but in terms of wisdom and thought as well. Ego aside, there was no one my equal.

But with my infinite power came an infinite amount of paranoia and questions. What was I supposed to do? Why am I special? HOW am I special? I would spend an entire day observing something I had never seen before, and then spend the night observing another location across the world and still find myself coming back to my bed and wondering if tomorrow would be the day I needed to turn to someone and reveal myself, if only to get their help in answering who I was.

There were countless occasions when I wanted to come out and show myself to the world. I often thought about how I would do so. I toyed with the idea of being a hero and making myself known to the world while saving people from tragedy as the cameras rolled. Everyone would be shocked and before some authoritative figure could corner me, I would bark out orders and everyone would comply because clearly, I was the only one in control. When it was said and done, the media would surround me and I would get a chance to introduce myself in a positive light, making it harder for anyone else out there to reprimand me. I would have had to have chosen a superhero name for myself by then. That scenario had always been my favorite. The news would go viral and slowly but surely, the world would learn a lot more about me and accept me, hopefully.

Or I could introduce myself to the entire world all at once, sabotaging a world-wide event like a world cup or a presidential address. It would scare many people but intrigue just as many. The limelight would be on me and the conversation would be on my terms. I could provide a warning to the world, letting them know that I'm watching or maybe an olive branch, letting them know that whenever I'm needed, I'm ready to help.

Maybe not so public though. When I was in my teens and struggling with the questions of if I should make world changing decisions all by myself, I wanted to secretly seek out the help of the world's presidents and prime ministers. I wanted to get into bed with trusted scientists. Maybe they could guide me to what the world really needed. Maybe they would provide me with a way to help the world without it relying on me. It wasn't just that though. Maybe I would meet someone who truly understood me and would listen to the experiences I have had.

But I trusted no one. As much as I would find goodness in people's hearts, whether it was rescuing a child from a building or countless other situations I've been in where someone had landed in dire straits, I found people to be inherently selfish. I saw

222

people run into burning buildings and later, I would observe their lives and more often than not, it boiled down to wanting to be a hero, or a simple matter of guilt. And that turned out to be my motivation too. The times I reacted, it was out of not wanting to experience the guilt of never taking action in the first place. I treated all human actions as a matter of self-interest. I hoped I was wrong. Some would call that empathy and thus a good thing. I still called it a desire or deed borne of a selfish desire to not feel worse for or about yourself.

The most powerful person in the world and no one to share my experiences with. Back in the day, I used my powers to become the popular kid on the block. But as time went on and I got too busy discovering the wonders and shortfalls this planet had to offer, the more I isolated myself. I spent less and less time with those whose friendship I valued. Sure, people would enjoy my company but eventually, I'd disappear on them. I always did for weeks or even months at a time.

Thus, I went through my magical life alone.

My isolation continued to deepen even more when I would be surrounded by people who appeared to know things. It was easy for me to spot when someone had no knowledge on a worldly subject or were acting worldly by practicing some random ritual that had become the new fad. It was easy for me to verify things and my experiences around the world forced me to create quick labels for many people around me who I thought had no idea what they were talking about. The most popular ones continued to be pretentious and misinformed. I couldn't stand being around such people, much less engage in conversation. My social life continued to suffer.

Maybe I should have been one of those same people I hated. Clearly, I judged everyone around me too much.

Chapter 28

Excerpts from my Life

Time: Sometime in 2004

Location: Cottage on Lake Tahoe

Event: A Forced date

I hated driving. The reasons were quite obvious. But pretenses had to be kept up, so at times, I had no choice. This was one of those moments and as usual, I was trying to impress some girl. Now it's true that when I was thirteen, I was just your average kid and my life did not behave like a work of fiction. However, my limited time and my sketchy lifestyle created some very erratic social needs for me. On the one hand, I continued being popular because I just happen to know so much about the world or people's personal lives without sounding like a geek or a stalker of some kind. On the other hand, I had a very active life no one knew about, which limited how much I interacted with people. It put strain on any relationship I tried to create and while most of the time I was okay with that, there would be moments where I longed for companionship. Even more so, I wished to see the world with another person and share the joys of discovering what it had to offer for the first time.

So, I was easy prey for anyone looking for short term attention. I was almost desperate and it took little for me to try to impress someone. It wasn't like I would fall in love or anything. I just wanted a shared experience with someone. I had lived a very lonely life.

This girl was clearly upset and I didn't have the heart to tell her that she was an idiot. I was in university now and a few of us were visiting Lake Tahoe during one of our breaks and all was going well. I wasn't there for Lake Tahoe. I had seen it before from above and below, from its banks and any other angle that existed. I had seen it in every season. I was just here to get away from myself and pretend to have some kind of normalcy in my life.

Either way, right now, I happened to be sitting in said car rental listening to this girl complain about the most trivial of things. She and her friend had a disagreement, to which she felt the proper response was to simply storm off. We all had a bit of a laugh about it but as time went on, she didn't return. I had been keeping an eye on her. She was half a mile away and continuing to walk towards the city. I pretended to call her and then informed everyone that she was taking this all quite seriously and that I would grab the rental and take her out for a while. One of my friends thought it was for the best. Another, not being able to help himself, sung out my name and hers being on a tree followed by the dreaded spelling out of the word "kissing." Just as well, though, as that little act of immaturity discouraged anyone else from following. I sat in the car and drove away and quickly teleported to within a short distance of her. I pulled up and stopped the car, and pretended like I had been searching for her for a while. She was touched. This idiot. This gorgeous idiot kept walking because she thought no one would ever bother to come look for her. A part of me wanted to leave her right there. Another part of me didn't care much because I was twenty with raging hormones. And you know … very lonely. I would make an awesome creeper one day. I picked her up and kept driving away from the cottage as she bared her soul out to me. I really didn't give a damn about her problem.

The truth was that before this incident, I actually thought she was very nice and currently, I was trying to ignore her annoying attitude. I was trying to get her back to a point where we could have a normal conversation and I would forget that this part of her even existed. I hoped it was just the alcohol talking. It took time but things returned back to normal and we just spoke about life. She had expressed it to me very clearly that she was not interested in returning back right now but I wasn't quite sure where to take her. I was scanning the route for any points of interest but I was finding none. And as we talked more and more, the afternoon caught up to her and she rested her head. I wasn't sure if she was sleeping or if she just had her eyes closed. I didn't care. She needed to be distracted and I wanted to see the world with someone. I teleported her, myself and the car onto Interstate 80. I knew where we were heading but it was a bit of a drive. As long as she kept her eyes closed, she wouldn't know what I was doing.

She was clearly out and every chance I got, I teleported

further with the car, ensuring I maintained a straight line. A journey that would normally take over a couple of hours was made in less than an hour. She was waking up and I decided to drive normally the rest of the way. She was wondering where we were and I told her that I wanted to show her something special but to do so, we may need to break a few rules. She was nervous but adventurous, like me. We kept driving for another fifteen minutes after which I finally stopped and we got out of the car.

She couldn't understand where we were. She saw a large fence but everything else was a barren wasteland with random pools of water that did not look worth swimming in. I told her to wait as I approached the fence and walked around. I waited for her to look away for a brief second and as she did, I teleported a couple of miles away, my foot attached to a couple of feet of dirt. I teleported back instantly, her being none the wiser and called out to her. She walked over and looked at me oddly as I climbed under the fence through the hole I had made. She asked me how I knew about the hole and I told her it was something I had read on a forum. She crawled through as well and a few paces away, I directed her attention to a marvel I had only discovered a couple of years ago. It was definitely not as big as the pictures made it out to be but it was still a spectacular sight. She held her face and ran over, watching the water spray up. I asked her not to get too close. She stood there for a moment. I could tell she had questions, not just about what she was looking at but how I happened to know about this one obscure little thing in the middle of the desert. I convinced her to sit down and as she proceeded to stare at it, I proceeded to answer her unasked questions.

The Fly Geyser was not a natural phenomenon. It was created due to a well drilling accident and what a beautiful accident it was. It was on private property and thus, the fence. There were other geysers created nearby but this was the marvel. The rainbow itself had given its colors over to it and the water glistened as it sprayed out. She laughed and smiled and finally, she looked at peace as she stared at it, as if nothing else existed. And I looked at her. I had hoped this to be a great moment and it was but not for the reasons I had expected. I saw in her right now what I had felt countless times over the years and I smiled, too. Someone finally knew how I had felt all those times when I discovered something new and beautiful. Now, this feeling was shared and I was there to witness it. She commented on how something so small continued to exist as the world just trudged along. She mentioned how only a handful of the billions of people will ever get to look at this small but wonderful spectacle. I continued smiling as she echoed thoughts and reactions I've had over the years. I finally looked away from her and we both stared at the geyser while I explained to her more of its history. She listened to every word and asked me if there were other places just as beautiful that I knew about and if so, if I would take her. I said yes, though I never took her to them nor did she remember to ever quiz me about them once we returned to the university.

At one point, she ran out of things to ask and as the sun started to set a little bit, we shared an unspoken bond for a period of time as we lay on our elbows watching the water fly in whatever direction the wind was pushing it in.

As the light diminished, I finally asked her if she was ready to head back to the cottage. She nodded and a part of me felt she too realized the triviality of her discontent from a few hours ago. We got back in the car and drove off, and at some point, she thanked me for the experience. I pressed the accelerator and soon, I was well above the speed limit. She looked at me, asking me how many more laws I was hoping to break today. It was in jest. She enjoyed our little journey into the world of rebellion as I was easily going well over a 100. She was nervous and excited, surprised no one was honking at us or pulling us over. I had my filter on for cop cars. There were few, not that it mattered, but I had to keep up appearances. I would slow down if I happen to see one and then speed up again. She was awake and would not be slumbering off. A high speed journey back to the cottage would be the only way to get back at some sensible time and not make her question how far we had travelled today. I could no longer teleport unless she looked away and every time she did, I pushed us a little closer to home.

My intent to go look for her may have started off with wanting to earn some brownie points but I returned back with a whole lot more. I felt a bit of my loneliness go away and for the first time I felt connected to someone else. She could talk to me about the sunset, the colors of the rainbow and how she felt when she saw it and I could do the same. There were thousands of experiences I wouldn't be able to share with anyone but this one would not be one of them.

Pulling into the cottage, I was happy. The day had been perfect for me. The others came running, worried sick that we had neither picked up our phones nor returned in a timely manner (I of course, had skipped bringing my phone altogether in case my GPS was being monitored). She apologized for her behavior and proceeded to tell everyone about the geyser. Plans that would never materialize were made for tomorrow to go take a look at it again as everyone got ready for a barbeque. She was the last to chase after the group but before she walked away, she turned around and came back to me. She gave me a hug and thanked me for a very special day. I got a peck on the cheek and then she turned around once more to catch up to the rest of them. I looked at her, and smiled. She had been none the wiser that not only had she spent the day making small teleportation jumps, she along with me and the car had been invisible and ethereal for the entire journey home.

Chapter 29

Excerpts from my Life

Time: 2003

Location: The Arctic

Event: Me with bear

Animals had always been a good alternative to people in sharing experiences. And as I've mentioned before, on countless occasions, I have followed the lives of various living things around me, be they human or animals. One such animal was a polar bear I named Polly. Judging by the location I first encountered her in, she had been with her cubs in her den not too long ago. But here she was, a great big polar bear with no cubs to show. I had scanned the area and sure enough, the cubs never made it out of the den. I had felt a sense of sadness. To have labored for so long and then sacrificed an entire winter only to suffer such a loss felt devastating. I could not tell if the bear shared in such sadness or if this was considered a part of life for her. Maybe I projected a lot of my own emotions on her but she felt distant. While I was seeing countless other bears traversing great distance, she was more lethargic, spending precious hours lamenting on the ice. Time was of the essence. She had to get to safer ground before the polar ice started to melt and from a distance, I would urge her on. But she remained sluggish through her entire journey and I felt in her what I felt in myself.

Loneliness.

I observed her for a week moping on one mound of snow and ice or another. She would sit for a while and then get up and walk for a bit, showing no sign of haste. For no reason whatsoever, she would then stop, standing in the same place for moments on end only turning her head back from time to time to see where she came from or what she left behind. When luck would have it, she would continue her trek but, usually, she would eventually just lie down. My frustration with her turned to a shared connection, at least in my head. I would often lay right next to her wondering what she was feeling. We would do nothing special but just hang out with each other. Well, I did. She had no clue I was there. At least, right now she didn't.

Environmentalists and conservationists say to not get close to dangerous animals. It's for your own protection as well as that for the animal. My protection was never an issue but for the longest time, I remained hidden to the bear, frightened that I may change her life in some fashion. But with each passing day, I felt like she wasn't making much progress and I did not want her to spend the last of the summer swimming without the possibility of finding refuge on ice or land. I wanted to push her along instead of merely transporting her. And maybe I was once again just projecting my needs on her but I felt she needed a companion after her ordeal. A safe companion.

I had surveyed the area and knew there were no people here. There were no cameras of any kind, hoping to trap the bears in a photo moment. One day, as she lay around, I made a decision and became visible to her. I wasn't sure what to expect. I had created a few scenarios in my head but as most situations turn out, you never prepare yourself for the most anti climatic moment. She didn't notice me at first at all while I stood there bracing myself for a face to face. But slowly, much like countless dogs and cats I've seen before her who suddenly tune in, looking up and confirming her visuals. She was not aggressive at that moment but confused, wondering what was going on. I did not move but stayed where I was, letting her absorb the shock of seeing a human this far into the arctic. She slowly got up and moved a little closer but kept a safe distance the entire time. She was inquisitive but also careful. Apparently, this was a moment she had not prepared for either.

The situation did not last long. It turned out that she preferred not to engage in a confrontation and moved back, eventually walking away in a direction. I decided that this was enough for today and proceeded to follow her under the cloak of my powers. She made little progress this day too but I did not push. I returned the next day for the time I had allotted myself with her and repeated the exercise and her behavior remained unchanged. She investigated me once more but she would not risk coming any closer than last time. A sniff here and a sniff there, she managed, but did not assume a threatening posture. I let this go on for another couple of days and eventually, on the fifth day, as she turned back to walk, I followed, remaining completely visible to her eyes.

She noticed her stalker and her body language modified. She looked bigger than usual, puffing in more air into her lungs while trying not to slouch anymore. Her movement remained constant with brief stops to reaffirm her posture and look my way. I heard a grunt or two once in a while until she eventually would turn around and openly threaten me. I would stop but not leave. After about half an hour of us playing this game, her tune started to change. I experienced a couple of false charges, no more than a two or three aggressive steps in my direction but they meant little to me. I realized I had bothered her enough and left for the day letting her continue on her journey. I returned the next day and the song and dance did not last too long. She attacked.

I had expected her confusion and frustration to last longer than it did when she slashed right through me. She tried a few more times as her movement became more frantic but she stopped quickly. She slashed again but this time, more gentle, as if testing a theory. She would jump at me and I would have to turn around so I could face her on the other side. She would circle me and a bit of aggression would return occasionally. She interacted quite often but eventually, her curiosity gave way to caution again as she must have realized that this exercise was not worth the potential risks and proceeded to walked away. I walked with her, too. She swept at me from time to time but eventually, she would be reminded that she had to keep a distance. So the final slash would always be followed by her strutting away in a hurry, ensuring a safe gap was maintained between me and her. I was definitely making her nervous. I was definitely making her feel a lot of very different things.

A few more days passed by and amongst my many travels, I would find my way back to her. She would grow more accustomed to me as each day came and went, to a point where she ignored me when needed but also chose to look for me when she lost sight of my position. I hoped she enjoyed the temporary companionship she received every day and there was some evidence of this being true. She would look back from time to time to see where I was and sometimes, wait for me as she traversed a rather difficult trail. I would simply teleport from one location to another and once assured I was still around; she would continue on her merry way. She still paused during the day but I could tell her daily treks were getting longer.

Soon came the days when she could be seen raising up her head from time to time to see if I had returned. When I finally appeared in front of her, her gaze would lock on and her body would tense up as if the anticipation was over, like a child happy to see a parent come home from work. She would gallop over and growl. She would try to touch but that was not possible, at least not at the beginning. See, I finally succumbed to her companionship too and let the outer part of my skin leave the ethereal plain. The first time I touched her, she was taken aback and there came the slashing again. My skin ripped but I was unharmed, phasing in and out to quickly heal the damage. I felt comfortable enough running my hands through her fur and after some time, she got used to that too. I never understood her thoughts, but she would talk to me and push me around. We became buddies and when I was not following her, she would follow me, curious to see if I had discovered anything of interest. I took this as an opportunity to help her considering her late start to this yearly migration. I would never lead her directly to her main source of food but if there was a seal around, let's just say that we did not always stick to the course that we had plotted. I tried to avoid her always expecting my independent movements to correspond to a possibility of food but I wasn't very successful at it. Hence, I let her lead us for the majority of the time.

I was of course, worried. Even though she was now moving much faster, and more fed than the average polar bear on such a trek, the ice was melting and there eventually came a time when we came across the broken ice, far later than the other bears. There were other stragglers too of course, not just her and they had not been as fortunate with feeding as she had been. I would often disappear during these times, as to avoid a misunderstanding and create a confrontation. But I would continue to watch her and monitor her progress. More importantly, I would make sure she knew I was disappearing. Earlier I had done so without her knowledge and realized that she had spent a considerable time looking for me. Bidding her farewell avoided a bit of this though she still looked around for me but not as much. In a sense, we set up a bit of a goodbye ritual that worked more often than not.

My next few encounters with her were no longer on solid footing. We had been companions for an hour or two every day for the last few months and as I looked ahead while she made her way, swimming from one ice platform to the next, the situation up front looked bleak. A tremendous swim was in store for her and the other stragglers and I had difficult choices in front of me as well.

By helping these animals get across, I was messing with the evolution of this species. An argument could be made that while a lot of the issues with the polar ice cap melting were works of humans, some other species were thriving because of it while the polar bear suffered. Were Polly and the rest now part of a chain reaction that was too late to reverse and the polar bear species doomed and succumbing to natural selection? Was I interfering with a pretty important event here? Then again, we caused this problem to exist. It's only fair that we fix it.

These two extremes kept pulling me apart but for now, I continued to follow the trail and took small liberties where possible. These animals were no longer in a position to hunt and each swim, which now lasted more than a mere dip in the water in between two ice sheets were getting tiresome to even watch. I would find ice from other locations and teleport them near the bears to provide much needed rest for them. I kept this going for a long period of time, but also forced the bears to swim for reasonable periods of time as well. I had interfered enough that I had given the majority of them a fighting chance, including Polly whom I would swim alongside. It appeared to give her strength in my own mind and that in turn gave me hope.

It was an arduous journey and thankfully, I was glad I was never put into the predicament of outright teleporting these bears. My interference may have been a violation to many but I treated it as a gray area and I could live with that. Polly had made it and she would spend the summer fattening up and getting ready for the next litter. The bears had still experienced a hard journey and they were in a position to understand the perils of their trek next year.

Polly is still alive today and every year, I continue to go back and follow her. She recognizes me every time and comes running back to me like a puppy. I've escorted her cubs too but I made my appearances less with each passing year, letting her go on with her life. We were both there for each other when we needed it most and now, she needed me less. But I would never forget the times when Polly and I just sat around and did nothing, or played in the ice or stared at the stars in the middle of nowhere somewhere in the Arctic. I would never forget how she once queued her cubs to touch me and they experienced the same level of confusion her mom did in years past. It may not have been a person but I was glad I had my furry companion to share in some adventures.

Chapter 30

Suffice it to say I hadn't ever actually had a steady healthy relationship with anyone. Even more so, I hadn't really been in a position where my relationships ever had to end in a negative way. I guess that was one thing in life I could be thankful for.

You know that one person on a TV show that was considered a supporting character and ends up becoming a fan favorite? This person never really had an episode dedicated to themselves and usually wasn't even a major supporting character but worked well only for a few minutes here and there. People created memes after this person and demanded an episode fully dedicated to them. Once I had gotten too curious and spent time with people less and less, that person in any friend circle or situation had always been me. Everyone enjoyed it when I'm there. But I did not ever have strong bonds with anyone.

But on the occasion that this side character did have an episode centered around them, no one quite enjoys it because the character only worked in small doses. And each time a girl showed interest in me, it resulted in a few dates or a very casual relationship. But it would never go anywhere. I was quite sure I was probably always classified under "not relationship material" but my breakups remained amicable. I was either considered to be somewhat boring because I did not share much about my life or was unavailable when others desired my company. Sometimes, I found the person needier than my life would allow me to cater to their requests. Ultimately, the issue was always me but instead of rash break ups, my relationships mostly died slow deaths. We always continued to be friendly long after on the few occasions I would make contact with them.

Caroline had moved on too eventually. It was a few months after that birthday party but eventually, she realized there were more fish in the sea and she had no problem catching one. The spark always remained. It was too bad we never got anything going. She often made me wish I would just grab her one day, ask her to trust me and take her on the most insane journey of her life. With every passing second as I would speak with her or remain merely in her company, the desire to do something like that would get stronger. We would eventually say goodbye and I would stand there telling myself I did the right thing while still wondering how much I could have changed my life in that instant.

It was the same with friends as well. I'd never really held out hope that one day, I'll be the best man at someone's wedding or get to plan out someone's bachelor party. I no longer know what Manuj and Mustafa are up to. Once we went to our respective universities, I never attempted to stay in contact. The few times we ended up running into each other back in our home town, I'm sure I asked them about what was going on in their lives but never cared to remember what their answer was. The few people I got to know over time remained active in my life only through social media as opposed to on a more personal level. And it made sense I guess. I'd always been around for events but

I'd never had a reason to walk home drunk with someone or drive them home. I had had no reason to take part in what I consider the "accessorization" of socializing due to my situation. I'd always been there for a movie, or a lunch, or shown up at someone's house. And once that engagement was complete, I'd missed out on all the other stuff that people did. From what I noticed, those were the times the true relationships formed and throughout most of my life, I had been too naive, pre-occupied or impatient to wait around for those moments.

The girl I took to go see the fly geyser? I remember that moment vividly. But I sure as hell don't remember her name anymore. I don't remember a lot of names anymore. For me, these people just came and went. I wish this wasn't the case. At some point, I reached a stage in my life that my desire to have friends or someone to care about was strong but I was no longer willing to sacrifice my lifestyle or allow anyone into it.

The one place where I did end up making an exception was family, if not always for the right reasons. When I moved away, my interactions with them grew less and it was evident that it had an impact on the happiness of those who had helped raise me. While I enjoyed my freedom and originally, made sure that I made it back for the holidays, over the years, I noticed how selfish I had been. I would make my presence felt to limit the number of questions I would receive on my whereabouts and disappearances. I kept away for the same reasons too. I was trying to find a balance, yet ignoring the fact that they were my flesh and blood and deep down inside, I should feel something for them just the way they felt something for me. Thankfully, over time, I realized that and I felt the weight of not being around them. When I finally made a true effort to spend time with them, I would find myself missing them more. So I would make surprise visits and spend more time during the holidays, limiting my personal travels to venture out into the world. I took a greater interest in large family gatherings, realizing that as my uncles and aunts got older and more relaxed, they were more enjoyable to be around. For a being who has seen the entire world, the one thing I cannot witness unless I see it through another person's eyes was their lives and their stories. I found myself enjoying them. I could live and see everything in the world today but I could not re-live history.

And the more I enjoyed these stories, the more I found myself listening to the stories of others too. The entire world did not live the fast-paced life I was accustomed to and in various places around the world, life was much slower. People still lived as large families and every once in a while, they would get together. I followed these families for years, having chanced across them intentionally or accidentally over the years. I would watch and observe the kids gather around a matriarch or a patriarch to hear tales, either about someone in the family or the community. I did not always understand the language but the expressions on the faces of the children let me follow the highlights. The interruptions from other family members, what I assumed were objections to some embarrassing details of said story made me laugh just as much as the members physically sitting there. These were important family moments to be cherished and I got the chance to share in them like I was one of them.

Except I was not one of them. I had never been one of them no matter which other family we spoke about. I was a stalker, trying to find joy in the communal life of others because I had none of my own. I was a fearful man, knowing that there will come a day when I'd be just as old but I would have no one to call my own to impart my life experiences to. So I continued to invade the personal space of other people and breached their privacy just so I could feel a little good inside for a few hours. I continued growing these one-sided relationships with complete strangers and become far too involved in their affairs. I was not one of them. I would never be one of them. In fact, they had no idea I even existed or was sitting just a few feet away from them with knowledge about them that no outsider should know. Deep down inside, I knew I was a horrible human being.

Chapter 31

Excerpts from my Life

Time: 2005

Location: The Midwest

Event: A second rescue

Continuing in my tradition of invading people's privacy, I often followed certain people around from time to time, trying to keep tabs on their lives. I didn't visit these people every day. If they had some profound effect on me, or I felt I needed to keep an eye on them, I would frequently visit them in the beginning but over time, I would limit my visits to once every few months. During these times, some would move and if I felt curious enough, I would track them down. The majority of these people were those that may have touched me in some ways but a few were made up of people I had rescued and were at risk of not living a normal life.

The events of 1999 still haunted me. Every once in a while, the warehouse with all the children would flash in front of my eyes and I would be reminded of those poor souls. I had followed every single one of them around after the incident to see how they adjusted and to make sure they got proper care. They all pulled through with varying degrees of success and over time, my need to stalk them lessened. They would forever remember the incident and it will have a permanent effect on the events of their lives but those kids still ended up going to school and were able to fit back into society. They all did, save one.

I only knew she was part of the group of children in that room because I had tagged every single one of them the second I had stepped into that dungeon. But I still cannot recall if I had actually seen her in there, nor do I remember when she stepped out, cradled in the arms of her rescuers on the day of the incident. All I knew was that following the incident, I had started tracking each kid, getting hold of their addresses. My first real encounter with her was the day I went to check on her the first time. She was no different than the rest during those early days, suffering from the same terrifying nightmares and getting similar treatments as the other children, whether it was to treat physical wounds or emotional ones.

She was named Claudia. I would love to say that she was the sweetest little thing but that would be untrue. I had never had a chance to observe her before the incident and what I saw of her now, well, it was difficult to watch and I limited the amount of time I would spend with her. As the other children adjusted and relived their nightmare a little less every day, her symptoms never improved and she continued to regress. I had hoped that she was just taking her time but the weeks turned to months and the months turned to years. In all my time, she turned out to be the only one I had to continually keep watch on. Whether it was the kid in the Philippines, the child I was only able to rescue after two years, or a lot of the people from some of my untold stories that

248

I had rescued from unfortunate events, they all somehow found a way to pull through. Not her.

She must have been seven when the incident happened. Being left alone since then had not been an option and frequent meetings would be required for her to ever gain trust in any new person in her life. Her parents remained her sanctuary at the beginning and her dad quit his job to take on something more part time so he could spend more time at home with her while the mom continued to work. Dad tried his best, continuing to homeschool during the evening while the girl, against her will, attended school during the day. As her experience forced her into a position where she could not socially interact with anyone normally, she got stuck in a never ending spiral of misery.

Kids are assholes and the ones around her were quick to label her a weirdo, making matters worse. By the time she was twelve, she turned to the only thing she could. The Internet. I was happy for that. She had a safe escape where she satisfied her curiosity about the world. She would read stories about the tragedies that had befallen others but I ensured she was never browsing and posting on forums. I did not want her to engage in any interactions with people that she would regret, at least at this age.

She finally entered her rebellious teenage years and the situation continued to deteriorate. My hope for her to find some solace on the web turned to concern, where I could tell that she was reading up stories about people experimenting with other means of escape. When she wasn't around, I would go back to those sites and leave them open, hoping that one of the parents would stumble across but they were oblivious. Her rebellious nature forced them to give her space as advised by a doctor who I could only label as a hack. Soon after, her behavior changed too and the warning signs were there. I felt like I was at a loss, not knowing how to communicate with this girl. Even if I did communicate, it would make matters worse. Nothing like knowing that a complete stranger has kept watch over you your entire life especially after being kidnapped at a young age.

So I would continue my passive aggressive methods to get through to her, leaving magazines, articles and pictures strategically in her view throughout the day talking about the ills or mishaps associated with recreational drugs. My efforts were all in vain as she continued to do her research and she continued building up her courage for that one day.

That day eventually came and I was ready to step in. It had been sheer luck that I had decided to check in on her that winter. She hadn't been at school or at home but she was a teenager without wheels and tracking her down wasn't hard. I found her standing around having a nervous conversation with a gentlemen much larger in stature. I wasn't sure if she chickened out or if her distrust in people and phobias forced her to turn away from that impending sale. She didn't try to make another attempt and I breathed a sigh of relief. The guy looked annoyed but fortunately for him, he decided to walk away from the situation too. I continued to watch her from time to time but my visitations became less frequent. Part of me hoped that she had learnt her lesson.

I waited too long. It was my first visit in 2006. She must have been fourteen going on fifteen but when I arrived at her place to make a routine stop after months of avoiding her, she wasn't there. Her parents were, however, which was strange, since she rarely left the house without her guardians. It was late but I still decided to check the school and there was still no sign of her.

Had my wish come true? Had she gathered the courage to make a friend and was currently at some mall doing whatever young girls do? I left for the evening, hoping to return a little later in the night to find out what was up. When I found her room empty a few hours later, I knew something was wrong.

That's when I noticed the parents acting differently. They weren't talkative and the dad appeared to have a perpetual gloom over his face. The two shared dinner in silence and after cleaning up, while the mother tried to sleep, he sat on the computer, running internet searches. I was not noticing them initially till the websites started opening up. My fears deepened with every click. She was missing again and I did not wait another second in that house.

It took only a minute at the precinct but I was able to go through all the data I needed. She had been missing for five weeks. There was no evidence of a kidnapping. She had been getting more and more secluded and all signs were pointing towards her having run away. I didn't understand it. She had been increasingly confrontational with her family, yet they catered to her every need. I read in her case file that one counselor said she had wanted to get back to a normal life without knowing how to do so.

I dreaded the worst. I knew about the time she tried to buy drugs. Sounded to me like she was using.

A small part of me tried to find a silver lining. If she had turned to drugs again, chances are, she never made it out of the city. If she was as terrified of unfamiliarity as she had been all her life, she probably didn't even attempt it. I looked to the sky and teleported below the clouds, using my brief seconds of hover time to locate a suitable building to start my search. The area was gridded out and I worked my magic. It took less than fifteen teleports but I had locked on to her. I breathed a sigh of relief at the exact moment I prepared myself to expect the worst.

It was a scene out of a clichéd setting in a movie. An old dilapidated building, crawling with junkies. The rooms and corridors suffered from questionable hygiene issues, but no one cared. Not the people occupying this building calling it home, not those who walked by it every day and not the government officials who promised every few years to make this world a better place for all the future generations to come. I did not teleport to the room she was in. I merely walked this time, delaying the inevitable. I did not want to see what was on the other side of that wall. I was already resigned to the fact that I would not be able to prepare myself for what was coming.

The thing is I cared about her most of all. She was another stranger I had elevated to the status of family, a stranger who had no idea that I even existed and whose life I had obsessed over for years; another unhealthy relationship that was one-sided on my part.

Still, I loved her in my own way. How could I face seeing her condition?

I went around the wall, biding my time when eventually, there was no more avoiding it. I was at the door. I passed through and I saw her. I watched her unable to move. She was fourteen, yet I saw the seven-year-old girl in front of me who hadn't taken a bath in days. She hadn't changed her clothes in forever either, showing signs of wear as portions of her top had been ripped in countless places. I hoped this was a natural wear and tear phenomena, given her state of existence. She had the syringe in her hand. I zoomed in on her arms. I saw the track marks.

How was she paying for this? I immediately regretted asking that question to myself as I did not want to know the answer to that one. She was crying. She was not enjoying this life but for some reason she was now stuck here and unable to break away from the cycle she was in. I could just transport her away but what good would that do? It would change little and in a few months, she could show up here again in the same situation or worse, venture out even further into the world making it harder for me to track her down. She needed a little push and I decided to do the unthinkable.

It took a while for her to notice me. She was still wrestling with the idea of sticking that needle in. This wouldn't have been the first she had today and in some sick way, I was relying on that. I started the theatrics for her, teleporting side to side, switching between visible and invisible and passing my hands through physical objects. She was confused, scared and curious. I had to make sure I did not push her over the edge. As I did that, I kept talking to her, asking her how she felt and if she was enjoying this. Would she like to break the cycle? As time went on, her focus changed from bewilderment over the trickery in front of her to the situation she had put herself in. At some point, my words took precedence and she cried some more. She threw the needle and covered her face, sobbing as she cried out that she wanted to go home. I walked over and held her hands, removing them from her face so she looked at me directly.

"Is this the life you want?" I asked her.

She looked around her, as if noticing for the first time the filth around her. She looked down at her clothes and I heard a small sob, as if she saw her disheveled appearance for the first time. She looked back up at me with eyes that were slowly turning glossy.

"No," she murmured, shaking her head as silent tears streamed down her dirty cheeks. I lifted one of my hands and wiped the side of her face, revealing more of her natural skin tone. My finger came back dark with dirt.

"Do you want help?"

She nodded.

"Let me take you back home." She sobbed some more and lay her head on me. She was tired and exhausted and ready to pass out. I waited for a moment, listening to her sobs slowly dying down and then teleported. I put her name and her parent's number in what was left of her pocket. Gently, I laid her down when the prompt in my HUD indicated there were no cameras around and stood up. She was now visible again to the real world and I slowly walked away, knowing that she was in the path of a security guard making his way back to the entrance. As I continued to walk away, I heard the concerned calls of a security guard requesting for help. Soon, she was carried by one of the guards through the hospital doors while another rushed with a stretcher. She was finally in safe hands.

She detoxed and eventually went home. Surprisingly, her latest experience helped improve her social skills. I guess that was what happened when you had far worse things to worry about. In some ways, I could not see this as a net positive. She was now even more damaged and while I think it helped her open her eyes to what she had been doing to herself, I couldn't say she knew how to rectify her situation.

I pitied her but more so, I pitied the parents. They could take comfort in the fact that this could have been a lot worse but I knew, looking at it from their end, that life was getting unmanageable and their pain and concern only seemed to grow.

Any parent would give up anything for their child and these parents were no different. But they would remain helpless and the more they would try to help her, the more they wouldn't know what to do. I would need to remain as her guardian angel, watching from above, ensuring that no harm came to her again.

Setback

Chapter 32

Excerpts from my Life

Time: Fall of 2005

Location: Hollywood Mansion

Event: The terrorization of a producer

I was perched on top of the 18th century antique armoire. It was made out of pretty sturdy wood, most likely a French creation, which had seen better days. I stretched my neck and glanced around the room. This master bedroom was larger than my entire apartment. Hell, it was probably bigger than my parent's first floor. The marble floor took on neutral earth tones and original paintings covered the walls. The current situation demanded the curtains to be drawn.

The young boy, dressed in casual jeans and a T-shirt depicting a man fighting a shark, seemed nervous. The door had shut behind him and he was now in the room alone with the older gentlemen, dressed in the crisply starched white shirts with cufflinks that were probably more expensive than my car. In his hand nested comfortably between his fingers was a glass of whisky, a single malt 18-year whose fragrance was overpowering me even from this distance. He was complimenting the boy on a job well done today and as an afterthought, extended his arm holding the glass in a gesture to ask if he would like to partake.

His eyes hinted that if he did, it wouldn't leave the room. I smiled. Even after all I'd put him through, his desire for young flesh was far too much of an addiction for him. This man was smooth as hell.

The boy tried not to look uncomfortable and reply back as nonchalantly as possible.

"No, thank you. I'm not sure if I'm ready for whisky yet." He was definitely uncomfortable. Rumors of others finding themselves in this situation were common.

"Nonsense. Have a drink," replied the older gentlemen, who had proceeded to pour from a decanter without waiting for the boy to respond. The boy looked around. He had talent. He had a singing voice that would grace the world two years from this moment and sky rocket him in the charts. He didn't know that yet, though he dreamed of it. He was wrestling with a dilemma. If he walked out now, would that dream come to an end?

"Hey, I'm not feeling too well today. Mind if we talk more about the contract tomorrow?"

The man was busy putting the lid back on the whisky. He hadn't flinched, though his facial expressions seem to show a hint of anger and frustration. Followed by nervousness. I smiled again. Maybe he had learnt his lesson.

The look of anger went away replaced by his judgmental eyes and a look of ultimatum.

"Child. There are many boys and girls who have walked

into this room. You know who they are. Many are living in mansions just as big as this not too far from here. When I asked them to sip this fine whisky, they all hesitated but the ones living in their fine homes today with their pools and Jacuzzis made sure they didn't walk out until I told them it was time to walk out. They still smile at me when we jog past each other on the street. Those who did refuse a drink, however, don't have their names chanted by teenagers everywhere. They don't have nice cars and I make sure that the only job they'll ever get is one that pays even less than minimum wage. So, when I tell you to take this glass, you will take it. Once you are done, if I tell you to do something else, you will do that, too. Have I made myself clear?"

The boy had clearly been intimidated. I chuckled, not because I was some kind of sadistic monster. Well, maybe I was but for completely different reasons. A part of me almost wanted certain events to play out the way I had imagined them in my mind.

The boy opened his mouth, attempting to make a final plea. It was a little heartbreaking.

The man cut him off mid-sentence and looked down, with a look of disappointment on his face. "You're not making me very happy. You don't want this night to end with me feeling a little disappoi ..."

A bulb on the chandelier burst. The boy looked up, half covering his face in fear. No such look on the face of the man. He knew what had happened. He knew what was coming. His waking nightmare was about to begin.

He turned to the boy and pleaded with him to stay. He screamed and he shouted, a deranged man who appeared nothing like his former self from mere moments ago. The boy was completely taken aback, having no idea what to make of any of this. Crazy was something he could not handle and, as the man reached out towards him, the boy backed away and scurried off through the doors, never to turn back. The man ran forward as well, hoping to reach the doors in time when they suddenly slammed shut.

He stopped in his tracks. I cracked my knuckles while still ethereal. It's time for my performance. Oh, how cocky I had gotten. That's the life you lead when you can do anything you want.

The man kept staring at the door, taking a step back slowly, as if not to wake up someone in the room. Suddenly, he lost sense of all orientation for a couple of seconds. I counted the time in my head. Three seconds in and he finally realized the surroundings I had familiarized him with. He splashed his hands frantically as a wave went over him, never once touching or ruining his beautiful shirt. From the right, a Great White jumped out right towards his face. I could not have planned it better. As his head disappeared inside the mouth of the shark, he was back in his room, sweating bullets. He was on his knees, gripping his heart as he panted and cried in desperation. He was looking around, as if hoping to anticipate where the next nightmare will come from. He saw his chair and rushed towards it, but only managed to crawl haphazardly. He gripped the arms of the chair and pulled himself up, leaning back as if he was preparing himself. He gripped the chair tightly, which worked out pretty well for me. I gripped the chair myself. Welcome to the Narcisse snake den.

I did my ritual of counting the seconds. It only took a few seconds for him to realize what happened. His eyes adjusted to the dimness and his head swayed violently back and forth as snakes coiled themselves around the chair. They were harmless of course, but the sight of tens of thousands in such a small area isn't for the faint of heart. A few were on his leg and he tried desperately to kick them off, screaming no at the top of his lungs. Moments later, he was back in his room kicking his shoes as hard as he could. I made sure these episodes never lasted more than seven to ten seconds. Any longer and he may not believe that he was delusional and going crazy.

He was sobbing openly now. I could hear commotion outside the room. Someone was climbing up the stairs. Time to call it a night for me. But before I went, I added one final new element to the ritual. I stood in front of him, watching him as he sat there stripped from all the power he had just a few minutes ago. I was the boss now. I raised my foot up and kicked his chair. As it came crashing down, his crying momentarily transformed into more desperate pleas. He was clearly willing to negotiate with his demons. The doors flew open and two men showed up at his side. He hadn't noticed. He just lay on the marble floor cowering in fear. His hired help looked at each other. This was the third time in a fortnight they have found him this way. I could tell they were ready to take some action. I'd heard there was a great institution not too far from where he lived that dealt with psychiatric break downs. I chuckled a little more and left. I would be back here again, I thought. Maybe it was time to replace the sharks with something far more menacing. Crocodiles?

I walked through the walls of his room only to enter into mine, a somewhat humbler setting. I was ready to call it a night. Looking at the sheets of orders I had piled up for tomorrow, I realized I could probably sleep in. My phone was blinking with messages and missed calls. Probably more clients but I decided to check anyway as I crashed on my bed for a moment before teleporting away to a finer location to spend the night.

I sat back up as I scrolled through one message after another. I switched screens to find multiple missed calls from my dad. I felt a little panic as I finally decided to check my voice mail. My dad usually left getting in contact with me as a job for my mother. Seeing his cell phone number show up so many times did not bode well.

Chapter 33

Excerpts from my Life

Time: Fall of 2005

Location: Hospital

Event: Mom

That Hollywood bigshot wasn't the only one who had all his power stripped from him in moments. Dad gave me the grave news on the phone: it was Mom. She was sick again.

After talking to my dad, I was the one who felt helpless. Now, my dad and I sat in the waiting room at the hospital, waiting for news.

My dad was one of the most aloof, stoic people I knew. He was a walking cartoon character. But right now, he looked like a man who was scared out of his mind. Many had come and said things to him, from family members to doctors. I had spoken to him, too, but he had largely remained silent through all those episodes, his face always pinched with worry.

All the time growing up, he never showed how much he cared for my mother. He wasn't the type who would make her breakfast in bed or secretly plan a romantic evening. But I knew how he felt about her and right now, the love of his life was lying in a hospital bed just a few yards from us, hooked up to wires and IVs, monitors beeping by her side.

The hospital administrator was back and calling out my dad's name. He snapped to and walked hurriedly over to the desk, hoping for some good news. It wasn't. Given Mom's weakening heart and her general prognosis, another heart transplant was out of the question.

He just stood there. He neither nodded nor protested. The administrator, realizing the awkwardness of the situation, looked at me. She immediately regretted it. Unlike my dad, I was filled with rage and anger. Before this was all over, everyone involved in that decision-making process would feel my wrath. She walked away, hoping to avoid a confrontation but only after offering us the deepest of condolences and a half-hearted attempt to extend us an olive branch by letting us know they will do all they can to make her comfortable in her last days.

I escorted my dad back to our seats but he resisted, preferring to go back in her room and sit with her. I obliged and walked him over, remembering to open the door instead of merely walking through it. I could not stand the sight of her connected to all these tubes. I could not allow it. He walked over, apparently ignoring all the things that were driving me mad and sat down on the chair by her side. She was sedated with her eyes closed, and remained completely motionless except for the rise and fall of her chest. He slowly reached over and folded the palm of his hands arounds her. I resisted the urge to cry. I told him I would be back in a few. He nodded, though I doubt he registered anything I said.

Nothing is impossible for me. I am the most powerful entity in the world. I could displace this world with the blink of an eye if I chose to. The universe had played many games with me but when it comes to my family, I stop playing ball. I walked through the corridors with a purpose making my way to any place where I could find the doctors I had earlier seen swarming around my mother. Eventually, I saw them through a glass window in the door. When the timing was right, I disappeared and made my way into the room.

They were still discussing her. In front of me were x-rays, medical books and a bunch of people discussing alternatives on what they could do. My anger partially subsided realizing that these people were still doing what they could. I owed an apology to the administrator. I looked around the room only to find drawings littered on the table of what I could only imagine were blocked arteries and blood clots. Then, it hit me.

Heart surgery. I went browsing through every medical book to find one picture of an artery that was clogged and pictures of what a clot would look like. It wasn't hard to find one and I returned back to the room where my dad was still gripping her hand. I did not hesitate. I had gotten so accustomed to my strengths that I never did stop twice anymore to plan out my moves.

I looked at my mom's face. She looked peaceful. I raised my hand and slowly lowered it towards her chest. I half expected her to react but as my hand slowly moved through her skin and entered inside, she didn't even flinch. One by one, my HUD started tracking hearts, arteries, blood clots and every other organ I was aware of. Labels showed up all over her body and I guided my hand relying 100% on what my powers were telling me. I found the blood clots. They were outside where I had expected them to be, judging by all the medical books I had scurried over in the past hour.

My finger was now on top of one of the clots. I looked at my mom once more and silently spoke to her. "I should have done this a long time ago, Mom."

I let a tiny part of my finger leave the ethereal plain. It was not even enough for me to be able to feel the substance surrounding me. I looked up my dad who hadn't moved an inch. His eyes were closed with his head resting on his hands and hers. I closed my eyes to and locked on to the surrounding area around the tip of my finger. I opened my eyes and prepared to teleport.

The sound of the room blared with different warning beeps. What had I done!? How could I have been so stupid. A blood clot is still blood. I never selected an area to teleport with me, just what constituted the makeup of the clot. I had come very close to teleporting all the blood out of her body. As nurses poured into the room, I backed away, horrified.

What had I done?

More people flooded the room and surrounded her. My dad refused to let go off her hand, anticipating that this may be the final time he gets to hold her while her body is still warm. As they separated his hand from hers, two orderlies pulled him away while she was wheeled off for an emergency surgery.

All I knew was, I'd tried to help, but I may have killed my mother.

Chapter 34

It turned out that she did not die that night. She survived, but barely. She would continue to live but medical science will never understand what happened. At one moment, her heart appeared ready to give up on her. The next, it appeared to be healing itself with the help of the doctors who went in for emergency surgery. However, her entire body had suffered some kind of trauma that could neither be explained nor understood. Her blood vessels were all slightly damaged and incapable of ever fully recovering. If anything, a wrong move from her would make matters worse. My mother would get another shot at life, as long as she was willing to sacrifice the majority of the things she wished to do with it.

She spent the next three months in the hospital. It was possible to have discharged her sooner but my parents had agreed to let them run countless tests. This was a first for medical science and they were both only too grateful to have the chance to spend more time with each other. I watched them smile and hold each other, looking into each other's eyes lovingly.

I felt a pang of jealousy. I'd never know that kind of love. I'd never get that close to anyone. When the time came when the doctors, residents and all other hospital personnel who had taken an interest in my mother's case could not justify keeping her around for another day, I drove the family car over to the entrance to watch my mother get out of her wheelchair and get escorted by my dad to the back seat. The entire ride home, my dad kept asking her what she wanted and if there was any place in the world he could take her. She just smiled and thanked an entity somewhere out there that she gets to see her two beloveds for a little while longer. They both smiled at each other. I die inside from the guilt.

I had almost killed her. Even though she was not dead, I had now severely limited what she could do. Working was out of the question. Carrying heavy loads was not going to happen. While my dad wouldn't think twice, she would forever be dependent on my dad now. That was my fault.

Me. Who was so cocky, he would mess around with the lives of the rich and famous. Me. Who swum amongst the fishes and can lay claim to being the only human in the world to have laid eyes on a true sea monster five thousand feet under the surface of the Indian Ocean. Me. Who could destroy the world in an instant.

Destroy. Even when I make things right, it's because I have the ability to destroy, not to fix.

I stayed with my parents for the next month, running every errand that needed attention just so my dad could continue being by her side. She called me into the room often but I never knew what to say to her. If she only knew I was responsible for her current state of affairs. I could not face her. I could not talk to her. I just lay in bed with her and hugged her a lot. This made her happy. This is the most attention I had given her in years. I sickened myself.

The month went by and it was time for me to go back. I visited them every weekend for a while but I needed some distance. I had a lot to think about. I would spend many days and nights just lying in my own bed. It had been a while since I had teleported to one of my beautiful hotels. It had been a while since I had utilized any power of mine at all. The universe had found a way to slap me right across the face just when I had gotten too cocky. Right when I thought I was invincible, capable of any feat, it punched me in the gut and made me human again.

I'd tried to make the world a better place. But in doing so, I'd taken too much joy in it. I'd tormented people. When things got difficult, I paid no heed to what was right or wrong. I merely did what I wished to do. In doing so, people lost their lives or worse, I've intentionally put a few in a position where I've acted as the judge, jury and executioner. Whether they deserved it or not was a different matter. I wasn't a being that could heal the world. I was a being only capable of destroying. My true essence was violent.

None of this sat well with me. I spent weeks sitting around moping. The more time that passed, the more I had trouble with this realization and the higher the motivation that I needed to change and prove myself wrong.

I was not going to give the universe a chance to teach me a lesson ever again.

Philanthropy

Chapter 35

Excerpts from my Life

Time: Spring of 2006

Location: Great Pacific Garbage Patch

Event: The great f**k up

Every time I've tried to turn my attention to helping people, I've had to live with unintended consequences. My destructive nature has taken over more than once in these situations.

Yet I never experienced this when I was out there being one with nature. Since the very early days of going ethereal, I'd been trying to clean up the rivers and oceans of the world. It was one of the few things I could do easily that didn't involve me worrying about getting caught or confronting other people. If I continued to focus on them, maybe I won't end up accidentally getting someone killed, whether it's some low life criminal or my own mother.

Hence, I continued the job of ridding the lakes and oceans of foreign contaminants and as I gained my HUD ability, the job only got easier. For every new type of thing I found in the ocean that didn't belong there, I added it to the list of filters I would activate when under water, whether it be something as large as the pacific or jumping into a very dangerous Pink Lake in Gatineau, Quebec. My radar allowed me to find things quickly and in moments, I would sort between what should be left on land and what should find its way into the mouth of volcanic hell. This activity continued for lengthy periods of time until the sinking of the Prestige, an oil tanker that now finds a home over 13,000 feet deep beneath the water near the coast of Spain.

I had mostly recovered from the events from six months ago and was determined to prove myself wrong. If I could only solve the world's problems without having to question my conscience, maybe I would find a way to redeem myself. So, I decided to take a more active part in philanthropic endeavors, hoping to get the same feeling of pride and satisfaction countless others get each time they venture out. I had not heard the news of this spill initially, not till reports started trickling in about the massive oil spill that was ruining the many beaches across the Mediterranean. The Prestige had been an oil tanker and capable of causing the largest spill in the history of the region. I sprang to action, not knowing what I would do but knowing that something had to be done about it.

At the end of the day, I was not able to avoid the spill from getting the aforementioned title but I was able to somewhat reduce the amount of spillage. I immersed myself into whatever continuous streams of oil particles I would find within the hull and outside of it and simply transported it out. It wasn't an easy thing to do. Oil wasn't something I was willing to just throw into a volcano. I honestly had no idea what the ramifications of that may be.

It also wasn't like I could simply transport the oil to some location on earth. The environmental impact of such a thing would be immeasurable. Oil was also a liquid and in order for me to transport it, I needed to bring it to a place where I could deposit it right away as I would not be able to keep it ethereal with me for longer than a split second. So I was forced to remove it in smaller chunks of quantity and transporting it to other parts of the world where tankers would normally be filled up. I had to keep the amounts at unsuspicious levels, though I doubt any oil producer would ever say no to having extra oil. I had no idea the grades would ever mix but there are some things in life I never cared about.

The incident with Prestige was a disaster but it was a great learning experience for me and opened my mind to the possibility of doing more to clean up the world. I researched the problems associated with the world's water supplies. Some of the issues were out of my hands but others not so much. I would take a snapshot of sewage spilling into rivers and lakes and promptly add it to a filter that allowed me to start removing it from the water. I would monitor the world for other spills, trying to minimize the damage before it got worse. It was easiest for me to always solve the issue at its source, before the spills would disperse. The issue that I always had to deal with was where to transport such a thing. Sewage was easier to handle. The majority of the developed world had ways to cope with such a thing and I would simply add more sewage to the amount these countries had to contend with. Other types of spills were harder to contend with but over time, I found the right locations for those too. Things were going great till I accidentally read up on the Great Pacific Garbage Patch.

Residing in the Pacific, this patch of garbage contains the highest density of plastic in the oceans, accumulating for years from pollutants in the seas and oceans as currents slowly divert it to this one location. This area is massive, with a range of hundreds of miles and I was hell bent on cleaning it up. I made my way to the coordinates and was left confused.

I definitely saw the debris but it was nowhere near the scale of what I had imagined. I had expected to see a floating mess, one I would simply be able to place my hand on and transport to any part of the world in chunks. But what I saw was scarce and spread out. I cleaned what I could and made my way back, trying to read up more on it and that is when I found out that the plastic had degraded to a microscopic level, dangerous to human and marine life but quite invisible to the eye. I was at a loss of what to do. It was impossible for me to tag this. I had no idea what microscopic plastic was supposed to be. I tried commanding myself to look for it but my HUD could not translate what it did not understand.

I eventually visited various laboratories where I tried to find pictures or any studies on the subject. My initial investigation yielded no results and it was simply by chance that I happen to come across a single study which happened to show some microscopic pictures of what I was hoping to see. Others, too, were determined to clean up this patch and in doing so had already done a level of research I had ignored doing for myself. Reading up and looking through all samples and pictures they had to offer, I arrived back to the patch with my newfound knowledge and searched again. The ocean turned into a river of tags, no pun intended, but I made a big mistake. Through all my research, whether it is true or not, I had convinced myself that while these particles are countless, they were not continuous. I dipped my hand to transport them out but I was not able to create the daisy chain I had been expecting. The failure I had felt only months ago in a hospital room returned. I was reminded once again that I was not omnipotent.

I spent a couple of days trying different tricks to rid the saltwater of its alien parasite in measurable amounts but nothing I tried worked. All these years, if I wished for something, it would happen but even my powers were not able to fool my mind on this one. Had I never had the knowledge of how the particles were dissolved, I would have never had to deal with this particular issue. I realized now that all these years when I had been cleaning up rivers away from their origin, I followed massive blobs and assumed a continuous connection between any contaminants I wished to get rid of and my powers had worked. A sense of nervousness kicked in and I made my way to a river I would routinely purge. My power continued to be useful as long as I could physically see the dirt, firth or the hazard but I was now powerless to simply make an assumption on cleaning up everything anymore. I kicked myself.

I returned back to the patch on the third day. I might have ruined my plan to make the world's bodies of water completely pure but I wasn't going to give up on this garbage patch just yet. Eventually, I made a decision I did not like but I felt like I had no choice. This would require a little planning on my end and I set things in motion. I inventoried the active volcanoes around the world and returned back to the patch. The only way to remove the plastic was to simply remove the water. I was very hesitant. Can one really remove so much water? How would the volcanoes of the world react? Was I once again going to solve an issue by simply using brute force without understanding the consequences of my actions? I decided to ignore that last question completely. I had to be very cautious. Not knowing what would happen if I just removed a sizable amount of water from the system, I was determined to limit the amount of cleanup I would perform on a routine basis. Each day, I removed tens of thousands of gallons of water and deposited it evenly over the volcanoes. The volcanoes reacted little to this and I would observe to see if I was making any impact to them. Thankfully, to this day, I haven't seen any negative repercussions, but I worry still. Each day, I would return back and scan again. For the first few weeks, whatever I removed was simply replaced back and I noticed no difference. But slowly, the quantity of plastic I found started to thin out ever so slightly and I could confirm I was making some progress. I continued my efforts and branched out, prioritizing my focus on the denser areas of plastic. A few more weeks passed and I reached an impasse.

I had made a decent dent in the patch, one that I could personally be quite proud of. However, with that came the problem of sparser quantities of dissolved plastic. I had definitely reduced the area that the patch covered and also reduced the density of the dissolved particles but for me to continue further with the removal of the saltwater itself did not seem to give me the same cost benefit as it did before. I was already worried about removing all this water from the eco system. I was not willing to continue further without a much better plan. Deep down, that horrible feeling of helplessness came over me again.

The truth was, unless I was able to overcome the original problem I had created for myself (which I never resolved), there would be no better plan. I hung around the patch for a few more days, not really doing much and then proceeded to simply leave and find other patches in the ocean that could be cleared up to a point. I'd never really been sure how I feel about what I did here. It was disappointing I was never able to fully recover the ocean back to its original form. It had seemed like such a clear winner in my books but at the same time, I had achieved somewhat of a success. I took solace in the fact that the next time someone conducts their own research on the water, they would be treated with a pleasant surprise and maybe find a solution to fix the rest of the problem. At least I had made the task of the clean-up less daunting.

However, I created more of a doubt in my head that I would ever be able to prove the universe wrong.

Chapter 36

The Great Pacific Garbage Patch wasn't the only thing I was unsuccessful in fixing completely on my own. I ran into the same issue with the ozone layer, too, when I attempted to do something about the giant hole in it.

But that's how it is, right? You mess up once and it appears that your losing streak would never end. With each failure I experienced, I came to accept with a heavy heart that at times, my powers had limits. It was certainly disappointing but I had to keep pushing myself. I just had to reprioritize where my efforts could be utilized.

Other than cleaning up the rivers, seas and oceans around the world, I continued to concentrate on disaster relief whenever it felt like my services would be beneficial in time sensitive situations. I'd been there to assist during hurricanes, earthquakes, tornadoes, avalanches and mudslides. I'd been there when forest fires have broken out or buildings and bridges have collapsed due to a lack of proper maintenance. Lives were saved, belongings were secured and damage to personal property and infrastructure was minimized. I'd probably saved the world a lot of grief and money over the decade. The level of success I was experiencing in this domain was certainly more of a highlight for me during these years.

Before my mother's near rendezvous with death, I had also taken a special interest in something that became a bit of a pet project of mine. After the 2004 tsunami, I kept a special eye on the Sentinelese tribe in North Sentinel Island off the coast of India. They captured my curiosity like no other people in the world. Uncontacted for thousands of years, they were the world's most remote tribe and after a research mission was launched to verify their status after the tsunami that provided back inconclusive results, I took it upon myself to do my own research. They were still alive but much like everyone in the region, had suffered but were up and about and trying to build back. They were a resilient group, but I had a hard time figuring out if they chose to ignore the rest of the world or were oblivious and scared of the giant machineries they would see flying high in the sky. Regardless, they wanted no part of it and would threaten anything foreign from coming close, be it man or machine. I visited them once more in 2006 hoping their population had remained stable. It brought me great joy that indeed, it did.

It was around that time however that remote Islands in general became more of an interest to me. Another such island was Tokelau near Samoa with a small population and reasonably remote, serviced by a single ship that could only move between islands if the weather permitted. Towards late 2009, when the local government discussed possibly powering the island with solar power, I took it upon myself to introduce the islanders with that clean energy, hoping to generate interest and continue to push for its funding. Doing such a thing was not easy though. I had a few devices sneaked in bags of others and once on the

Island, would conveniently move the devices around, allowing others to experience them. I may have frustrated many with the game of hide and seek with the devices but at least it has helped in making a power station on the island in the near future a realistic hope.

And in this manner, I continued with my efforts to make this world a better place to live in. I undertook the task of creating an artificial barrier reef near Tuvalu, an Island that will be amongst the first to suffer the impact of climate change, in the hopes of giving it a few additional years before the rising tides force everyone off the land. Carterets Island, another chain in danger of vanishing due to climate change had taken up relocation for its inhabitants, and I provided assistance where I could, making sure families did not have to leave any belongings behind. Relocation was not the solution I would want but for the majority of these islands, there was no other choice left. Some had passed the point of no return and some will get there soon enough. That is what happens when self-interest and profits take precedence over the lives of people and nature. Depression would often set in and on many occasions, when I decided to take action, I would remind myself on the vow I had taken countless times to remain non-confrontational and simply, help the world.

Thus, humanitarian efforts would continuously find themselves with far more medication, blankets, and equipment than they had started off with before distribution, wells across Africa would find themselves dug a little deeper each morning people would wake up, and additional rocks would be found at dangerous river crossings, making it easier for people to cross over or to even construct a better mode of crossing.

I could have just built a reef, or transported all the medication that was needed or help put up bridges and roads but my role as far as the universe was concerned was to assist, even if I wanted to do more. While my anonymity continued to be my guiding principle in making such decisions, other more philosophical reasons occupied my mind. The world must continue to exist without me and that I was not and should never be a get out of jail card.

Of course, I was always nervous about messing up again. My mother was closest to me but she was still a single person. What if my actions took away countless mothers from young girls and boys such as myself? My wish for anonymity during my philanthropic endeavors as well the philosophical debates in my head were often trumped by this one thought. But a mix of failures coupled with the nature of my passiveness by simply being reactive to world's issues kept taking a toll on me. As time went on and on, holding to my philosophies continued to be harder and time and time again, I would involve myself a little more, becoming a more organic part of this world. The fear of messing up was always something on my mind. But I guess power truly does corrupt and try as I might to constrain myself, I felt I had to do something. Even if I made mistakes along the way.

Chapter 37

Excerpts from my Life

Time: Fall of 2007

Location: An impoverished region of the world, run by warlords

Event: Pirate Booty

Gold, gems, artifacts and salvage. A lot lies underwater and up to that moment in 2007, I had spent the majority of my time trying to cleanse the world's oceans. My focus changed a little bit when I happened to locate a debris item I had selected as part of my filters some tens of feet under the sea bed. The navigation was difficult as once I went beneath the sand bed, my visibility was completely impaired. I came back out again and looked around. I was pretty deep underwater and the closest reef was a bit of a distance away. Disturbing this sand at the bottom should not have any significant impact. I thus removed portions of the sand in small quantities, just to be extra cautious, slowly digging a hole to this piece of garbage I had wished to remove. I was mostly curious as its removal was inconsequential at this point. What I ended up finding however during the process was carved wood. I stopped. I added this particular type of wood to the current filter and I proceeded to remove the sand around it. The remains of a boat could be made out and I felt a sense of excitement creep up on me. This was fantastic.

I did not have the patience to do an entire excavation so

I touched the boat and teleported it out of the area, though leaving it in the ocean, a few hundred yards out. This wasn't a boat. It was a portion of what must have been a ship. This particular portion appeared to be the stern, approximately twenty-five feet in length and ten feet wide. I teleported out to a dive shop and grabbed a light. Accessing the inside of the hull was not much of a problem. I did not even have to go through it. There were enough holes to just crawl through and that's what I did. No dead bodies. I breathed a sigh of relief. But I found old instruments of navigation and various other tools I could not recognize. This ship must have been buried in the sand for ages. It belonged in a damn museum. I did a quick scan for anchors in the immediate area, specifically one that wasn't situated next to a regularly used buoy. There was one a couple of miles out and I put my plan in motion. Quickly, the ship was transported and partially buried around the anchor point. It took a few adjustments but I managed to place a small portion of the ship around the anchor.

I teleported up to the boat only to find a bunch of people with way too much money fishing for marlins or whatever deep sea fish they hoped to catch. I did a quick check for the usual suspects and chuckled. There was absolutely no noteworthy fish to catch in the area and I figured the locals were probably scamming a bunch of tourists who have never seen a marlin in their lives. I hung around for fifteen minutes, watching one guy gripping a fishing pole as if at any moment, he was going to reel something in. One of the girls was hitting the cooler pretty hard to the point where the tour operators looked a little concerned about her movements. I was growing tired. These guys were not going to catch anything and I had better places to be. I would be doing everyone a favor if I forced this boat to move.

I teleported into the middle of the ocean and teleported back, a small distance away from the boat. But this time, I wasn't alone. Twenty five feet on each side, the ocean water teleported with me and right away, lost contact. It was brought back into the normal plane of existence, causing a mini tidal wave. I wasn't worried. I was there to save the boat had my plan gone wrong. It wobbled, throwing a couple of people off their chairs and induced nervous laughter from everyone. The girl who had consumed more beer than she should have, laughed the loudest, even as she barely hung on. Clearly, one such incident wasn't going to deter anyone. Every minute, I repeated this same action. The crew got a little concerned before the tourists, probably caring for the safety of their livelihood and gave the signal that they were going to move to another location. The anchor was pulled but not without resistance. Eventually, it broke through and made its way to the top and I teleported back down to make sure everything was okay. It wasn't. The piece had broken through but did not remain attached to the anchor. I grabbed it and placed it gently back on it, escorting it and nudging it back in place every time it would move around a little. It was about to surface and I gave it a final nudge to keep it in its place. The locals and the tourists gathered, confused by what they were seeing. A life jacket was thrown out into the open water and one individual jumped into the water to help dislodge this monstrosity from the anchor. However, the sight of a small desk with navigational tools stuck on it resulted in exactly what I had hoped. The crew exchanged dialogue in their native language while the tourists tried to get their heads around what was going on. They pulled the table back up and spent some time investigating it. They were unsure of what it was and where it came from but everyone agreed that the fishing trip was over. The possibility of finding an ancient wreck got the occupants of the boat excited and they raced to the shore. A couple of days later, the wreck was confirmed and work was underway to see if the wreckage could be pulled up.

I was rather proud of myself but wondered what else was lying on the ocean floors. On the one hand, I was the only person in the world equipped with locating all that the ocean bed had to offer however, while my HUD continued to function, I had no recourse for darkness. Traditional lights could only go so deep and trying to get something that worked thousands of feet underwater would draw attention, even if removed for only a brief period of time. I made a decision to scour closer to the coasts. It made sense. Back in the day, most seafaring vessels wouldn't dare go too far from the coast anyway. The results were almost immediate and so were the problems. I could not suddenly unearth so many ships at once or the booty they may have dropped during their travels. It would draw far too much attention. The reason why I spent so much time underwater trying to make a difference was because it had limited scrutiny, yet now, this is going to become problematic. I needed a way to select the ships I wanted to draw attention to.

But what was the point? I would probably be helping a museum or enriching the life of a historian. How was I really bettering anyone's lives by spending my time doing this? That's when it hit me. I started looking for gold and gems and once again, the results were immediate. It was almost something out of a movie, with entire treasure chests lying around and in the cases where they had broken, all this wealth lay dispersed over and under the sea bed. I would gather them all up and transport them to my hiding spot within the Lechuguilla Cave. I kept gathering for days, often finding certain artifacts that I was sure belonged in a history class but for now, I kept them in the cave, hoping to one day get them in the hands of the right people. I also found salvageable metal and I gathered that too and stored it in the Sahara, as it was much too big for the cave.

Once I was done, I looked at what I had in front of me. I was in a position to be the richest person on the planet. One of those treasure chests alone could buy me a small country. I always kept a small supply of this wealth in my cave for myself and an emergency supply in a far more accessible place just in case I lost my powers one day. But the rest of it was not needed by me. I emptied out large amounts of gold from one of the chests I had excavated only days before and conducted a quick test. I selected a small fishing village and placed the chest with a limited amount of gold within a noticeable rocky area by the sea. It took a few days for it to get noticed but it didn't stop the children from grabbing it and bringing it back with them as the adults gathered around to see what bounty they had found.

Soon the news spread across the village and more people gathered. This was a small community and a very homely one. There had been no squabbles over whose kid found the treasure and how it needs to be divided. After ensuring that the chest did not belong to anyone in particular and no one had any knowledge of where it may have come from or what its purpose may have been, the gold was placed under the care of a trusted villager and in a few days, it was easy to tell that they were planning on figuring out the best way to spend it to help out the entire community. Some of the elders had been traveling to find new boats, others were finding contractors in nearby villages to fix problems that had plagued them for a while. I was happy. This was exactly what I had wanted and a difference was being made. More importantly, it was reaffirming my faith in the goodness of people but only briefly. Things always had a way to go south just when I get my hopes up.

I returned a couple of days later and noticed something was very wrong. This wasn't the village I had left. Some regulars appeared to be missing as well and there appeared to be a gloom. I scanned for the gold and it wasn't around. Nor was the chest. They wouldn't take all of it for any kind of a transaction and it was safe to assume that events may have transpired that did not end favorably. I switched my scanners on and I found them all in each one of their respective homes in horizontal positions. I found that odd, given the time of my visit. I decided to stroll over instead of teleporting, hoping to observe and see if I could understand the reason for why the air around the village smelt so different. The women felt more at guard and there was little activity at the stores. Those that happened to have people around were not really being used for commerce. They just happened to be the location where most people had congregated and indulging in deep conversation.

As I got closer to one of the homes, I noticed one last thing that was oddly peculiar. A lot of windows were shut. Doors that were normally open were held ajar only by a bit. This didn't appear to be the inviting village I had been spending my time at and upon entering the first home, I understood why. There were bruises all over this first villager with signs of fracture. Family members tended to his needs but overall, the mood felt grim. That feeling that had been haunting me for the last few months came over me again. I tried to shake it off as I hurriedly made my way to the next house only to find a very similar situation. My walk to the next home had a sense of purpose and upon my arrival, I could only find one way to deal with my present failure. With anger. It was apparent to me that the bounty I had left here somehow caught the attention of the wrong crowd. I was to blame for what had transpired in my absence. There had to be retribution for this.

I could not understand the language they spoke so it was hard for me to decipher the true nature of what had occurred here and who it had involved. I spent a few hours looking for old gold coins around the region but it appeared I had conducted my search in the wrong direction. Coincidentally, I arrived back at the village at the same time some questionable looking people were getting out of their dusty and rust laden pickup truck. There was terror in the faces of the villagers, with people shaking their heads and pleading with these men who held rifles in their hands, as if to convince them that they had nothing to offer. The most vocal one received the butt of the gun to his face as others tried to close their doors and hide inside. The gunmen spoke loud, like giving a speech of sorts, casually pointing their weapons at men, women and even children who were quickly shielded by loved ones. I stayed prepared. I had to follow these guys back but no one was getting hurt today. I wasn't prepared to allow another punch to be thrown.

First things first, there were lethal weapons at play that required neutralization. I walked alongside these gunmen. A quick swipe and I removed any bullets that the cartridges may be loaded with. A quick swoop and the chambers were left empty too. Extra ammo was removed and a couple of handguns were displaced. I located the wife of one of the men lying in the infirmary and I could see the fear and the anger in her eyes. If it wasn't for the helplessness she was feeling, it was conceivable that she would have engaged in something really stupid. I was counting on that and decided to take a very calculated risk. I left a loaded handgun close to her. I kept the other gun with me for the moment.

Another guy, well past his retirement age, was smacked in the head as well. He fell to the ground. Some around him momentarily reacted, reaching out for him but none dared get any closer. The wife I was counting on was losing her sense of fear, now completely engulfed in hatred for what she was witnessing. I nudged the gun closer and it caught her eye, completely eliminating whatever hesitation she had left. I hoped she would be smart, that she would shoot before warning them. I did not expect her to be a good shot but I needed them to be taken off guard. That's when I can make my entrance.

She fired the first shot alarming everyone within earshot. The gunmen prepared for battle yet in the chaos, were unsure where the bullet was fired from. Pandemonium had ensued as the majority of the people ran in different directions while others cowered in the hopes of dodging bullets. The gunmen screamed out what I assumed were profanities as they finally turned to this charging woman who didn't give two fucks about her life at this point as she continued to empty out her clip. They fired back, hoping to stop her in her tracks and make a quick example of her. But her charge continued with only a few rounds left in her handgun and the men, in a fit of confusion, played with their guns while looking for cover. She was almost out of ammo but it was enough to frighten the multiple gunmen. This was my moment.

I dropped the other gun on the ground and kicked it closer to a man who had decided to seek refuge next to a wall. He noticed the gun, and must have assumed that it fell off one of the men during the retreat. The same look of determination was in his eyes that I had previously witnessed in the wife whose husband lay on a bed with broken fractures. He shuffled to the gun and picked it up, firing it blindly in the direction of the antagonists. With the gunmen unable to figure out what was wrong with their rifles, their slow retreat turned into a full-fledged sprint back to the truck. The wife was all out but continued to run and as fear was replaced by a small sense of victory and defiance, others joined her in her forward march towards the pickup truck. The gunmen could still hear bullets flying over their heads and refused to turn back. I managed to trip a couple, removing the weapons from them once again, and throwing them closer to the villagers who appeared to get bolder by the second. I deposited the ammunition close to them as well. The bullets mostly missed their marks but the village had a stash of weapons and ammunition to defend themselves for a short while and a small victory in their belts to bolster their confidence. I knew that wouldn't be enough, though. The last of the tripped gunmen got back up and made a final run, getting into the truck in time and racing off. I followed close behind. I had no choice. I knew how this area of the world worked and a handful of guns would not be enough until I took more drastic actions. For now, I forgot about my mother. For now, I forgot about my code, my guiding principles and the methods and philosophies I had decided to adhere to.

I sat on top of the truck, listening to these men nurse their superficial wounds. With each passing minute, their voices grew bolder, as if revenge was already being plotted. I grinned. I missed this. It took another half an hour but we finally made it to camp. There were also a lot more of them enough to frighten law enforcement in even a large town. As the truck pulled in, some commotion began as the story of their latest raid was narrated from one person to the next. Someone of authority was summoned and the story was repeated once more. The authority figure was not too physically intimidating but his demeanor told another story. The reactions of those around him implied he had earned his position. Questions were asked and those returning were screamed at and kicked for incompetence. The leader turned around and screamed out instructions. Gestures and grunts of battle were exchanged as this army mobilized. Individuals picked up their own rifles and ammunition and proceeded to step into their cars, hoping to exert their dominance over those who were defenseless against what was coming to them.

Not on my watch.

I scanned the area and once I had confirmed there was no one else around in the immediate area, I began. I knocked a tree down over one of the newer unoccupied vehicle just as one of the younger lads was about to step into it. As everyone's attention turned to the spectacle of a crushed jeep under a large trunk, I touched the next one and teleported 50 feet off the ground. Gravity took over and this all-terrain vehicle found its way back to the ground. I did not check to see if anything or anyone was underneath. I wasn't in a caring sort of mood. I was not interested in knowing if anyone got caught in the explosion of the gas tank that occurred right after or if someone had happened to be in the way of the flaming tire that had been dismembered from the jeep and was now speeding towards the crowd of shocked men.

As panic and pandemonium broke out amongst these heartless souls, I started knocking down people one by one as they ran in no particular direction. Some started shooting for no reason either, with bullets flying into the air, trees, buildings and those they had called comrades just moments ago. A few were trying to get control of the situation, barking out threats and orders and I grabbed one by the neck as I ran and teleported a few feet up in the air and let him go. He crashed into a trash can as he landed, his body going limp after jerking like a ragdoll. I grabbed another couple of guys who were running next to each other and teleported them back to where the jeep I had previously thrown had exploded and was on fire. They almost ran into a fiery death. I flung a few more vehicles up in the air and made them land around the perimeter. By now, all sanity was lost and the men started converging back, hurtling around each other in a circle, not sure where the next attack may come from. They were close to a wall that I intentionally decided to teleport into. Chunks of brick and metal flew in all directions, smashing against the back of heads as more bullets were fired and more fell to the ground.

I wasn't trying to kill anyone but I wasn't intentionally trying to keep this little battle of ours safe. With every passing minute, I made the playing field a little more dangerous. The spectacle of flying vehicles was now joined by rolling tree trunks, exploding bricks, littered fires and people constantly getting teleported back to the same position they had started running from moments ago, again and again. More and more of them either fell or gave up trying to run, succumbed to the mental and physical exhaustion. The leader was left intentionally unharmed. His face had lost all color and his arms trembled. The demeanor that commanded the respect of all his peers was now replaced with one that was waiting to beg whoever was in charge right now to stop and go away. I walked over to him and he looked right through me at the destruction I had caused, hoping that he could somehow vocalize to himself what had just happened. A wet spot had begun to form in front of his pants and it brought me a little joy. No. It brought me a lot of joy. I grabbed his shirt and flung him. I'm not particularly a big guy and it didn't push him too far but an invisible force pushing against his chest had a far bigger effect on him. He fell to the ground chaotically punching and kicking up in the air hoping to make contact with his unseen opponent. I let him continue for a while as he kept connecting with nothing. His punches became more and more erratic as his will ran out to fight back. A sad expression came over my face.

He was giving up too quick. I was hoping he would embarrass himself a bit further. It was time to have a little more fun. It was time for the final nail in the coffin. I raised my arms to my side like a bear and then waited for his reaction.

His feet, ass and arms were all on the ground as he was looking forward. Suddenly he jerked and moved back even further, trying to desperately crawl away while facing the dismembered forearms and hands that made their way towards him. They moved around unsupported in the air side to side, disconnected from anything else that he could see that was organic in nature. As I got closer, I reached down to his head. He watched these hands from hell surround his face and he closed his eyes, muttering what sounded like either a prayer or a call for forgiveness. I gripped his head and followed it with a head butt. I let go.

My arms were by my sides now and he continued to stare at them, waiting to see what my arms were going to do next. After a momentary standoff, I moved in close once more. With one last desperate attempt, he pushed his hands forward and gripped my wrists just as I came down on him. Success! His determination grew. He had no idea what witchcraft was at play here but as God was his witness, he was going to fight back. How I loved the idea of giving him some false hope.

Atom by atom, my forearms and hands started to go ethereal while still remaining completely visible. The fighting spirit in him started to fade slowly as his grip over my wrists began to get wobbly and eventually, my arms slowly moved first, through his hands, followed by his wrist and his arm. He was paralyzed. As my fingers came to rest around his throat, my skin lost its ethereal form. He felt the warmth of my flesh around his neck and now the only thing left in him was pure terror.

I punched his face.

I punched it again.

I punched once more.

Then another time.

I waited another second and jabbed his face again. As tears rolled down his eyes, he opened his mouth to let out a plea but only blood emerged. I was done listening. I punched him some more. When I was done punching him, I kicked his shin. I kicked it again. I felt a calm over me, the warning sign that I had been trying to avoid but any sense of care had left me at the village. As his body remained motionless yet breathing under the patch of red that had been forming over the course of the beating, I stopped. I left him alive but I had beaten him to a point where he no longer had the will to move. I pulled him to the car with little resistance. I grabbed all the guns I could find and the gold they had stolen. I grabbed anything else I felt the village could use. I transported the entire vehicle back, with him in the driver seat unconscious back to the village. Once I knew the vehicle had been noticed, I turned around and walked over to the rocky beach and sat down. The village sounded like it had surrounded the car. The gold and the guns sounded like they were being carried away.

I heard a final loud cry from a defeated man followed by angry voices that may have been kicking something around. I never looked back. For now, street justice appeared to be the right course of action. I continued to stare at the ocean, humming a tune to a song I no longer recognized.

I was well aware of what had just transpired. After months of trying to help out the world while keeping my powers and emotions in check, I finally let myself go. I could blame it on righteous anger, but I knew that a part of me had been yearning to do so for a while.

I would have never allowed what I had just described a decade ago. I'm glad I wasn't the person that I was slowly becoming now. The truth was that having power or superiority over others was an addictive thing and if you exercise it too much, you did it for the sake of wanting to be better than the rest. But even when I decided to punch that man's face in repeatedly, I may have been enjoying what I was doing, even if it felt wrong to do so. It may even appear that I had snapped and was responding to my base instincts but the truth is that my actions were quite deliberate. For years, I have practiced my reactions to various different situations and in this particular moment, I had exercised one that I had gone over in my head countless times. My punches were premeditated and served a purpose. The theatrics were deliberate and served a purpose too. I was in control of myself.

Being superior also implied that those around you could be made to feel like they're in a position of inferiority and I used it to my advantage. I knew how it made others feel when they could not understand nor control the events around them and during those moments where I felt like confrontation was inevitable, I used this advantage to the fullest extent. I used it just the way I had premeditated them. My confidence was returning and it was difficult to ignore that in only a few short months, I was coming close to becoming the same person I had been hoping to avoid.

I spent a lot of time reflecting after the events of that day. Much like a bad habit, I could not shut the doors on who I was or how I felt. I had my moments of weakness but I could not ignore my strengths either. In moments of confrontation, the results normally ended up in favor of me. But I still feared what I was and what I could become. I feared failing at the wrong moment because my ego had outgrown my abilities.

Moderation felt like my only key.

Philanthropy. The more I tried to make a difference to the world, the more I continued to come in conflict with others. For a few years, I ignored this reality even though the thoughts were always present at the back of my mind.

It wasn't until 2007 that I finally started thinking about philanthropy from a different perspective altogether. While I still avoided taking action if only to figure out what I wanted for myself, I started observing the lives of whalers, hunters and poachers. I watched deforestation occur across the globe as people hoped to develop new markets. I observed towns like

Kivalina in Alaska in its losing battle against climate change and I kept a watchful eye on the industries that polluted. I knew it was only a matter of time before I wouldn't be able to hold myself back and the best thing for me to do before I enter this new phase in my life was to go back to my roots.

If I was to moderate my actions moving forward, I had to create a new set of rules and guiding principles in relation to direct and intentional confrontation. I started to study not just the subject matter that had my attention but also the players involved, ensuring that I understood the innocence and the guilt of all those that would be affected by my actions. I was entering into an area of gray, even if to a lot of people, it seemed very black and white.

2007 was going to be a year of learning. 2008 was the year I had to ensure all hell didn't break loose. It was the year where I could achieve great success and set myself up for terrible failure when it mattered the most.

Confrontation

Chapter 38

Excerpts from my Life

Time: Spring of 2008

Location: Africa

Event: The hunt

I had selected my target very carefully. I had been stalking her for a while now, even before she left her resident country. When I put this particular plan together, it required me to do months of research. It started with me spending a lot more time in the field observing the efforts people put into hunting an animal. I had to work my way backwards. I would locate those with guns, which was never the hard part. If anything, I initially thought my job was quite easy and the first time I came across a man holding a rifle, I almost decided to act right away but something held me back. I knew nothing about this poacher and what his intentions were. He had been hunting an elephant, so each time he came near one that seemed like a worthy target, I merely moved the massive bull to another location within the park. I'm sure I left it pretty confused but that was the price of saving its life. But I did not follow the animals around. I followed the people this time and while this particular man had been very focused on finding an alpha male with big tusks, I occasionally observed him admiring the rest of the wildlife and I was forced to stay my hand. I had to remind myself that I had just entered that gray area I had been so afraid to approach all these years.

After an unsuccessful day, he returned home to his disappointed family. This activity of his helped bring in the bread and butter. His priority was his family and their well-being. Would he have chosen this life had he been given another opportunity? I couldn't know. I observed many more poachers and their stories appeared to be somewhat similar. Many were trying to get their kids through school, often driving a handful of children with them to another village or town that offered better education. This was not the type of evil I was looking for. What if I focused on the source of the issue?

Saving an animal meant it was a little harder for me to trace the source of the poaching. But once in a while, I would be too late and the remains of the animals were already making their way to the end buyers. Even here, I met more gray area, with most growing up in cultures where prevalent beliefs were held to a higher level than the life of the animal itself. Such traditions were difficult to break and it was hard to simply classify such people as evil as well, even if they were ignorant. I could put an end to these activities but without breaking the belief system, the practice would always continue in some shape or form. There were definitely a few who were taking advantage of the situation but these were in the minority. I had still not found my target.

That's when I honed in on hunters. Surely, this wasn't a gray area at all and these people were well aware of what they were doing. So, I followed the hunt and even here, I wasn't too sure about my initial analysis. I was frustrated not because I hadn't expected to find a gray area but because so much of our world was being destroyed by people who were not trying to do so. I found youngsters being brought into this life and made to think that this was okay. I found others who truly thought they were helping with conservation efforts and the worst thing was, it did help. But there were a few who just enjoyed killing an animal but I decided not to focus on them for now. I was ready to get my hands dirty but still wanted to try a slightly passive approach to it.

This girl I ended up targeting was sixteen years old. I'm unsure if she had been on hunts before, but I had established the fact that this is the first time she was getting ready to bring an animal far larger than herself down. She was excited and her family fueled this excitement with words and gestures of encouragement. I had located her by back tracking her as well. I went after the local hunters and listened in on correspondences, reading invoices and emails where available. Her age and experience caught my eye and I traced her back to her house where she had been preparing for her trip, not just by learning how to handle a gun but by spending nights on the Internet reading up on the animals.

Her first day out did not involve the hunt at all but a safari as she observed the game at the park. The whole family enjoyed looking at the animals, making me feel even more perplexed at the idea of why they would like to take one of these same creatures they are marveling at down with a bullet. The entire thing felt rather foreign to me. As the day continued, she observed the diversity of wildlife while her guides told her anecdotes of the time they had hunted a particular animal. Questions about the wildlife were asked and answered, while the daughter was briefed up by the more experienced hunters, including the guides on what she should prepare for tomorrow. She showed her excitement and expressed her own impatience. She wasn't the only one who was being impatient. I couldn't wait for tomorrow, either, and I returned back to one of the many destination hotels. I sat by the beach enjoying the wind on my ethereal face and listening to the ocean sounds. I played the many different scenarios that could take place tomorrow in my head again and again, hoping that in each of them, my objective does not fail and no one gets seriously hurt. I finished sipping on my last mojito and eventually, went to bed. My alarm was on for early morning. These guys weren't going to waste their day.

There was another reason why I picked this particular hunt. For reasons that failed to make any sense, they were going to hunt a rhino. Either the family had a genetic intellectual disorder or were highly experienced and cocky. A rhino hunt was particular advanced and quite dangerous, and it could go on for multiple days and could not be done from the safety of a Jeep. They would have to get down on the ground and track. Doing so could lead to various dangers, the least of it being the aging bull itself. I woke up quite early, grabbing some food from the buffet and making my way to their camp. They were already up, inspecting their equipment and receiving a final set of instructions on the day's events. The briefing was simple. Only a small set of rhinos were eligible for a hunt. The scouting parties were already out looking for the tracks. Instructions on when to remain in a Jeep and how to traverse the terrain were reiterated and a warning was provided not to touch any other wildlife. The safety of the family was the responsibility of the guide and should the girl not make the shot in time, the guides would bring the rhino down themselves. All was understood. This was an extremely experienced family who knew the routine.

I, myself had already scanned out the surrounding areas, where the scouts were currently located. One had found the right set of tracks and scanning further, I had already spotted the unsuspecting bull. It was an older one as expected and quite large. More so, he was in the thickets and hard to spot. This is the beast I would need to keep my eye on. No other rhino met the necessary requirement in this area.

It took an hour till the family arrived and met up with the scouts. The girl showed no signs of fear or hesitancy. She had been prepped and was ready for whatever nature was going to throw at her. All but me, that was. I had already perched myself far away at a vantage point. Tall areas were hard to come by in this plain and I found myself pretty far away but still, I had already zoomed in on the girl, the scouts and the rhino as I tracked each one on a separate frame. I started tracking another couple of animals as well. Their whereabouts were crucial to me and without them, my plan would definitely not work as well.

The morning remained largely uneventful as was expected. This was going to be a long hunt and from time to time, I would return back to my home to send out texts and make a quick call here and there to a friend or client, and then I'd check back in with the poachers.

The Jeep followed close behind where it could as it looked for certain that today won't be the day they will be firing a shot. From time to time, some of the travel continued in the vehicle. The family looked tired but the girl looked quite disappointed. All the prepping probably did not prepare her for the realities associated with hunting at all. I bet they were all relying on the adrenaline and thrill of the payoff to compensate for the exhaustion and boredom that came with the stalking.

They retired for the day when the light started to fail. They had made some good head way and I was quite sure that by tomorrow they would be on top of the animal. I had to be extra vigilant tomorrow. I did not go back to a local resort just yet. I decided to spend some time with the rhino. I wondered what his life must have been like. He was definitely older than I was. Did it ever get bored by the repetitiveness of his own existence? It often disturbed me that the average human had a routine they follow, they could still watch shows on TV, listen to music, socialize in various ways with people and partake in eating a variety of food while engaging in sports. Their daily work brought a different experience. Yet, almost all animals lived by the same rules every day: wake up, find something to eat, protect the young and sleep. There was no variation from the rule. How had this rhino survived so long and not gone crazy from boredom? Having spent as much time as I had with these animals, I no longer believed any of these creatures were self-aware. Maybe I was projecting my own humanity on them. I would smile every time I would think this as this wasn't the first time I'd had these thoughts go through my head. The rhino, too, looked tired and was going to rest for a bit. I bid adieu and left.

The morning came and with it, much excitement. The girl had woken up early today and so had I. The cook who was part of this expedition had put together an incredible breakfast of eggs, sausages and toast. It made my stomach rumble but I dare not break cover or leave to grab a bite. When the family congregated around the table to eat, I felt like this is the first time I actually observed them as people as opposed to a family hoping to end the life of a beast.

She was dressed up in stereotypical khakis. Her hair was a tad below shoulder length and as she stuck a fork into her sausage, her family made a little fun of her for being so impatient. She flicked the sausage at her dad who appeared to be picking on her the most and laughter erupted all around. Breakfast was interrupt at this point as auspicious news reached the camp that their target had already been spotted from far away on one occasion. The last of what remained on everyone's plate was gulped down and the father who had spent the morning

315

bothering his daughter was now alongside her, letting the teenager brief him on safety and rules of the hunt. He couldn't look prouder. For me, it felt like the weirdest, warmest family moment. I thought about my own dad at this point. He and I would never bond in this way and a part of me wished for what these two had. You know, without all the killing and blood and stuff.

The family took off, using the Jeep to get as close to the animal as possible. I continued to monitor the situation tracking everyone from a distance. The father was inspecting his own weapon along with his daughter's and going over the years of training she had received in a few minutes. I knew nothing of these weapons at all but they looked reasonably formidable to me. One of the guides even remarked on their marksmanship. The mother remained vigilant, appearing to be one of the better trackers and very alert. They kept a firm grip on their rifles and they mostly traveled in silence and followed cues. It was the right thing to do as the moment of truth was almost upon us and I finally got off my perch and teleported closer, but not before taking care of a few things on my end. Much like this family, I had to prepare everything as well for all this to go down without anyone or anything getting hurt. Well, getting too badly hurt. Everyone, excluding the bull, were aware of the showdown that was about to take place.

The walking stopped as a gesture was given by the lead guide that the rhino was in his sight. The shot was not clear and he instructed the girl along with her dad to come closer. Slowly, the others gathered around them, so as to provide the extra security if something went wrong. The rhino was enjoying the shade but their vision was partially blocked by a boulder and some trees. I looked at the girl, who too, could see the animal in the distance. She was still calm and collected, which was impressive. For the first time, I realized that the family was indeed, quite confident. The idea that anything could go wrong hadn't appeared to cross their mind. They had little reason to think that anything would. At no time had the family exhibited arrogance and in fact, they had shown a lot of respect to the local guides along with the animal. They had trained very well as well. These guys were professionals and not a single wrong move had been made. Too bad there was no guide on how to handle a situation when a supernatural being such as myself decides to interfere.

The guides remained patient. In whispers, they explained that there was no clear shot and they risked the animal going west where they would have to continue tracking it. It was more important that the animal continued north, which would bring the rhino closer to them but also, in an open clearing. For now, they had to wait. The dad placed a hand on the girl's shoulder, who followed his lead. She kept the rifle aimed but did not take the shot. She was playing by the book and her mom and dad appeared to be very proud of her who also continued to keep their guns aimed at the innocent 3,000-pound behemoth. I wasn't too worried for him though. My actions from a few minutes prior had already made him safe from the guns. My only worry was the guy with the bow. A single arrow wouldn't do much damage to the rhino but it was still of concern to me.

The guide alerted everyone and motioned the girl to steady her aim. In the distance, the bull had stood up and after appearing to toy with the idea of moving into the bushes, eventually decided to walk in the direction of his stalkers. I teleported even closer. I had imagined various scenarios and in each one of them, my timing had to be impeccable. With just a few yards away, the guides gave their signal. Her mom leaned in closer and whispered to the girl that she had a shot. She also reminded her to be patient and wait for what the girl felt was the right moment. The girl was not nervous at all, nor was she annoyed at the constant instructions. I could sense the adrenaline in her pumping, yet her breathing remained contained and her body remained completely calm. She waited for half a minute while the rhino stopped and looked around. It felt the danger yet hadn't honed in on it. At that moment, I saw the girl's eyes and I knew a shot was about to be fired. Time stood still for a second.

She pressed the trigger. An awkward pause followed. The dad looked at his daughter, convinced she had done everything correctly. The gun was to blame for not firing. The mom had already assessed the situation and realizing that there was still time, quickly took the malfunctioning gun away and handed her daughter her weapon. Nobody wanted to check to see if the rifle was in fact loaded, as that would make too much noise. I could sense hearts racing as the rhino appeared agitated but still at a safe distance. The girl had lost a bit of her composure but was still in control, this time trying to hurry with taking her aim. Everyone else already had their weapons drawn in case she took too long or attracted the attention of the animal. She fired again. A look of bewilderment was shared by everyone as this particular gun failed to fire too. Someone made a soft whistle and the attention was back on the animal. The rhino had noticed the trained guns on it and its demeanor became aggressive. The guides barked for the mom and daughter who were now without a functioning weapon to move back as they along with the dad took aim. I moved next to the rhino in time to see the first arrow fired. I waited for it to shear through my hand and at the right moment, teleported it slightly to the left, grazing the animal just enough to make it charge and make the angles believable. Triggers were pressed and the guides found themselves in a situation they had never been in before. Every weapon malfunctioning took them by surprise. There was no time to look for refills, not that it would matter because much like the ammunition they had all expected in their guns, I had left the cartridges empty as well.

People dispersed in every direction as the rhino pushed through. Loud and panicked orders were barked which I had been counting on and in the midst of all this, the girl who had held up quite well so far let out a scream. Nothing was worse than something happening to you that you hadn't expected at all and she became hysterical. As people jumped left and right as the rhino charged, my movements had to be even quicker. Small teleports here and there and I was moving people away ever so slightly from the horns of certain death. A couple of people managed to get into the clear but thankfully, these people still had a conscience. They came back for the girl and the family, who were now stationary, unable to move. The only person with a functioning weapon covered the young girl as he raised his bow and slowly started pushing the family backwards. A member of the guide team had already soiled himself as the rhino refused to let his hunters get away. This is the moment I had been waiting for. As the mother held her daughter waiting for the impending doom or a miracle rescue, the situation got worse.

I had been tracking a pride of lions purposely about fifteen miles away and had also transferred them to our proximity moments before all this went down. Attracted by the screaming and chaos, they were now part of this three-way showdown. The rhino had had enough and the sight of the lion was enough to deter it away as it raced off. The panic amongst this raiding party of humans only got worse. The lions didn't appear to be overly aggressive towards the humans, but they were still freaking lions. Three lionesses in fact. The girl at this point was in tears as she was slowly led back by her dad and mom. The dad had sustained a sizable injury from the rhino, by my design of course. It was imperative that a bit of harm came to them but I wasn't going to allow anything serious. As the guides slowly tried to get control of the situation and move back, empty guns trained and a bow ready, they continued backing away as one radioed home base.

The lionesses slowly proceeded in their direction, but kept a distance, enough to make the entire ordeal terrifying but not enough to be of real threat.

A couple of other men, whose guns were quickly rendered useless by me as well, joined them and seeing the tribe forming, the lionesses eventually backed off. They had fed for the day and were not particularly very interested in people right now. A little more backtracking and the Jeeps came into visibility. The girl tried to make a run for it but was slowly grabbed by one of the newcomers, ushering her to calm down and to not make sudden moves. There were other dangers around them and she was attracting them. She was already in a state of meltdown and as they finally got into their jeep and raced away, I smiled to myself.

Words were exchanged amongst all and accusations were thrown about. The inventory of bullets was examined twice and then, a third time and the entire experience had to be explained again and again to everyone as people tried to make sense of things. The girl was pretty scratched up, too, and so was the mother. It was later that I discovered that the girl had also sustained a minor concussion when she fell down. I smiled some more. I returned back to the plains, teleporting the pride of lionesses back to where they had been originally and checking up on the rhino. Its behavior was back to normal, as if the events of that late morning had never happened. If another family on a safari suddenly dropped by to see it, they won't even know from its behavior that it was staring death in the face. It reminded me of NPCs in video games who always went back to doing what they were programmed to do once the threat of a protagonist harming them had passed. It was unwise to try to touch it or appear in front of it like I do with most animals when people aren't watching. I picked up the guns the party had dropped and threw them into a volcano.

The family spent the rest of the time at the hospital waiting for the father to recover while simultaneously, contacting lawyers and speaking with the government officials to establish who was to blame for the mishaps from that day. The girl had expressed a very clear desire never to engage in that activity again and thankfully, the family didn't try to change her mind. Maybe they had all decided to reconsider their definition of a vacation.

Personally, I felt proud. This was the first time I had proactively gone after the problem and not simply tried to protect an animal or person. I had entered a new phase in my life and I believed I was about to make a lot more difference even as I struggled to navigate this new world of gray.

Chapter 39

Did I feel bad about putting a teenage girl through that ordeal? Not really. She didn't deserve it but I may have scared her from ever attempting what she did for at least a lengthy period of time. While there were some hunters out there who really didn't give a damn about the animals they targeted, a lot of them didn't feel what they did was necessarily wrong or worse, actually felt they were protecting the environment.

By paying big bucks to hunt a limited quota of animals based upon age and gender of the animal, hunters justify their need to hunt by stating that they were, in a sense, saving a species of animal from extinction. And the results compliment that theory. A lot of animals out there were and are being singlehandedly protected by the strict rules that protected the hunting community.

The reality was that these people were not conservationists. They were exploiting the situation. They were exploiting departments that were underfunded or countries that do not enjoy the same standard of living where they come from. They were willing to give money as long as they get something back in return. Saying these people are conservationists was to me, equivalent to a person saying that they'll protect a group of women from getting raped as long as they themselves, could rape a couple of them once in a while. Sure, the majority of the women wouldn't get violated but I'm sure many of you reading this probably felt a certain level of uneasiness at this thought.

I had determined that reasoning with the majority of these people would lead to no gain at all hence I decided to simply scare them. That one girl had been my proof of concept. With the success I achieved on that hunting trip, I managed to sabotage countless more and I felt a level of success had come with them. The stories were circulated through social media and forums about horrible experiences. In addition, it painted many local guides in a bad light, making it look like the breakdown of the trucks, ammunition, rental equipment or the planning around the hunt was their fault. As we all knew, negative reviewers were notorious for not taking any part in the blame themselves. I had already noticed a decline in the number of hunts over 2008 and 2009 since I started my crusade. I couldn't use the same MO each time though. On a few occasions, I teleported the animals around to make hunts unsuccessful. Sometimes, Jeeps would run out of gas at the most inopportune moment. I continued to sabotage the actual weapons but the most fun I had was making the hunters feel they were horrible at their hobby. Through no fault of their own, they constantly missed their aim or fired when it was obvious there was no shot to take, resulting in the animal running away or charging. Blame was always thrown around in each of these scenario and across review websites, credibility of certain tour operators was constantly getting called into question. In almost all of these situations though, the biggest deterrent continued to be putting people in the direct line of danger. Most hunts, even when the animal of interest wasn't around ended that way when I got involved.

For those that I considered to be total dicks, however, I always made sure they got hurt. And if they ever tried to continue going on a hunt again, I made sure they got hurt even more the second time around. Bastards not only deserved it but it greatly discouraged them from trying a third attempt at least for a lengthy period of time. Recently, I'd also heard of countries wanting to pass stricter legislations around hunting due to the bad reputation they have been garnering in the media. My antics had been making the front page and every time I read about them, I chuckled.

Judge. Jury. Executioner. The voice in my head reminded me what I was becoming. I ignored it.

But while I was out there making a difference in the lives of those who could not speak for themselves, I realized that animals around the world weren't the only ones getting hunted. Whether for profits or land grabbing, people's selfish motivations were putting others less fortunate or simply different from them at risk as well. It is hard to believe in this day and age but there are still tribes and communities around the world that have had little to no exposure to the rest of the world. In an age where I'm completely aware of what one of my friend's sister-in-law's gardener had for lunch this afternoon because people feel the need to overshare their inanest experiences, entire tribes exist in complete isolation. They'd enjoyed a level of autonomy, much like the folks in the Sentinelese Islands. Yet, around the world, with room having to be made to expand residential or commercial industries, forests were being torn down and this is bringing expanding populations of people in direct conflict with indigenous local tribes that had not only occupied a piece of land for centuries but are quite unaware of the outside world. The majority of them still live as hunter-gatherers and are no match for bulldozers, semi-automatic rifles and technologies, which were utilized for getting rid of them.

I found the entire thing unbelievable. It was hard for me to fathom why entire tribes including men, women and children would be wiped out to simply gain access to pieces of land. But human selfishness knows no bounds.

By late 2008, I was out there, defending these tribes and punishing those who refused to show any value to life. I was involved in much more than sabotaging guns and vehicles. This was one of those occurrences when the local and federal governments were on my side, at least on paper, and I created situations where I would bring these murderers in direct contact with the local police or military. Arrests would be made and in cases where a battle would break out, guilty lives were lost. During this time, a very special government initiative caught my eye and I discovered one of the most unique tribes I had ever heard about. I made it my life mission to defend this tribe at all costs.

Chapter 40

Excerpts from my Life

Time: Fall of 2008

Location: Rondônia

Event: The man of the hole

Remnants of holes five feet deep were littered around the area that I was currently scanning. Around the holes existed the same markings. Remnants of a thatched shelter, some still in very good condition. If I wasn't native to the area, I would have passed right by them without giving them a second thought. I also found very rudimentary tools not worth salvaging and tiny clearings made for outdoor fires.

This was all that was left of the tribe.

The camp was made by a single person, and I was trying my best to find him. No one can ever be completely certain of what happened. Was it active poaching? Was it simply an encroachment on the territory, a disease or even less likely, an internal conflict. But at a minimum, for the last 14 years, all that remained of this uncontacted tribe in the forests of Brazil was one man who day after day, continued to exist while watching his back. It is not surprising at all why I felt drawn to him. Could there be a lonelier person in this world? I was instantly reminded of Polly the polar bear and our escapades together years ago and a part of me wanted to experience that feeling again, but with an actual human being.

Brazil had taken some great steps to ensure the continued survival of this man. Laws were in place to protect all uncontacted tribes in the region (of which there were many) including but not limited to a ban to deliberately contacting these tribes without the tribe first showing interest in dialogue and possible assimilation. Our one-man tribe had a protected area and there were plans for expanding this area even more to provide the necessary space for him to live, a move worthy of applause but not without its critics. Many around the area wanted the law repealed and others engaged in direct physical antagonism to flush out a man who was the last of his kind and provide the government with a reason to no longer make the area inaccessible for development. The way people's minds work baffled me.

I was pretty determined to ensure that the land he walked would not be destined to become a plantation or a ranch any time soon. After I had researched all I wanted to know, I made my way to his territory. Finding him was simple but confirming that it really was him took a little longer. He was dressed much like the other tribes in the area, at least to my foreign eyes, as I was not able to tell the subtleties in the clothing. His primary weapon appeared to be a bow and arrow, something he carried around with confidence. Melee weapons were on hand as well. As I followed him around for the next few days, I noticed his diet was mixed, ranging from local fruit to the animals he hunted with his quiver. As night approached, he always made his way to one of his huts where he lowered himself into the hole and covered it up. This appeared to be his routine day in and day out for what must have been decades. My heart broke as I watched him going about his business and I was struck with the realization that I had not heard him speak once. How anyone would spend years without having a reason to utter a word was beyond me and I continued to feel drawn closer to him.

As I followed his routine, I would encounter others in the area inhabited by him and I would grow tense. If he sensed anything as well, he would go on the defense, grasping his arrow while looking for suitable cover. Some of the people were harmless and completely clueless as to the danger they may be putting themselves in by encroaching onto his territory. He had seen his fair share of tragedy at the hands of foreigners and a misunderstanding would not end well. On other occasions, though, it was clear to me that those entering into these lands were well aware of the person who walked there. Their intentions were not always the best but thankfully, in the majority of the situations, the limited visibility in the forest favored our guy.

I would routinely follow these ranchers around to see what signs they were looking for in order to locate the man. As I picked up on their cues, I would plant fake ones of my own to draw them away. In situations where a conflict occurred, which was rare, the man could hold his own and my respect for him grew.

I grew angry at the ranchers, who seemed determined to

persecute him. These ranchers would often experience an accident on the way home from a fallen tree branch or by coincidentally running into an insect or animal with whom, an encounter would be less than pleasant. Anyone who repeated the behavior of trying to shoot this guy would see himself transported closer to one of the local forest checkpoints where they would be apprehended by the proper authorities based upon the suspicion on entering into the restricted area with ill intentions. The forest was so thick, the majority of the people weren't even aware of the teleportation while they scrambled. But they always questioned how they got so close to a checkpoint so quickly.

When things were peaceful however and he wasn't running around gathering food or building a new place to call home, he sat around and I watched him. For days, I watched and I felt uneasy. There was something very wrong with the picture and I always had trouble putting my finger on it. Not till one day when I was so focused on him, that I hadn't done a scan of the perimeter in a while and he stood up, alerted by some sound that had completely escaped my hearing. Quickly, I checked to see what direction he was looking at and turned. His senses were good. He had isolated the sound towards the correct general direction as I observed a posse of five ranchers slowly making their way towards him. In fact, they were in visible range and chances were, he was already spotted. This was confirmed a moment later when shots were fired as he jumped off the rock he had perched himself on. He did not fire back. He was hopelessly outgunned and he knew it. Without stopping to turn or to make any unnecessary movements, he ran in a deliberate path, quickly putting distance between himself and his attackers. They followed, but I knew they would never be able to catch up to him. Not that it mattered because once again, someone had pushed the right buttons and I was ready to make my own moves. I smashed my foot against one guy's shin and he fell to the ground, writhing around in pain. The others stopped to pick him up while trying to figure out what had happened. As he reached out with one hand to accept the help, I grabbed his other arm holding the rifle and smacked two of his friends across the face. The time for exchanging words was over. As the one who was subjected to my wrath stood staring at his hands dumbfounded while slowly motioning with his other hand to everyone to not come any closer, the beatings began. In the commotion, I teleported the guns away from all of them and fired a few shots myself.

The panic began. With no knowledge of where their guns were and an unseen enemy, the ranchers dispersed. One of them ran into a conveniently positioned log I had placed, instantly cracking a bone in his leg. His travels back to civilization would be problematic. Another tripped over my foot and went flying, landing on an unforgiving rock. Two that happened to be running together ran into one of the traps set up by our friend. As his leg fell into the hole that was dug up to capture a small animal, he shouted in pain. He held his friend for support, who lost his own footing and fell on a barbed plant.

As for the final guy, I made his life miserable for the next half hour. The sounds of the shots I was firing constantly behind him encouraged him to make haste. My constant teleporting of him deeper and deeper into the forest was making it impossible for him to get out. At this point, he had lost all bearing and I expected him to take hours to make his way back, if he even could. I fired more shots near the checkpoints and slowly led the authorities in, giving them enough clues to move in the general direction of our five trigger happy men. I made my way back to our man of the hole, which is where he was currently hiding. At some point after he felt the danger passed, he came back out again and sat and I looked up at his face again. I finally understood.

Yes, he was lonely. But he wasn't me. For the last few weeks, I had been projecting my loneliness onto him. The truth was that this man wanted someone besides him but this someone was no longer anyone who was a part of this world. This person was long gone and he had no more room in his heart for those who were left on Earth, especially not after the way he had been treated and the things he was made to endure. Whereas I was looking for any kind of companionship, he desired none anymore. We were not the same and somewhere inside me, I felt lonelier. I smiled at him and let him be. I continued to look out for him but I was no longer going to invade his privacy for my own benefit. It was the least I can do for a man that had everything taken away from him and wants nothing from this world anymore.

War

Chapter 41

Excerpts from my Life

Time: Jan 2009

Location: The Midwest

Event: See the world

Claudia's drug use had finally done its damage. She lay hooked up to the dialysis machine. Family sat on a couple of chairs next to the bed as the parents held each other outside the room, being briefed by the doctor. The wife had to physically support her husband. He had been a broken man for years now, seeing his daughter never recover and continue down a path of deterioration. From time to time, there were improvements but she never truly recovered. A day when status quo was maintained was a good day but if one was to look at him, it would seem appropriate for him to be lying on a bed next to her too. There wasn't much more life left in him and given the news that was being delivered to him, there was not much for him to live for either

Complete kidney failure was on the menu, among other things. Due to the severity however, the kidneys took precedence, making all other problems a non-issue. Even if they replaced her kidneys, which the insurance companies would never likely fully cover, there wasn't much long-term hope. Dialysis wasn't going to do much at this point, either. The physical damage to her body was far too severe. The father tried to conjoin a few words of desperation together every time the doctor would finish, sometimes even interrupting her mid-sentence, somehow hoping that the next words coming out of her would contradict everything he had heard from her so far. His wife would hold him tighter, tears flowing down her cheeks as she tried to comfort him. His legs gave up strength and his knees came resting to the ground. She tried to support him back up but it was to no avail. She succumbed as well and they both remained on the floor dealing with their tragedy as family members and nurses rushed to their side.

The writing was on the wall. I shed my own tears as I walked through the wall and entered her room. I stared at her and gently touched her forehead. Of all the people I had followed throughout the years, she was the first whose life was coming to an end and there was not much I could do about it. Try as I might year after year to show her a different path, my efforts only ever yielded temporary results. She was on her way out and all I wanted to do was cradle her in my arms.

I was angry. Not at her, or her family. I wasn't angry at her kidnappers from 1999 or all those that facilitated her addiction. I was not mad at asshole teenagers in the community or at schools who are too busy berating others like herself in the hopes of climbing the social ladder. I was angry at myself. I was angry because it took me over a decade to start interfering and making a more conscious decision to help and try saving the world. I was angry that I had limited my visits to her purposely as I had been busy stopping robbers, poachers and hunters. I had ignored the people I had met who mattered the most to me. Specifically, I had ignored her.

It was easy to stereotype teenagers as well as drug users, even if one admits that their life was not their fault. But she never fell into those stereotype. Through her pain, mental illnesses and addictions, she had always been a good person. She had never stopped caring. I guess that was the big problem, wasn't it? She turned to that life to become immune to the universe around her and to not worry about the people she was surrounded by but her drugs never helped her gain that blissful indifference.

Her body was ravaged by needles, and while the drugs did their damage, they brought other diseases as well. The vast majority of the needle marks were from recent escapades, which would explain their absence when I last visited her. I had heard mentions that she was going to be kept sedated tonight. I retired, not to one of my beautiful and serene vacation destinations but to my apartment, infested with random parts from machines waiting to be built. I brushed many of them aside from the little mattress that occupied the corner of the room. I lay there for a while, motionless at first with my eyes opened. Over time, moisture built up around my eyes and when the weight of the growing tears around my eyelids could not support themselves, I felt them trickle down the side of my cheek. The floodgates opened and I weeped for hours. I had rescued her once from that dilapidated building and delivered her to a hospital. For a brief period, she was okay but her depression would kick in and she would experience minor relapses. On those occasions, if I was around, I would guide her back. If I wasn't around, she would always manage to guide herself. It always gave me hope that she knew at the end of the day what was best for her. Not this time around, though. My absence had been too long and the abuse her body had taken had been excessive. This child who I had treated like a little sister since I took an interest in her life was going to die.

I looked at the folder lying next to me, filled with work orders that I had committed to. I wanted to burn them all. At this moment in time, I cared little about keeping up appearances so I could file my tax papers at the end of the year and show a livable income. Keeping up appearances felt so trivial to me. I told myself to snap out of it. No matter the current situation, I had built this entire fake life for a reason.

I gently wiped my eyes and rubbed the residue on my pants. The folder contained a decent number of orders but not overwhelming. I could probably knock them all out tonight if I didn't stop. So I began, building one custom machine after another. Sometime during assembling, I changed my voicemail to say that I will be out for the next couple of weeks. When the orders were finished, I waited for the stores to open, tying up another few loose ends. I wasn't sure what my schedule was going to be for the next couple of weeks but I was going to be out for extended periods of time and I wanted nothing at that point to be a source of distraction. By 10 AM, the PCs were delivered and I teleported back to the hospital. She was awake and by the looks of it, she had been informed about her situation and her imminent demise.

Honestly, I hadn't known how she would react to the news. Would she be relieved? Would she be confrontational about it? Time and time again, what I've realized after looking at the reality is that it is never one thing or the other. As she held her parents, I saw acceptance in her face and even a bit of peace. I also saw tears and regret. Her voice was apologetic as she repented to her parents for never being grateful for all that they had sacrificed for her. They were all lying on the bed together now, holding each other tight and I just stood there, listening to every apology, the hopeless words of hope, the sharing of unconditional love and the crying. I never once looked away.

Hours past and at some point, the parents vacated the room, leaving her alone for the first time since I had arrived. During this time, all I could see in her eyes was a look of finality while she stared into nothingness. Her tears had stopped yet I could tell she was at the brink of losing control of them at any point. I felt her take another breath, more pronounced than the previous few, like she had experienced some kind of an epiphany. Slowly, she mouthed, "So this is how it ends," as she closed her eyes, letting the last of the wetness around her lashes clear up, trickling down all the way behind her ears and onto the sheets.

"Claudia," I said, as my invisibility wore off and my voice returned back to the realm of the living. She jerked up, not having expected anyone back in the room. How could I have been such an idiot? Why would I suddenly show up in front of a girl who had been traumatized by the sight of strangers her whole life? Just as I was regretting the decision I had made to reveal myself, I saw her tilt her head, still looking at me like she was trying to fit me in to a certain memory from a past life. Her eyes must have opened a bit more. Either that or her pupils dilated, but suddenly, there was a marked difference around her eyes.

"Have I hallucinated you before?" she asked. Her words took me off guard. They were very specific as if she had a very vivid memory that she had accessed. I waited a second, choosing my own words wisely as well.

"Hallucinated? No."

She smiled cautiously as if to indicate she was comfortable yet acknowledging this entire situation is rightfully quite awkward. "So, you were real then?" She continued after another pause, "At the risk of coming off as delusional, which shouldn't matter much given my current predicament, are you a guardian angel because if so, you may have dropped the ball this time."

I choked up and chuckled at the same moment as tears continued to remain a recurrent theme over these past twenty-four hours. I wanted to apologize and beg for forgiveness for not being there for her but I stopped myself. Regaining some composure, I replied, "I'm not your guardian angel though I'm glad you appear to recognize me. And this isn't the first time I've dropped the ball with you. For that, I apologize."

She continued looking at me, like my confirmation of somehow knowing her puzzled her yet made her curious about my identity even more. My scans went active, and I started monitoring the movements of all individuals of interest and their distance from this hospital room. Slowly, I moved closer to the bed. She did not feel threatened. I had passed the point of no return and oddly, I was okay with this. I smiled and told her that what she was about to hear would scare her, interest her, make her want to stop me so she could ask an endless amount of questions or press that little button on her bed that will likely cause people to rush in so they may take me away. I requested that she be patient with me and hear me out. To make things a little lighthearted, I reminded her that it's not like she has anywhere to go right now. She smiled back. I died a little inside.

I had rehearsed this a million times. A million times, I had turned to an imaginary person and had tried telling my story. Each time, the story started differently emphasizing the same elements of my tale at different moments in time. Sometimes, I would imagine myself not even speaking but simply performing like I was the feature presentation at a theater or a circus. But now was the moment of truth when I finally get to tell someone my story and I was again at a loss of what I wanted to say. Should I tell her about myself or should I start with my first encounter with her?

Should I make up a persona and continue to hide who or what I truly am? As she continued looking up at me waiting for me to start, I opened my mouth and let the first thing come out of it. I told her about the bus ride I took almost twelve years ago and about a dog that chased me and changed my life. As I told her about my ability to teleport, I did so in front of her. Her head jumped back a little bit from shock as her face got far more attentive and surprised, similar to how I would react to my own abilities over a decade ago. She however, did not show any signs of being scared or nervous. I saw excitement and for a moment, she had forgotten about herself. She was now completely engrossed and waiting to hear the next chapter in my fairy tale. I grabbed a blank notebook someone must have left and as I continued to describe to her what my teleportation ability entailed, I did some tricks with it. She laughed and she squealed in excitement, like a child seeing a magic trick for the first time. She tried to speak up a few times but remembered my request, yet I could see the nerves and her muscles all tensed up, like she couldn't hold things in much longer. Poor thing. Teleportation was the tip of the iceberg.

I continued to move forward and told her about my invisibility as I was setting up the appropriate demonstration. She saw me disappear completely and then materialize without my arms. She saw my hand appear out of nowhere as one of them floated up to a glass of water someone had left behind for her. I took a sip from it as the rest of my body disappeared, selectively choosing to let her see the water traverse my alimentary canal. As she stared back at me with an expression that looked like someone in front of her had just been run over by a train, I continued to speak to her, this time telling her about my vision and what it could do. I looked around the room and provided her measurements of how far everything was in relation to me and other objects. I let her know the whereabouts of the doctor and her dad. I explained what I could do with some of my other visual features. She remained transfixed, absorbing every word coming out of my mouth and hoping to see another trick. When I was done, I knew it was time to show her what would be the hardest ability for her to grasp. I looked at her and told her to trust me and not to get scared. I asked her to hold my hand.

She was nervous at first, not knowing what my latest gimmick would be about and slowly reached out. As her hand started to overlay over mine, I asked her to stop and look but most importantly, to not panic. It took her a moment to notice but when she did, her fascination with the experience took over. I had expected her to pull her hands back but instead, she slowly moved her hands around more as they glided right over mine. She looked back at me and moved her hands over to my face, her jaw remaining slightly ajar as her hand went right through it. She pulled out and as she did, I took my hands and clasped hers. I explained being ethereal to her. She wanted to speak but I didn't give her a chance. I walked right through a wall and back. She looked satisfied with the answer to the question that never got asked. I sat down next to her again and she continued to stare at me. I stared back, choosing to not continue the story further. I wasn't sure which tangent to go down. An awkward silence ensued until she lost all patience.

"Can I speak now?" she asked.

"Yes," I replied.

"How …?"

I stared at her in silence and eventually looked down. The question that had haunted me for years.

"I don't know," I answered back.

She asked me about what caused them again, as if I may have misunderstood her first question. I told her about my years of investigation into government entities, hospitals, family tree, sinister lab experiments and my need to look over my shoulder to see if others were watching. I shook my head at her and she understood, while looking disappointed. She saw a similar expression on my face and probably realized this line of questioning troubled me greatly and switched gears. There was much to discuss about my powers.

She inquired about each ability and I answered all her questions. With each new bit of information, her inquisitiveness and fascination with me grew. My ethereal abilities caught her eye the most initially but switched more into invisibility and teleportation as she inquired about my experiences. She had completely forgotten about what she was going through right now, instead choosing to immerse herself in my life. After sharing a few stories, she kept returning to previous subject matters, ranging from how it felt every time I used my ability to continuously asking how any of this was even possible, as if subsequent inquiries about the same subject seconds apart would somehow lead to another answer. Sadly, she was straying very far away from the one question I had thought she would ask and at a point where I realized that I probably did not have that much more time to spend alone with her before someone returned, I interrupted her.

"I was there, Claudia. I was there when you were rescued along with those other children."

The silence was deafening. She didn't say a word. She just looked at me, expressionless, but I knew I had her complete attention. I told her about what I did with my life once I gained those powers and those few occasions during the early years when I had gone down the line of helping others. I told her about the entire warehouse incident and the part that I had played. I described my feelings as I had walked into that room and seen them all chained up, and the accidents I caused to ensure the culprits would be apprehended by those that were waiting outside. I paused but she continued looking at me, once again showing no signs of being angry, mad, scared or sad. She just wanted answers.

So I continued. I told her how I had followed her since then and how I've tried to manipulate situations to stray her off decisions I felt she may regret or push her in a direction that I approved of. I confirmed that I was there that one night when she magically found her way to the hospital. When I had seen her finally express an interest in talking to this one boy, I had been there to create serendipitous interactions between them. I told her about last night and how I had ignored her too long these past few months and arrived a bit too late. Finally, I said I was sorry. I said sorry for not doing enough and I said sorry for constantly interfering. There was another pause. My story was over save one last statement. I told her that she was the dearest of all the people I had encountered throughout my life.

She continued to look at me and but I didn't have the courage anymore to meet her eyes. Eventually, I heard her voice.

"Are you et .. ethee .. damn it ... can I touch you right now?" she asked, while moving her fingers around as if to inquire if they will just glide over my body again.

"I'm not ethereal."

She reached out with her arms as far as she was able to extend comfortably and I took her cue. I leaned in and she placed my head on her shoulder. We stayed that way for a while with the silent understanding that this was not the time to share any more words. An overwhelming amount had already been said and the emotional toll was significant. She had just learnt about an entity that had followed her around her entire life. I had for the first time revealed my true self to another person. Neither of us had any intentions of breaking away from this moment.

Sadly, I noticed that I was about to overstay my welcome

as I saw the approaching nurse. I let her know that I had to go because my existence must remain a secret. She quietly understood. I looked at her and she nodded her head, letting me know without saying a word that my presence in the room would not be communicated with others. She asked me if I would return. I let her know that even though she cannot see me, I would be here the whole time. When she was alone again, we'd talk. She smiled and asked me to disappear. I did as the door opened.

I was a little nervous at first. Would the others notice a subtle change in her behavior? Would she be able to keep such an incredible thing to herself? Every once in a while, she would look around the room, like she was expecting to see a hint of me somewhere. Every time a person in the room looked away, she stared at the window, as she expected me to be there. I would remember this. She shared a few brief moments alone during which time, she would call out to me. I would reply back with a hush, asking her to trust me and to be patient. She would smile, taking comfort in the fact that I was in fact still there and more importantly, not a figment of her imagination. When it started getting late in the day, she used her own condition to manipulate her family into going home for the night or to at least, stay out of the room. She mentioned wanting some time to herself before falling asleep. Her parents were unwilling to not honor her daughter's requests during her last few days yet still reluctant on not spending each waking hour with her. Slowly, they made their departure. Extended family members convinced them to rest for the night at the house, assuring that one of them would remain at the hospital to keep a presence. Once I had confirmed that they had left and the remaining person was doing everything in his power to avoid awkward conversations with a dying teenager, I returned back to the room.

She was lying on the bed looking dejected. I assumed she had been looking and calling out to me and had given up once her calls were not answered. I went and stood by the window and reappeared.

"Missed me?" I asked

If she could get off the bed, she would have run over to embrace me but for now, that dejected look turned into a smile as her eyes lit up. I walked over and she didn't miss a beat.

"Where did you come from? Are you insanely rich? How come no one knows you exist!?" The questions were spewing out of her like a runaway train. She paused for a second and gave me a naughty look. "Do you look at girls when you're invisible?"

I smiled back. "What would you like to hear about first?"

She paused for a moment again, as if prioritizing what she needed to know the most.

"Who else have you revealed yourself to?"

There were certainly animals out there and a bunch of people whose lives I had made miserable but I don't think that is what she had meant.

"You're the first."

She took some joy in that. Everyone enjoyed feeling a

little special. I hoped I wouldn't be fielding the question around spying on girls again. I breathed a small sigh of relief when she didn't push it.

"How does no one know you? You must be like, this insanely rich dude living in some mansion with all the different powers you just showed me."

I told her that was not how my life worked. I explained to her that my powers allowed me to live a life devoid of most limitations. I had access to the best of foods, and balconies overlooking oceans and mountains every night. I had no need for fast cars, or TVs as I had an entire world to explore. The need for money or a noticeable upscale lifestyle was not required. I had caught her off guard, as if she had never considered something like that. She however, remained transfixed by one detail that caught her eye.

"You have travelled the world?" she asked.

I replied back with an affirmative.

"Have you ever seen a baby elephant?"

It was my turn to smile. Through my years of checking up on her, I knew that she loved them and I started telling her about my various encounters with them on the African plains and the Indian forests. I shared stories with her about how I had rescued a few abused ones over the year and returned them back to a herd that appeared to be accepting new members. She especially enjoyed listening to stories about elephants I'd seen. I even saw one born right in front of my eyes. Every story ended with another question about another animal or a place as she went through the list of things she had always fantasized about witnessing for herself. With each question came another affirmative leading to another story she wanted to hear regarding the subject. For an hour, she lived her life vicariously through me till I could tell she required rest, even if she denied she did.

"Claudia, I realize you don't have much time but the little you have left, I want to share it with you. Let's make the most of it. I need you to rest and tomorrow, I will tell you more. In fact, I will tell you about places the world is unaware of or species that I helped rediscover when the top scientists of the world thought they were extinct. I will tell you about the various festivals I've seen around the world and rituals of tribes that most outsiders had never witnessed. If you can continue to send your parents back home every night and request some rest a couple of times a day, I will be there waiting. This, I promise you."

"But you are real, right? I'm not hallucinating again?"

"When you wake up tomorrow, I will return. Your days of hallucinating are behind you."

She nodded and let go of my hand. I kissed her on the forehead and said my goodbye. However, I didn't leave. Whether out my own selfishness or a desire to ensure she actually got some rest, I stayed behind, unknown to her to see what she did next. She stared around the room, as if her mind was on overdrive. I could tell that she was collecting a list of questions and turning them into a list, ready to pounce on me tomorrow. She was fighting to stay awake but eventually, I heard the silent snores. It was my time to go somewhere and reflect on my day as well. Falling asleep on a balcony from where I could hear the ocean waves crashing onto the beach seemed appropriate even if a little indulgent.

I kept my promise and continued to visit her. Each day, she listened to me tell her about some place I visited. She wanted to know the people, the creatures, the culture or the terrain. She wanted to know how the food tasted like or the strangest thing I had ever witnessed. I brought back a star nosed mole for her once for a few minutes. She held it in her hand for a brief moment till she couldn't handle how weird it was. Impulsively, she'd ask me about other things I could go and find. If I knew where those things were, I would excuse myself and return with another creature or a trinket. The night I brought back a baby elephant for her straight into her hospital room required the most amount of coordination, even with her. It could only be for a few seconds while the animal slept but seeing the look on her face made it all worth it. For everything I brought back, she wanted to know which adventure first introduced me to that creature or thing and for the first time in my life, I relived all of them again while watching her every expression. Somewhere deep down, I knew that telling her about my many adventures brought more joy to me than it did to her.

A few days later, I arrived to find out that she had made a decision to get off the dialysis machine and had convinced her family to allow her to do so. She wanted to be back home and spend the remainder of her days in the company of loved ones. In a couple of days, she was back in her home and I was by her bedside every night telling her more stories from my life. Soon, she started inquiring more about the less beautiful side of the world, as if she was trying to come back full circle to her own tale. I shared stories with her that were less than pleasant. From my attempt to clean up the oceans to the people I have encountered through the years that deserved nothing short of death, I held back nothing. She would start off by letting me speak but eventually, gravitate towards how I felt, the type of actions I took and the type of actions I wanted to take. As time went on, our discussions became less about my escapades and more about what and how I had felt through the years and I shared everything with her. I expressed my frustrations about sticking to my guiding principles and I told her how the world could be so great yet horrible at the same time. She didn't interrupt, letting me list one thing after another that I had witnessed. One day, she finally went down a line of questioning I had been hoping to avoid.

"You can fix all this. From everything you've told me, you could step right in and put the world in its place. You've attempted to on so many occasions. Why do you always stop so suddenly?"

Where should I begin? In the most chaotic way possible, I spurted out one thing after another. As I tried to explain to her my side of the story about how I felt the world should try to sort out its own problems and how the sudden appearance of a being such as myself would in itself create an unpredictable future for the world, I realized that I was having a hard time convincing myself of my own arguments. It was difficult to judge who should be at the receiving end of my attention. I paused when I mentioned that. She continued to look at me. She could tell that I needed to justify myself a little more.

"I try, Claudia. I try so hard to convince myself to make this world a better place. It may look like I've done so much but it always comes at a cost. I've gotten people killed. I've purposely left them to die. I almost killed my mother. When I thought I was the most powerful entity in the world, I managed to put myself in positions where my powers were rendered useless. I'm too afraid of what would happen if I truly went down that path and have it all blow up in my face. What if I manage to mess everything up and left it worse off than it already is? What if one day I was just truly fed up by it all and teleported everything into the sun?"

I went quiet. I had never admitted that last part to anyone before. I leaned in a little and she grabbed my head, gently pushing it closer to hers as she ruffled my hair. She didn't provide me with a rebuttal. She held me close as if to imply that she didn't judge me. For the first time, I was actually voicing the thoughts or discussions I've only had with imaginary people in my own head. For this, I was uncomfortable yet grateful. But she pressed me no further on that topic.

As the days passed and her end was coming near, we had

made full circle. She became more occupied with herself again. She wanted to know the names of the other kids who had been in that room with her and wanted to know how their lives turned out. She was glad to hear that they had mostly recovered from the incident. She would get depressed often though, wondering what happened to her that was so much more different. I had no answers for her. Time after time, she would ask me to tell her a story of her and my encounters over the years and as I would finish one story, she would quiz me on what she could have done differently to make her life turn out a little more like the others. Every night, I would leave with a sense of guilt, having not helped her with the information she was seeking or having made a difference years ago when it would have mattered.

It was a Thursday night. She looked very tired yet chirpy, speaking to her parents and joking around with them. The dad looked happier seeing his daughter show some improvements in her condition. I watched them banter for a while. For a moment, they were a family again. I walked over to her side table and flipped a frame towards her closet. It took her a while to notice but when she did, she started her subtle nightly rituals. We had come up with that signal a while ago so that she doesn't always have to worry about if I was around or not. As they kissed her goodnight, her dad remarked on if she wanted anything special tomorrow. She looked like she was caught off guard. She paused for a second, as if trying to think of the first thing that came to her mind that wouldn't sound absurd and eventually replied back her want to taste some hazelnut ice cream and watch a movie. She wasn't specific. I got very nervous and impatiently waited for some time to fly by after her parent's departure. I became visible and moved towards her bed noticing she looked a lot frailer than she had been just moments ago. She could sense that I knew there was something wrong and volunteered a reason.

"I doubt I am going to make it through this night. Starting tomorrow, you'll need to find another dying girl to share your stories with."

I knew this moment had been coming for a while now but I was still unprepared for it. I just stood there, not knowing what to do or say. I wasn't feeling anything, either. She motioned me closer and I sat down on the bed next to her. We still weren't sharing words. I held her hand and she held mine. With such few precious moments left, it was ironic that neither of us knew what the appropriate conversation should be. An hour went by and she finally broke the silence. Much like myself, she had been gathering the strength and courage to ask me something.

"You've allowed me to live a life through the stories you have told me. For this, I can't thank you enough. I know more about the foraging nature of insects than I should and you have named and told me about places I didn't know existed. You have brought me back things and let me hold them, something that I would have never done had I lived a normal life. However, I am going to die tonight. Do you think there is any way I can see the world with you before that happens? Would you like a companion for one night?"

I was unable to answer. Her request had taken me completely off guard but I could not think of a better way to spend tonight. Any night for that matter. With one statement, she had found a way to make both of our wishes come true.

I scanned the house and her parents were sound asleep. I held her hand and asked her to close her eyes. As she did so, I sat down cross-legged and pulled her over me and placed her arms around my neck. I laid her head on my chest and reiterated to keep her eyes closed. She complied and ten seconds later, requested for her to open them. She found herself surrounded by the strangest forest covered by a rocky canopy. I identified the location to her as the Son Doong Cave and quickly her eyes lit up, remembering it from the descriptions I had provided to her just a few days ago. She had little strength to stand up so I stood up and held her in my arms as we gently spun around. She looked at it for only a couple of minutes while I pointed out certain landmarks to her and she eventually spoke again in an impatient voice, "I do not have much time. Show me more."

We stood atop Angel Falls that night as she observed its beauty under the night sky as the water fell all around us. I kneeled over to provide her with a view no one had ever experienced before. I momentarily let the top part of our bodies leave the ethereal plain so she could feel the water rush all around her. She laughed and I smiled.

I clenched her tightly and wrapped a string around both

our hands to make sure we didn't separate for even a split second as I took her underwater and showed her the marvels of the reef that lay adjacent to Pemba Island. All around us, trigger fish pretended to charge us before suddenly turning away. Above us, a pod of dolphins swum by.

Next, we traveled to the busy early morning market in Fez followed by a quick trip to Polly's Den in the Arctic. That stop made her especially happy and I allowed her to touch the bear. I transported her to buildings and facilities that the world had forgotten about and she observed how nature had fought back and turned these locations into an industrial garden of sorts. Every two minutes, we ended up in another location where she observed the local wildlife or the culture but with each stop, I could tell that while her spirit rose, her body deteriorated. She could sense this as well and turned to look at me, acknowledging that this could not go on forever. She resigned to her fate that in fact, I would only be able to show her a portion of what she had requested. I was not ready to accept that and out of nowhere, I was reminded of a very foolish thing I had tried back in 2007.

"Did you say you wanted to see the world?" I asked.

She nodded her head.

"I want you to lay your head on me and close your eyes one final time then."

She was not sure where I was going with this but she did what I asked and I teleported us to the last stop we would experience together. I asked her to open her eyes and she did, staring straight back into mine. Her field of vision was obstructed by me holding on to her but she was able to observe the clear sky behind me and the complete desolation of the terrain under my feet. Slowly, while still gripping her hand tight and ensuring the knot I had tied with the string before going underwater was still intact, I sat down and asked her to turn her head. She did and gasped a couple of seconds later, her mind taking its time to fully comprehend what she was seeing in front of her.

"Is .. is that …" she was unable to finish the sentence.

"Yes, it is," I replied while helping her sit on me. "Congrats on being the first woman to ever sit on the moon."

She stared at the Earth in bewilderment trying to spot the edges of different pieces of land in order to identify the continents. I could tell that she was going to ask the obvious question and I volunteered an answer before any more words would come out of her mouth. The moon was the furthest I had ever traversed, still uncomfortable with the idea of teleporting to areas that my mind had trouble comprehending. The silence kicked in again but I welcomed it. We both just wanted to stare at the world and share this moment together.

The stop lasted more than two minutes this time. Her back lay on my chest as I placed my arms around her. We had been like this for well over an hour. I had spent that time reliving old memories in my head and wondering how all the moments had somehow led to this beautiful yet tragic instance. She had been thinking about things as well as she finally broke her silence.

"In all these days, I never asked you what your name was. I assumed you didn't want me to know but I would like to have that knowledge now before I die. Will you give me the chance to call you by your name?"

I told her my real name and she whispered it back. A couple of minutes went by, as if she was trying to formulate a thought that she wanted to share with me. She broke the silence once more.

"How often do you think about teleporting that thing in front of us out of its orbit"

I remained quiet for a minute, not because I felt nervous but because I was preparing to finally utter the answer out aloud for the first time.

"Every damn day."

She did not flinch, as if she had expected to hear that reply.

"Don't worry. You never will," she said calmly. I was hoping to reply with a very clever comment but she didn't give me a chance to speak up.

"The first time we met, you asked me to be patient and to listen to you while you told me your story. I would like you to extend the same courtesy to me. I want to thank you for saving my life all those years ago and keeping an eye on me. I wish I had gotten to know you far sooner and in much better circumstances. I would have gone on every adventure with you and maybe, would have avoided this fate."

She stopped momentarily to catch her breath. In front of us, I could see lights going dim over a certain region of land.

"I have heard you apologize to me several times over the last couple of weeks for not having done enough. When you tell me a story about an injustice you see or a side of the world that is not as pretty as the sights you showed me today, I can see it in your eyes that you want to rectify it all. When I question you about your lack of taking any actions, you find reasons to justify what you do yet you hesitate, like you somehow know they are all excuses. You blame yourself for not taking a more active role in safeguarding the rights of the weak, the disadvantaged and you blame yourself for the fact that I will cease to exist before the light finds a way to sneak through my curtains tomorrow. The fact that I just felt you tense up against me is a testimony to it being the truth.

"And you should blame yourself. You had the ability to stop it all but you didn't. You made a conscious choice. I'm not saying that I'm not responsible for my own fate but you could have saved my life. You could have continued to actively interfere with events happening in this world but you didn't and because of you, a lot more children never got a chance to make it back to their loved ones, many others have died needless deaths and people continue to live in poverty and subjugation because you were unwilling to fight the good fight against the oppressors. The guilt that you live with every day is real and it is just.

"You make up silly excuses. You come up with hippy

stories about somehow handicapping the world. You sound like you're somehow concerned with people's opinion of you, which I think is bull considering you've managed to live separated from everyone for over a decade. Worst of all, you try to convince yourself that you fear failure. That you will somehow leave the world a far worse place than when you started."

She paused. I could sense her mouth was running dry. I wanted to stop her now. I didn't quite understand why at this moment she would do this. I did not understand what she hoped to achieve by putting me down. I did not want her to die angry with me. As I prepared to speak up, she cut me off again.

"You're not scared of failure. You're not scared of what people have to say and even you do not subscribe to the idea that the world will somehow come to rely on you to solve its problems. You're scared because each time you've achieved success; you think you've embraced a darker side of yourself. Your sense of justice and action is tied to violent and rash tendencies. You keep blaming yourself for what happened to your mother yet deep down inside, you know full well that you saved her life and you did so by taking matters into your own hands, even if there was a cost associated to it. Your problem is that you're too scared of becoming the villain in your own story!

"I'm not trying to be mean. It is my goal to make you feel guiltier. You need to understand that you are a good person and the only way you will make up for the decade of inaction is by finally snapping out of this thinking that you are somehow not part of this world or that one day, you will in fact stare at yourself in the mirror and meet your arch nemesis. But that will never happen. I have seen your heart and it is pure, even if you are capable of failure once in a while and human enough to make a mistake.

"You need to embrace yourself. You need to start interfering. If you do, maybe the next Claudia will live. Nobody can predict what would happen or how the world will react if someone such as yourself was out there making a difference. They may turn against you or look at you as the scapegoat for solving all their problems. They may be inspired. You may leave the world in chaos. I don't know. You don't know either. So stop speculating. What we do know is what did happen when you did nothing. What we know is that you had the ability to solve these problems. What we know is that you waited too long and we only got two weeks to be together when we could have had an eternity.

"I love you. You've tried to look after me your whole life and in my final moments, I want to look after you. Go out and save the world. That is what you want to do. That is the noble thing to do. Become the hero that the universe is constantly pushing you to become. And just the way you've taken care of me my entire life, take care of my family. I'm not sure how my dad will survive the next few days.

"I know you want to reply back to me right now but don't. Let me enjoy the last few moments of my life knowing that I may have just made a significant difference to yours and in doing so, made a significant difference to the world. Now let's shut up and stare at that miserable place we both refer to as home."

Even if I wanted to reply, I had no words and no rebuttal. At that moment, my heart just felt heavy so I continued staring back at Earth, not once looking down to catch a glimpse of her. In a few minutes, she had stripped me down and I was left here with no response. As her breathing slowed down, I gripped her tighter and with whatever strength she had left, she pressed down ever so slightly on my hand with her palm, as if to tell me it was okay. Moments later, the sobbing began as I squeezed her lifeless body in my arms.

Before daylight broke, I returned her back to her bed and kissed her forehead for the last time. She looked peaceful and I wanted her dad to see that. My heart no longer had the strength to stay longer and witness another two people live through the tragedy I had just endured. I gazed at her one last time and each time I prepared to leave, I found it hard to move. I just wanted to look at her for another minute. This continued on for a while till I heard some stirring in the other room. In mere moments, someone would come to check on her and this room will be filled with pain again. I came to accept that this had to be the final goodbye and held her hand once more.

"Thank you for your words. They won't be in vain." I kissed her hand and gave it a final squeeze.

Chapter 42

Since her death, I stopped exploring the world. I stopped trying to seek out new life or attending the regular festivals and events that took place each year that I enjoyed so much taking part in. I spent a lot of my time staying in or staring at a beach for hours. I visited that spot on the moon often too, as long as I could see Earth from it. Initially, the time was spent moping. Once in a while, I would check on her family to see how they were. The mom coped though I would often find her in a back alley behind her place of commerce smoking a cigarette, a habit she only picked up recently. The majority of her time was not actually spent smoking it but merely, holding it in her hands as the other end continued to burn. She would stare into nothingness. Between you and me, I think she had accepted the death of her daughter. This new ritual of hers was her way of coping with her husband who was an entirely different coping mechanism. He was a drone, doing the bare minimum to get by. When he wasn't feeding himself, he would spend the entire morning and afternoon in Claudia's room. He would clean it or read a book or a clipping he would find, even if it was nothing more than an old school text book. By the time the wife would arrive home, he would grab dinner and only talk about his daughter. She listened to everything he would say, even if she had heard the same story every day for the last week. I kept an eye out. He didn't appear to be in danger yet but he was still just an empty shell showing no signs of improvements.

I needed an outlet too. I never provided them with any explanation but I went back home for a few weeks. It had been years since my mom's surgery and she had managed to gain some of her strength back. I told them that I just wanted to spend more time with them. They probably thought I went through a bad break up. My dad acted like my dad and within a day, pushed all the chores he was supposed to be carrying out over to me. My mother was happy to have me around, insisting that she cooks me meals even though she was not capable of spending much time around the kitchen.

We spent a lot of time in the living room. During the day, my mom and I watched stupid movies and laughed a lot. I would make her tea while she would ensure there were always packets of crisps lying around. For her, I was still that teenage child who snacked through the afternoon and spoilt his appetite for dinner. She seemed to not care as much anymore.

When my dad would return though, we would eat a meal and my mother would retire to bed. The two of us would stay in the living room and I would sit and watch whatever documentary he appeared to be engrossed in. I caught up on a lot of David Attenborough. Once in a while, I would comment on a fact about an animal, insect or location, in an attempt to impress. His response would be limited to, "Huh ... how about that."

At night, I would spend time in my room reminiscing about my moments here. This was my first lab. My countless nights of experimentation had all been conducted in this very room. Damn place belonged in a museum, I thought. I would walk over to my window and see the city that had barely changed. I could spot all the rooftops that I would make my way to as I first initially took to teleporting, hoping to not materialize over another object. I would chuckle, realizing how far I've come.

One Saturday afternoon, my mom requested my dad to run to the store and grab some produce. I leaned out to grab the car keys, knowing full well that these particular instructions would be passed down to me. As I put my shoes on to leave, my dad put his light coat on and walked over too.

"You can drive a stick, right?"

"Yes, Dad. I've been driving your car for weeks now. I drive your car every time I'm here."

"Oh, that's good. You drive. I want to pick something up too," he said as he grabbed his wallet from the table and walked out. I blew my mother a kiss and followed him out. Across the street, there was no old lady watching the street. Ms. Farnsworth had passed away a while back and the house was still unoccupied. The chair she sat on every day was still eerily placed on the front porch.

My dad and I never really spoke for the duration of the ride to the store. As I grabbed the items my mom had listed down for us, I noticed my dad had nothing in his hands.

"What was it you wanted to pick up?" I asked.

"Oh? Yeah, never mind. They don't have it," he replied

rather unconvincingly.

He got to the car before me and opened the trunk for me. After depositing the bags at the back, I came and sat down, searching for the keys in my pocket.

"It's good you are here. Your mother's spirits are lifted."

I paused what I was doing, suddenly taken aback by the fact that my father was attempting to speak what was not just on his mind but in his heart. He was a caring man but words had never been his strong suit. That little phrase from his mouth, coupled by my emotional state was creating a very overwhelming reaction.

"Thanks, Dad. I'm glad to be here too," I replied.

"Good," he said. "But I think it is time for you to leave."

There was a moment of silence. I wasn't sure how to respond to that. He decided to continue. "Son, I don't know what you are running from but I'm glad you came here. It was good to see you again. Every time you came for the holidays, our hearts sank because we knew a couple of days later, you would be gone again. Having you here for so long felt like we were a family once more.

"It's been hard for your mother and me but we have survived through everything. We are both in a good place now. But you are not. I won't ask you what happened but time will find a way to heal all wounds. Look at your mom if you need an example. We love that you are here but your mother and I both agree that unless you don't go back, you will never move on from whatever happened."

He was right. When I came home, I needed to see my family. I needed to get away from it all to heal but that time had passed and now, I was avoiding facing the trials and decisions that lay in front of me.

My dad continued, "I hope you got what you were looking for back here at home my boy. You should stay a few more nights but then, get back to your life. Just remember to visit often."

With that, silence filled up his sedan once more. I turned the key in the ignition and drove off in the direction of home.

Chapter 43

As days became weeks, I tried to figure out what to do with the rest of my life and do justice by Claudia. Her final words remained with me even though I wasn't ready to face them. She was after all correct but I couldn't admit it to myself for a while. But she had pushed me in the right direction and I could no longer make any excuses in my head without feeling the guilt kick in. No more passive philanthropy. No more elaborate sabotaging to discourage certain types of behavior. I was prepping to take the world head on for the first time in my life.

It was fitting that each time I would think about where to begin and would walk myself through various different scenarios, my attention turned back to kidnappings and drug trafficking. If it wasn't for one or the other, she would have never headed down the path of destruction. Children, I felt, were in more immediate danger than drug addicts, so I turned my attention to global kidnapping rings. There was little gray area here as well for me to struggle with. In my mind, I had already passed judgement on all of them. In the months leading up to the fall, I started preparing for battle. The world was about to see a far more sinister side of me and I was not going to be settling for one offs. Nothing other than causing a significant stir in this criminal organization would cause me satisfaction.

Of course, I was simplifying the issue. There was no 'one' criminal organization. There were many. On occasions, their

371

motivations were quite different. Some operated regionally, and others on a more global scale. In many cases, these were just one off kidnappings, either politically or monetarily motivated. Still, finding a place to start wasn't all that difficult. It was the fall of 2009 and only a year ago, *Slumdog Millionaire* had graced movie theaters all around the world. I happened to watch it with a very specific interest and decided to validate if the child trafficking problem in India associated with beggars was a reality. The time zone worked well for me too. I was free to conduct matters where I resided during the day while spending the nights on the other side of the planet.

Finding the children wasn't hard. Bearing witness to their plight, however, was a different story. Right off the bat, I concentrated on Mumbai and New Delhi which all my research was pointing towards as the hub of most operations. I located many children with disabilities, ranging from severed limbs to visual and mental impairments. I started tracking over fifty on the first day but concentrating specifically on those that were in close proximity to each other. My problem wasn't tracking. I was far more interested in their interactions. While the majority of the crowd would be giving them money, I was interested in the person who collected it from them.

At the rate of over 40,000 kidnappings a year, an estimated 100 kids were going to be forcibly taken from their homes that day. A small portion would be rescued and recovered but the majority will be introduced to this life or one that was similar. My gut felt sick watching these kids but after thirteen years of living this way, I was able to muster the strength to watch without interfering. Some of these kids were seasoned; a couple looked like they had just been sent out on the street not too long ago. You could tell by looking at them that their predicament and their situation was still unreal to them. The veterans appeared to have settled and were sometimes, even part of the collectors or worse yet, snitches. It was all quite disgusting.

In a matter of a few hours, it was obvious there were multiple rings operating in the same regions. While a few children had the collection man show up every couple of hours, others had to wait for designated times during the day. There was one guy who had the money slipped to him. I was not going to pursue any of these people for now. My goal for the first couple of days was to merely observe and put a tracker on as many collectors as possible. The grand total came to twenty-four, all men in the late teens or early 20s. Were they brought into this life in a similar manner? Were they victims as well or was their recruitment incentivized strictly by money? I didn't care. Regardless, if they had no sympathy for these children, I had no sympathy for them.

A couple of days passed and I moved away from the children and started following the collectors. This was harder to do as they were all spread out and once again, I could monitor their movements but what I needed to do was monitor their activity. So I followed each one individually. These guys made a lot of stops along the way, finding the children, stopping for tea or chatting it up with some friends. They showed no remorse. My patience was running thin but I continued to persevere. Through them, I located and marked even more children that I had originally not picked up. Eventually, the drop would be made and I had my next set of people to follow identified. I wish I could color code all of them to be honest but alas, this ability was never given to me. Now that I had identified the need for it, I toyed with the idea that maybe I'll find a new prompt on my HUD in the coming months. I could only hope.

As the days went on, I tracked the small fish to the bigger fish. I was no longer only in Mumbai and New Delhi. I found myself camping in various places around Tamil Nadu, Kerala, Bihar and Kolkata. The networks were huge. The entire operation involved from the high two digits to a couple of hundred people, ranging from carriers to accountants and bankers. Government and police officials were involved as well providing protection. A network of doctors existed to carry out specific amputations for less money you would spend on food in a week. Drug traffickers were in the mix, providing a supply of opium to keep the children addicted. There were enforcers in the mix as well ensuring that the kids paid their dues. But that was only one side of it. A whole specific set of people existed for housing the new children, for actually kidnapping them and scouting for more to keep an eye out for supply for an increasing demand. A small population of these folks in these criminal organizations were abducted children to begin with. I struggled with this idea but kept firm on the fact that their fates were already sealed.

This all eventually got me to the ones profiteering the most from this venture. A few were well-respected individuals in the community. Others lived secluded lives. Some were known gangsters with the child-begging ring as one of their many lucrative investments. From the beginning, I was hoping I could simply put a familiar face on all these criminals I had encountered. But, the more I got embedded, the more I realized there was no pattern. From the rich to the poor, from men to women and all different walks of life and professions, a diverse group of individuals were involved and seemed to have no moral dilemma in the enterprise they were all engaged in. I was counting down the days before I would pull the plug on the entire operation.

It wouldn't come as a surprise to any of them, however. See at the point of finding the safe houses where these kids were located, I was forced into a situation of taking action else subject another child to a life of misery. At the beginning, I stuck to my subtle ways, gaining the attention of concerned citizens or people of authority to investigate and thus, freeing the children. I soon realized that with more and more safe houses being discovered, not only was this cumbersome and time consuming but sometimes the people just didn't want to get involved due to risk of repercussions or a well-placed bribe in the hands of the right person.

No worries. The bribe-takers were also added to the list of people I had plans for. I started warming up to the idea of more direct confrontations. Physicians and guards frequenting these locations were beaten to a pulp by an unknown entity. Guards experienced unfortunate falls while physicians encountered their own surgical equipment working against them by an unskilled hand. Doors were left unlocked for children to run away. It didn't take long but news spread of a vigilante. I continued perpetuating this by leaving everything but my top skin ethereal and donning a hoodie. My face and extremities remained only partially visible to give the semblance of a real person but making it impossible to identify me. There were still children in the pipeline that required a secure location to be dropped off by these criminals so temporary safe houses were provided or were simply rerouted to an existing one. They all met the same fate. This behavior of mine went on for weeks and it got to a point where unofficial contracts were being renegotiated so people would be willing to assume a higher risk with the vigilante about while others were simply not looking to partake in the business altogether. Authorities considered some of these easy wins and started taking credit for the recently liberated children and thwarting the recruitment efforts. I didn't mind. I felt this was only making the more pious amongst the law enforcers and those in the community more confident in taking action.

Eventually, the instructions I had been waiting for were finally sent down through the hierarchy. Supply of new children would be put on hold indefinitely while the situation with the vigilante(s) was fixed. Bad people, very bad people, were hired to carry out the job of finding and identifying those that had caused the disruption to their business. When the hit on my head was in place by multiple criminal families, I smiled. It was time. The total tally of people I had to take care of came to 2,181. The majority would meet similar fates. The rest would experience something worse.

A month after my first trip to Mumbai, I found myself standing on the desert fields of Rajasthan. I had picked a very specific spot, roughly twelve miles from the closest inhabited village. I felt the sand engulfing my shoes. I felt connected with the entire terrain. Another location had been scouted by me roughly five miles away devoid of any kind of life as well. I closed my eyes, and a split second later when I was sure I had locked on to everything I wanted to take on my little journey, I teleported thousands of feet above the second spot. Below my feet, 220 feet of sand and rocks had teleported as well, in a reverse conical shape with cylindrical sides that were over 200 feet in diameter at the furthest points. Most of the sand dissipated on the way down while stones and rock fell with a thud. I returned back to the first location. Some of the sand had caved in but the hole I was trying to create looked about right. At the bottom, it was still roughly 200 feet in diameter with the opening no more than forty feet. I teleported down. It would be very hard though not impossible to escape this. I walked around for a while and tried to climb on the sides. I teleported up to random spots and punched the walls. Sand would dissipate each time I did this but the integrity of the wall would hold. I was satisfied by this. I had no intentions of wanting this little prison to cave in and kill everyone right away. I brought back the limited amount of food and water I had been accumulating for this day from my cave over to this ditch I had created. Yup, I was going to give them some food and water.

2,181 people. One night. I moved region by region grabbing the majority of them in their sleep and the others by distracting them away from their social circles. As I teleported each into the pit I had created, ensuring I had left their communication devices behind, the confusion began, slowly followed by the panic. Little light was making its way back into the hole and each new group of people I teleported back was placed at a distance from the previous one. Most of these people had never met each other. They navigated blindly at first and then towards the calls of others who sounded like they may be in a similar predicament. Movements were cautious though and the lack of light intensified the distrust. Nobody could see the teleportation happening at all but every minute, the population of people in the hole continued to grow. Fights broke out and I could tell that those that may have been carrying a weapon may have already thinned the crowd a bit. It was my turn to turn a blind eye. While others argued, some investigated, eventually finding the supplies I had left for them. Some tried to climb the inverse wall failing miserably. Five hours later, a total of 1,973 people had been transported. They were all feeling the walls, hoping to find an entrance even if it was locked. The rational mind could not comprehend what was happening. I sat down and watched in amusement. In particular, their attempt to climb on top of each other's shoulders was the most inspiring. Their eventual collapse was hilarious.

I wasn't sure what the point of providing them with the supplies was. I wasn't sure why I left them where I did. Part of me wanted to kill them all but I wasn't ready to do such a thing. I was still haunted by the idea of taking lives, though the hypocrisy of the situation I've put them all in was not lost on me. I think I knew full well exactly how this was going to end. Their possibility of survival was quite low but the little hope I left them with for escaping comforted me. I wasn't a total heartless bastard. Or at least, I told myself I wasn't. I dropped a few copies of a note I had written so that in the case they do get out, they would be aware of what caused the situation to occur in the first place. The vigilante had shown them justice. I never returned back to that location.

Two hundred and eight people were still left. These 208 represented the worst of them. From those who pioneered the ideas to the ones who were put into position of power to safeguard against such a behavior, they were rounded up in one of the more secluded safe houses that I had taken the liberty of reinforcing. They were packed like sardines yet unable to break through the defenses I had set up to contain their population within its walls. Along with them, I had collected enough evidence and sent it to various reporting outlets across the world with their names. Confusion and panic ensued here as well but this time, I wasn't playing games. The sound of the first set of bones breaking caused the rest of them to run, but it didn't matter. The area was secure and when I finally decided to give everyone false hope and purposely allowed a section of the wall to get compromised, those who managed to break free were teleported back time and time again. It was a moment worthy of a great monster movie. By the time I left, the floor was covered with blood and the walls covered with bloody prints. Copious amounts of furniture lay in pieces, sometimes even through the limbs of one of these people. I can't deny that hair and teeth had been pulled out, fingers and tongues were made obsolete and some would even wake up to find portions of their bodies with second and third degree burns.

Judge, jury, executioner. Would Claudia still think my heart was in the right place? Would she have approved of what was happening here? At this point, I finally asked the one question that I believe she had been pushing me to ask. Was I okay with what had transpired?

See, these people were the worst of the lot. These were the financiers, the kingpins of these child-begging rings who had no excuse at all. They had the money, the education and a life that would have helped them separate right from wrong. These were the people whose disappearances would make headlines because the world only cares about those who are rich and famous.

I felt I was mostly okay with what had transpired. Mostly

okay was good enough for me.

I had now given them a fate worse than death. Within a day, this safe house would be discovered and within its walls, they would find carnage. A hard to miss message would be found as well, smeared on the walls with blood alluding more to a vigilante ring that was now seeking street justice. This blood would be tested for evidence but the only thing they would find is the mixed DNA of all those that will soon find themselves behind bars. There would be no bribing. There would be no behind the scene political deal. I had distributed the evidence to all the right places to ensure a quick backlash if any of those things were allowed to happen.

2,181 people. And this was only my first escapade. I had made a dent but that is all it was. A dent. There were more rings like these in India and extended into Pakistan, Bangladesh and a host of other countries as well. My routine became formulaic. I would spend a few days observing and eventually, strike, trying to target larger numbers each time. If I was bored with a pit, I would leave them 24,000 feet on an unclimbable side of Nanga Parbat. Some were deposited on the world's most remote Islands. All were made aware of why they encountered their fate. And for those who were too rich or famous to go unnoticed, they would be found trapped somewhere having seen better days. Evidence would always be made public in each of these escapades of mine.

It only took a few months to see the problem shrinking. Maybe I had made a dent large enough or maybe others were temporarily closing operations. I knew this was not going to last though. A purge of this kind had be conducted periodically.

Child trafficking rings operated all over the world, even in the developed nations of the world but thankfully, they all operated in a similar manner with a few subtle differences. Finding the children in India was easier. I knew what to look for. In other situations, I had to start with pictures of missing children and then try to locate them. Once found and freed, the formula remained much the same. However, child rapists, those who ran labor camps or utilized them for "parts" were added to the list of people who would be subjected to my wrath. By the time I was done with my first phase, tens of thousands of kids had been liberated and even more found who had been taken away from their families ages ago. In addition to this, I had also made countless people disappear and a small subset incapable of living a life again.

The world had taken notice. Agencies across the world were searching for people who had gone missing. A very well coordinated ring of vigilantes had been theorized not just by the media but also by private and government agencies across the world. As expected, the general public was grateful while the governments were left nervous. I made a final attempt during this time to eavesdrop in the hopes of hearing my name or seeing my picture pop up on a monitor screen or a physical photograph. It never did and for the first time, I was ready to believe that the world had never known about my existence. I was a mystery to them and for now, I was glad they were all busy running around trying to gain intelligence on an imaginary self-righteous band of faceless justice seekers.

Chapter 44

Taking down kidnapping rings hadn't been the only item on the menu during the fall of 2009. As I worked my way mapping out the supply chain that existed for trafficking children, I had started on a brief research into the cartels that plague the Americas. The interesting thing is that finding drugs for me is quite simple, much simpler than having to look for children. However, the drug business was a far grayer area, at least to me.

It was true. I did dislike drugs and Claudia's death definitely created a bias. One could take an economical stance or that of personal freedom and argue that the war on drugs shouldn't exist to begin with. One could even argue that alcohol could be categorized as a more serious gateway to drugs and its negative effects far superseded those of the majority of contrabands that are illegally distributed. I personally had little interest in arguing over the merits of the legalization of the drug trade. In this particular situation, drugs themselves meant nothing to me. I was more interested in those involved with their production and distribution.

Drug traffickers and cartels were responsible for heinous crimes. Many argue that if we simply legalize narcotics, the crime would fall but that in itself is again irrelevant to me. All it tells me was that a person's need to then engage in murder and other such crimes was reduced but their willingness to commit them still remains. These were not good people. This was the same reason why I was having such a hard time understanding how to deal with this situation. Unlike the trafficking of children, where I can point at anyone involved in such a business and pass judgement, the intent behind everyone involved in the drug trade was different. Some people were merely trying to make some money without having to get their hands dirty. Others engaged in the business out of fear of repercussions. Some weren't very nice people but still had limits regarding the type of crime they were willing to commit. Finally, there were the soulless bastards who had no problems profiteering off someone else's misery or life. Mapping the distribution of this business was not going to be a problem for me. However, trying to figure out what judgement to pass on those I tagged gave me pause.

Then, there was the fallout. What if I managed to disrupt the supply for an extended period of time? Will the shortage lead to even bigger issues? Will the innocent get caught in the crossfire? The number of variables were quickly adding up. I tried to remind myself that it was this exact issue that had made me be so passive in the past. It didn't change the fact that there were people in this equation that I still needed to bring to justice. For now, I had to concentrate on mapping out the movement of the drugs so I could figure out all the players in the game.

As I mentioned before, finding the drugs wasn't going to be that much of an issue to me. The quantity and the types of drugs however, made it much harder to isolate and figure out what to track so I decided to concentrate on a region. It was hard to ignore pop culture as well as the news so I had set my eyes on Colombia and Mexico. To get even more clichéd about it, I scanned remote areas and forests. My search focused on Sinaloa, Cali and Medellin but soon turned towards Michoacan and Oaxaca as well. From the looks of it, the industry around marijuana appeared to be slowing down, with cultivation slowly moving towards opium for the production of heroin. Cocaine supply still appeared to be strong. Meth was picking up, too, which made my life a little easier as tracking a super lab in a country I was already looking into was far more convenient than tracking down a cartel in the US amongst hundreds of home labs. Again, I had to remind myself that I was not necessarily after the drugs or those who made them. I was interested in those who had shown they were willing to go to any lengths to turn them into a lucrative business.

I only had to find a single lab or crop field per cartel. After that, I let their logistical operations do the bulk of the work for me. As trucks pulled up to carry away the crops, I followed them to the next phase of their lifecycle. I watched as the opium paste was crafted by people of all ages but more importantly, I also took note of the trucks that pulled in from other locations. This was all that I had needed. The routes did not run twenty-four hours so I had to be patient. It would take days till I found all the farms for cultivation. The same could be said for cocaine, except the production of coca leaves was not exclusive to its production. A decent amount of time was wasted following the wrong convoys of trucks to the production facilities. But soon, I was on the right course again and waited for other trucks to show up before locating other sources of coca leaves. While I waited, I would spend time in the meth labs to see where the raw material came from. Much to my surprise, the majority came from legitimate places so the lab itself needed to be my starting point.

Once produced, the steps followed were largely the same. All the narcotics were pre-packaged for delivery, like they were ready for wholesale. Before delivery, packaging would be added and I observed the most creative ways in which these same products would be packaged once more to be smuggled. They used plastic bags small enough for human mules to swallow, or put drugs inside the ceiling and walls of other products and within nooks and crannies of transportation vehicles. I had no idea cocaine could be smuggled mixed in with actual baking soda. Separation processes appeared cumbersome but in most cases, the users of these narcotics didn't seem to care. They snorted it anyway.

As you may have guessed it, it's the smuggling part that as usual employed the most amount of people. From those running logistical operations and protection to others who had either been paid off or got into the business to get others to turn a blind eye, the networks were vast and were not limited to the two countries that I had been targeting. From what I could tell, the majority of the cost when it came to running this business was absorbed by this particular step, even more so than the creative packaging I had come across during my investigations.

I was blown away by the entire thing. These was one of the most sophisticated operations I had ever seen involving tens of thousands of folks. Each additional day that I spent investigating the drug market introduced me to even more people I needed to keep track of and more areas that required visitation during my daily runs. Sometimes, I felt the burden so much that I completely gave up mapping out the movements of these drugs in the Americas and went back to concentrating on the child trafficking trade exclusively for a few days. It was certainly far more disgusting but the task of monitoring the extent of the problem was less daunting.

Sometimes, though, I would mess around with their logistical operations just for the fun of it. The US Customs and Border control was proud of the thousands of kilos of narcotics they are able to seize coming into the country, yet it was a dime in the bucket. I would help them out from time to time with the most juvenile of tactics, ranging from slapping an adhesive piece of paper on the side of the truck as it pulled in for customs that said "I'm carrying heroin" to removing the majority of the gas from planes and boats in the middle of their journey, causing them to either get stuck in the middle of the sea or make an unexpected landing in an area that was not of their choosing.

As my confidence grew, my antics expanded to other areas of their operations. One time, in the middle of the forest, I followed around the main enforcer at a wholesale packaging area waiting for the time he would walk close to where most of the produce was. It just so happened that the moment was extremely opportune. As a couple of others out there argued with him not to smoke so close to where the merchandise was housed, I happen to flick off the match he had in his hand onto the floor, where only moments before I had been able to put a believable amount of dry twigs and grass. Now to expect that to turn into a full-fledged bonfire in reality would be ludicrous but if it did, it would be a passable story. And that is what happened. I exaggerated the fire by forcing the flame to extend and very soon, thatched roofs were on fire as well. I knocked down a few wooden pillars and even a couple of walls to accelerate the process. They managed to get a few packages out but in the commotion, most people were interested in saving their lives. After all was said and done, the majority of the blame for the merchandise that was considered unsalvageable fell on that one guy as I had hoped.

I slashed tires, removed entire engines and on the watch of some of the people I really disliked during my course of observing them, made the cocaine, meth or heroin simply disappear. The cartels never took kindly to such a thing and a week later, someone else would always take their place. I did not seek out what happened to the person who I had set up.

Weapons. Oh, how I had fun with those. I never liked guns. They do genuinely scare me, which I guess qualifies them as the deterrent they're supposed to be. During these times when

I was messing around with these people, I would often empty out the clips that were already in the guns. A lot of these criminals were often found without their knives as well at the moment when they looked for one. A few of my favorite moments however were when I replaced shipments of guns and ammunition with obvious toy replicas. I still remember the look on everyone's' faces. No one was even mad, they just stood there in disbelief, not sure what to say as the situation was somewhat unprecedented and comical, even to a few on the scene who dared not openly smile about it.

It all started off as fun and games but soon I had an ulterior motive for my actions. While what I was doing wasn't creating any significant dent in their business, I was managing to frustrate and create a higher than usual level of distrust amongst the different partners within the cartel business. I was making them question loyalties, or the service provided by certain suppliers and questioning certain smuggling routes. I was making them question some of the business decisions and I could see that at times, the higher ups were beginning to second guess some of their plans that had earlier been considered routine walkthroughs. With more eyes heavily scrutinizing the entire business and some cartel bosses feeling the need to now micro manage certain portions of the logistics that had failed repeatedly, the tension and stress levels were higher than usual.

It had been almost six months since I had first turned my eyes on Cali. Back then, I knew nothing more than a single field and a few workers cultivating it for the following harvest. A 180 days later and I was tracking over 12,500 people. Out of these, I had narrowed my list down to about 600 that became my primary targets (though everyone in the supply chain would feel the effects of my plan). I noted where they lived, what cars they drove, who their closest allies were and most importantly, where they kept their liquid assets. I knew passwords to their bank accounts or had access to the keys of their safety deposit boxes. I was ready to make my move but I had never been this nervous. There were way too many moving parts, various different details to track, some time consuming operations that I had to personally and physically conduct and the scariest part, an unpredictable fallout.

April, 21st 2010, I took the majority of the unused weapons stash along with the ammunition that I was aware of and threw the bulk of them into an active volcano. I felt a little bad as the equipment could have been recycled. What was left over was taken to my cave to help out some innocent underdogs in the future when the need arose.

My second focus were all shipments in transit with limited visibility. The amount of time it would require to figure out that these items had gone missing would take at least a couple of hours. I raided the routes that were used for bringing raw material, carrying the produced drugs, those that were prepackaged and finally, others that were in the process of being smuggled. This was a time intensive process that required me to travel from one vehicle to another while trying to locate them on their routes. Planes and boats were even harder so I tackled them at the runways and docks before they would move.

I next hit the American warehouses, first the ones that were empty save a few security guards and then the rest. A silent vigilante once again took care of those that inhabited these warehouses. A couple of hours had already passed. An isolated call here and there would be unnerving for a few and expected, given the random disruptions that have plagued the cartels as of late but an escalation of call backs about missing merchandise would set a few wheels in motion that couldn't be reversed. I had little time left.

That night, meth labs exploded one by one. Packs of cocaine, meth and heroin burnt in fires at the various locations I had marked for months now. Hysteria ensued at all these locations. Risking to save the product would mean certain death. The fires I had set up burnt so intense that running in to recover the product would have been a fool's errand. People were seen dispersing in all directions and in more urban locations, certain authorities took notice. It was just as I planned. The more locations I could expose, the more the probability that an uncorrupt official would take notice and the higher the chance of finding the required evidence to put the cartel members behind bars.

My next stop involved the packaging facilities. This was perhaps the greatest challenge of all and till the time I arrived at the first of these many locations, I had still not decided on what I would do. Moving all the merchandise out of these locations would be cumbersome. Due to how everything was spread out and occupied, I couldn't just light everything on fire as I would risk casualties. As I stood in the central room of the first location I visited I made an impulsive decision to teleport. Everyone here felt a tremor. A few people laughed and told jokes in a language I could not understand. I smiled. I teleported once more, creating a larger jolt. Many were now convinced there was an earthquake in progress. Little did they realize I was merely teleporting the entire facility we were currently occupying by a centimeter or two. I teleported again, changing direction each time and every time I engaged in this activity, I could tell that the structural integrity of this building was failing.

As a column came crashing down, people dispersed. Many still tried to grab what they could but another couple of teleports later, the house was in freefall and collecting salvage was no longer an option. Don't worry, while some who had accidents from falling debris experienced injuries, no deaths occurred. The drugs were of course still recoverable but accessing them would be a challenge. I was not worried. I teleported and came back with a camera and took a picture. I made a note to drop the picture off along with coordinates in an unmarked envelope at the DEA's office tomorrow. One by one, facilities fell in a similar fashion and for locations that would go unnoticed, I continued to take pictures and associate coordinates to them, hoping to drop them off in the hands of the right people. With the destruction I had already caused, it was impossible to assume that these events were not manufactured by someone.

By this time, the news was definitely out and I was simply wrapping up. A few more controlled forest fires around production facilities and I was about to move on to the last acts of destruction and vandalism that I had planned for myself tonight: the removal of assets and money. Never had I seen so much money in my life. This was all accentuated by the amount of gems, gold and jewelry I came across. All this would make its way to my cave so that at some point, I would figure out a way of redistributing this wealth as I saw fit. I also found incriminating papers in security deposit boxes as well of a few people who were not as well versed with how to hide information. These too would make their way to the right people. In addition, vehicles utilized for operations or merely bought to display wealth were tossed over and rendered useless. A few were dumped into rivers and oceans while others would be found later lying on top of inconceivable places. Equipment was destroyed as well. It was vandalism at its finest.

Finally, my attention turned to the 600. Using their own personal computers, I started the long and arduous task of transferring money from their accounts. It wasn't to some charities or to some fake account I had created. I had no intention of this money getting lost. Hell, I had no idea how to even make this money disappear. What I had in front of me were a list of account numbers of people who had an uneasy coalition with each other and started transferring money into their portfolios. There was nothing subtle about how I did that. I then proceeded to find those whose accounts I had emptied out that night and set up accidents that were meant to fail.

It was six in the morning now but the industry was in an uproar. I could not understand the majority of the conversations but that was fine. I had anticipated this. I was mostly interested in who was provided with certain instructions to carry out the contingency plans. As always I took note. With only a limited amount of time and so many people to follow, I decided only to concentrate on those where I felt the reward would be the highest. I did not pass the opportunity to listen in on any conversations happening in English. The fruits of my labor finally paid off. Over the course of the day, I discovered more hidden reserves of cash, merchandise and other distribution nodes. My night would be busy again and the evening will be spent partaking in a short slumber. For now, I enjoyed the chaos that had ensued and while I could not follow the majority of the planning and actions that were being discussed, I could tell that the stress levels were through the roof and a number of people were trigger happy. I wasn't sure if the transfer of money had been detected as yet but I kept my fingers crossed and hoped the fallout was going to be in a manner I was expecting.

The following night was more of the same, taking out the few new locations I had heard of. This time however, I was more liberal as far as injury counts were concerned. This was all purposeful of course. In addition, I isolated out those people from the previous day who were trusted to carry out some of the contingency plans I had been monitoring. Almost all of them appeared to fall in my list of 600 and I couldn't be happier. They were loyal but they would talk to me.

See, a good portion of these people have seen death waiting for them at every turn. They were all familiar with the idea of incarceration or even torture. They were tough cookies. But I was a different beast. I could force the unexpected and no amount of preparation ever prepares you for that. I transported one to a high narrow tip of the Matterhorn where a single wrong step to the left or right taken by the person accidentally or forced by the strong winds would result in a splattering end to life. It was the end of April and the polar bears were out in the Arctic. Another one on my list happened to find himself outside the den of a female with three cubs. I toyed with the idea of introducing Polly to this human scum but decided against it, picking a far more aggressive mother I had come across the year before. Individuals were suddenly transported from their stress heavy yet comfortable setting into the middle of snake pits, edges of volcanoes, around komodo dragons, in drying pools of hungry piranhas and in oceans during a feeding frenzy involving nature's more unforgiving carnivores. I made myself known to them and asked a single question; to tell me all they can about the next steps and every contingency the cartels had. There was no moment for these people to think. Nature is truly the scariest form of intimidation and secrets spilled out in the hopes that I would show mercy. I didn't.

Judge, jury, executioner. The three words that kept repeating in my head like a blinking warning light. I no longer ignored them. I just remained indifferent to their existence.

I learnt a lot more that night and did not wait till the next sundown to put my plans in action. I had mostly heard about other hidden stashes of drugs, weapons and money and I was quick to dispose of them. Back up facilities had been named and over the course of the next few days, they would all be deemed inhospitable. In the last two days, tens of thousands of kilos of merchandise had been destroyed creating a void in the supply but more importantly, the actual operations had now been disrupted for weeks to come. Police, army and joint drug enforcement had begun mobilization. I had already witnessed one of many raids that were going to occur over the following weeks. These raids would result in countless arrests, some due to the noticeable destruction in property and a limited number of other locations through the photographs that I had been dropping off with GPS coordinates. Raids led to more clues I had left behind, pointing out other locations worth investigating.

Over the next few days, things mostly played out the way I had hoped they would. The truth was that I had never been able to figure out what I would do with all the people I was forced to track and at 12,500, the planning of separating out the grays from those who were black and white as far as their characters were concerned seemed like an astronomical undertaking. So I created the mistrust amongst those who were willing to kill each other and those at the top. Those at the bottom of the hierarchy were mostly ignored. These were usually the more innocent ones. Those enforcing operations found themselves either getting arrested or in conflict with others just like them. The accessories to the crime, the ones who either facilitated the work or turned a blind eye without directly involving themselves with the business would notice the disruption in the supply along with the lack of cash flow. Then there were those at the top. They waged war. The movement of cash finally came under scrutiny amongst the different cartels spanning different narcotics businesses and countries and nature played itself out. I supervised what I could to ensure innocents were not caught in the crossfire. Children who were part of these families were removed beforehand for their own protection. There were about 400 of them and they would find themselves waking up in the US near child care facilities. No one would believe their stories of being magically transported. The governments would theorize that there was a large scale war in effect and these children were smuggled. There would be skeptics but as long as a rational explanation is being offered no matter how improbable, the irrational would be dismissed.

I took the opportunity of this all-out war between the cartels to plant my own explosives on their real estate assets along with their helicopters and planes. Weeks went by and of the 600 people who were supposed to meet their fate by my hands, over 400 of them were no longer part of this world. Those who were left and considered themselves lucky soon found themselves on an unexpected date with me in environments that were neither familiar nor inviting. They too asked me for mercy and they too, were denied. Another fallout was taking place in the markets that were served by these cartels. The supply had run out and I had ensured that manufacturing and distribution would be hampered for some time to come. More battles took place on the streets fighting over what little supply existed and yes, there were more casualties. However, I felt strangely comfortable with all this. All these years I had spent worrying about the consequences of my actions and now that I could see them getting played out, I found myself standing around with a meh expression on my face.

I was tired, though. One had to respect the empire that existed just so people could have the choice to destroy their own lives. These were impressive people who had set this network up. You can call them criminals but they were smart. Give them a legitimate business to run and they would have made a fortune for them. Maybe this is how things were during the prohibition era or at a time when other things that are considered normal today were illegal for distribution. Maybe it's not a bad idea to legalize it all and then wait a couple of decades to normalize the market. I don't know. The more I was burdened with thoughts about how the world should work as far as narcotics are concerned given everything I have witnessed over the last few months, the more my head hurt and my will increased to not side with a political argument.

The dent I created would have a lasting effect but eventually, I knew that order would be restored. Much like child trafficking, others would pick up the pieces, forgetting how at one point, the entire industry was brought to its knees but someone would get up and say that it will be different this time. With it, we will see new faces who would be once again willing to hurt, torture, kill and exploit others in the name of profits. This was all going to be a cyclic gig for me and unless I changed my habits, I knew that every so often, I would have had to involve myself in creating yet another disruption. I hoped that the next time however, things would be easier, especially if I continued to monitor everything that will rise from the ashes, whether it's the narcotics industry, child trafficking or anything else.

Epilogue

Thirteen years ago, I experienced an event that has since then redefined how I have lived half my life. The thing about the event is that it resulted in a discovery. I hadn't actually gained any power that day. It appears that I had always had it or happen to have acquired it recently prior to that day. Every so often, I would be gifted with another power and it would reinforce my need to spend a good portion of my life investigating the cause of my predicament. Yet, thirteen years have passed and there are no answers and at this point, I have gotten so comfortable with the idea that my condition is so random that I fear the possibility that the nature of my powers is somehow manufactured and manmade.

I'm twenty-six years old. With the money I've accumulated by digging for buried treasure and my recent escapades with the drug cartels, I have enough wealth lying buried deep within a cave to buy entire countries. I have now seen and recorded every species known and not known to humanity and have traversed every piece of land and water, whether it's the numerous crevices of a cave or the deepest darkest parts of the ocean. I have observed festivals, events and rituals in every country or the remotest parts of this world. If one was to ask me about my experiences, the best way to reply would be to say that I have flavored all that the world has to offer.

But that's the problem, isn't it? I am a being that has no need for expensive cars, precious stones, real estate property or even an abundance of money. I've seen it all, the good and the bad that this world has to offer. From the very beginning, I had decided that I was going to maintain a very passive existence as far as this world was concerned but over time this kept getting harder and harder. Through most of my life, I attributed this to the fact that with each passing year, I've been made witness to more and more of what's wrong with the world that it makes it hard to ignore and not take any action but it's only recently that I've realized that I've had this all backwards. My problem wasn't that I was witnessing all the bad but it was the fact that every year, there was far less good for me to discover.

In the early years, I could easily distract myself away with wanting to explore a new animal or traverse another scenic region of the world I happen to come across in a magazine. If I saw a robbery in San Antonio, I could distract myself by going and witnessing a cultural event taking place in Mongolia instead of concentrating on the increase in crime in the state of Texas. But the more I witnessed, the less was left for me to explore. I've seen the aurora borealis so many times that I don't care for it anymore. I no longer look forward to seeing the ice melt in Antarctica to watch baby emperor penguins take their first steps into the ocean.

But eventually, I felt like I'd seen it all. I felt like there was nothing new. The problem with seeing things that are great is that you can only continue to experience them again and again just the way they are. There is no reason to modify or change them.

And when you run out of the good, you realize that you've seen all the bad as well and the thought that continuously goes through your head is that "I can fix it!" The only thing that had been holding me back in the last year or so was me. I was afraid of exposing myself and I was afraid of not understanding the long-term consequences of my actions and breaking everything. I was afraid of unleashing the true strength of my powers.

But, Claudia had been right also. My actions would not necessarily result in a world that is worse off either. The reality is that it was impossible to predict what would happen and the only true constant right now is that my lack of action continues to keep status quo. Those who are suffering continue to suffer. Species will still continue to go extinct. Maybe I needed to be that wrench that had to be thrown to break the entire system.

I have an immense amount of wealth lying around and I've only distributed small amounts in the fear of the economic situation I would create if I suddenly introduced it all into the system. As of this moment, I don't care. There are entire regions of the world where living in turmoil is considered normal, corporations find legal loopholes to questionably profit, and an environmental calamity may be on its way. I've been too scared to pick sides but I don't care anymore because I have no reason to pick a political, religious or cultural ideology. It's irrelevant. The world would be a lot better place if we simply concentrated on injustice instead of worrying about who is who. There are certain actions out there that are indisputable in their characterization regardless of what justification people want to make up. I don't care if you sell drugs but if you've harm a child, I will now be coming after you. I don't care if you're defending your country or if you feel a superior force has subjugated you. If you've intentionally killed an innocent person to profit from it or further a personal agenda, I'm coming after you. I don't care about the type of contracts you make people sign up for utilizing your services or gaining employment in your company. If you decide to be a dick, I'm coming after you.

I haven't decided if I will reveal myself to the world. Should I become that entity that once discovered, becomes a deterrent for all? Should I be what brings the world together, either out of fear or unites them in order to defeat a common enemy? Or should I just leave it up to people's imaginations while I continue to save the world while performing noticeable miracles. God has been identified as the culprit for things we don't understand in the past and on other occasions, ghosts, spirits, and aliens. Maybe I can continue to remain anonymous and hidden but perform fantastical feats and let the world debate over the existence of a supernatural being. Hell, maybe I'll become some kind of a deity worthy of worship.

To be honest, I have no idea what I'll do next. However, I do know that I am no longer ignoring the world's problems. I will no longer be passive. I could no longer be the person who is capable of dropping an entire ocean over a country or dislocate an entire mountain in mere seconds yet when it comes time for action, just sit around and hope mankind finds a way to figure it out for itself. If I'm capable of making a difference, whether it's through direct action or intimidation, those cards are on the table. The only thing I'm sure about is that the world is about to become a very different place and I have no idea what this place will look like. For the first time in my life, I'm completely comfortable with the idea of becoming the catalyst for complete chaos and then sit back and see how it all resolves itself. My intentions may be noble but I am quite self- aware. I am unintentionally sounding more and more like a supervillain.

My life is not a work of fiction. I was denied an origin story. I was denied love interests. Through the majority of my life, I cannot recall there ever having been a supporting character whether it was by design by me or my circumstances. And while I had no one around me who would end up playing the part of a supervillain, I still feared walking up to the mirror in the future and seeing the reflection that looks back at me. The protagonist and his arch enemy could still end up sharing the same set of boots.

I prayed I would avoid that fate.

About the Author

I have spent the better part of my life imagining characters and placing them in environments where they don't fit. When I'm not busy day dreaming about stories, you will find me planning trips to go visit places I have never been to before.

I live with my beautiful wife and our two adorable boys.